Praise for *Rules for Thieves*

"The world building is magnificent and intricate, and it would be a shame if there isn't a sequel, even if Ott does wrap up the key plot points; Alli and this inviting setting both deserve another outing."   —*BCCB*

"Alexandra Ott's funny, thrilling debut, *Rules for Thieves*, will have readers flipping pages from the very first scene."
                                               —*Shelf Awareness*

"This compelling debut fantasy novel with complex themes, lots of action, and a good cast of characters will appeal to fantasy readers across the spectrum."   —*School Library Journal*

"Alli's southern European–inflected fantasy world is built carefully and tightly, complete with class structures, customs, and a patron saint–centered culture. The ending isn't squeaky clean but provides a sense of closure as Alli makes a meaningful discovery about her heritage. A smooth debut." —*Kirkus Reviews*

Also by Alexandra Ott

The Shadow Thieves

Rules for THIEVES

By Alexandra Ott

ALADDIN

New York   London   Toronto   Sydney   New Delhi

ALADDIN

An imprint of Simon & Schuster Children's Publishing Division
1230 Avenue of the Americas, New York, New York 10020
First Aladdin paperback edition June 2018
Text copyright © 2017 by Alexandra Ott
Cover illustration copyright © 2017 by Eric Deschamps
Gold illustration copyright © 2017 by Thinkstock
Also available in an Aladdin hardcover edition.
All rights reserved, including the right of reproduction in whole or in part in any form.
ALADDIN and related logo are registered trademarks of Simon & Schuster, Inc.
For information about special discounts for bulk purchases, please contact Simon & Schuster
Special Sales at 1-866-506-1949 or business@simonandschuster.com.
The Simon & Schuster Speakers Bureau can bring authors to your live event. For more
information or to book an event contact the Simon & Schuster Speakers Bureau
at 1-866-248-3049 or visit our website at www.simonspeakers.com.
Cover designed by Jessica Handelman
Interior designed by Greg Standyk
The text of this book was set in Bembo Std.
Manufactured in the United States of America 0518 OFF
2 4 6 8 10 9 7 5 3 1
The Library of Congress has cataloged the hardcover edition as follows:
Names: Ott, Alexandra, author.
Title: Rules for thieves / by Alexandra Ott.
Description: First Aladdin hardcover edition. | New York : Aladdin, 2017. |
Summary: Twelve-year-old Alli Rosco escapes her orphanage, only to be hit with a deadly
curse by a magic-wielding, law-enforcing Protector, and with nowhere else to turn and
days to live, Alli learns to steal from a street thief named Beck and follows him back to the
legendary Thieves Guild, where she hopes to find a home and the means to save herself.
Identifiers: LCCN 2016052075 (print) | LCCN 2017026150 (eBook) |
ISBN 9781481472760 (eBook) | ISBN 9781481472746 (hardcover) |
ISBN 9781481472753 (paperback)
Subjects: | CYAC: Orphans—Fiction. | Stealing—Fiction. | Magic—Fiction. | Fantasy.
Classification: LCC PZ7.1.O88 (eBook) | LCC PZ7.1.O88 Ru 2017 (print) |
DDC [Fic]—dc23
LC record available at https://lccn.loc.gov/2016052075

FOR MOM, DAD, AND KATIE

Chapter One

Adoption Day is the worst.

Way too early in the morning, Sister Perla stands over my bed, her wrinkled face illuminated in the flickering candlelight. Wisps of gray hair frame her grim expression, a stark contrast to her white robes. I throw my blanket over my head, resolving that today, of all days, I will not get up. I close my eyes.

"Alli," she says, "don't you know what today is?" She yanks the blanket off me.

"Well, since yesterday was the fifty-second day of Ilaina's Month, I'd guess today is the fifty-third," I say without opening my eyes.

"Yes," she snaps. "Adoption Day. And if you aren't up in one minute you'll have kitchen duty for a week."

Now I look at her. The hard set of her jaw means she's not bluffing. This is not the day to test her.

I toss aside my blanket, shivering in the drafty morning air. The bare wood floor is gritty under my feet as I reach for a set of clothing. Around me, the other girls rush to put on their nicest clothes and brush their hair, frantically trying to look their best. With a muttered curse, I find my oldest, grayest uniform and throw it on. It helps that I still have a black eye from yesterday.

Sister Perla herds us upstairs to the chapel, where Headmistress Morgila is waiting to give us her annual lecture. We must be on our very best behavior, we must smile and be polite and use our manners, blah, blah, blah. I always roll my eyes and sigh as many times as possible during the speech just to remind her how I feel about all this. In the past few years, she's taken to ignoring me, and this year is no exception. She knows lecturing me is a waste of her time and mine.

Once Sister Morgila finishes her speech, we line up to leave gifts or offerings for Harona. People call on Harona a lot around here, since she's supposed to be the patron saint of children and families. And since Adoption Day is held on Harona's Day, the pleas to her are more desperate now than usual.

I haven't said any prayers or left any gifts on this holiday since I was eight. Harona and I are not on good terms.

With our obligatory gift giving complete, we all troop downstairs into the big playroom, where a few old toys are strewn across the juice-stained rug, and a drooping map of Azeland fails to hide the peeling puke-yellow paint that coats the walls. The first order of business is the distribution of simple name tags: stiff white paper with our names inked black. We're supposed to pin them to our clothes, like dogs with tags on their collars, so we can be on display for strangers.

Mine goes in the trash.

But right before I throw it out, I take a second to look at it. It's the only time I ever see my name printed out all official, in fancy script and sharp black ink: *Alli Rosco*. It seems legitimate, somehow, like a real name for a real girl, not an orphan. I run my finger over the ink, real quick, just to see what it feels like. Then it goes into the trash like all the other nametags before it. I don't even bother to hide what I'm doing, since the Sisters have other things to fuss over right now.

After my ceremonial Chucking of the Name Tag, Sister Morgila explains to the new kids what will happen on Adoption Day. The potential families will meet with the Sisters to discuss what kind of kid they're looking for, and the Sisters will try to match us up. The family decides if they want to adopt someone or not, and that's the end of it. If they don't, Sister Morgila promises that a "better match" will be found, but we all know there's no guarantee. Every year that we aren't adopted worsens our chances. The younger kids go quickest. And a lot of us age out without being adopted.

We're told to act naturally, to play like this is a normal day, but only the little kids actually do. The older, scared ones sit in a corner and pray to Harona. A few others who have been here awhile just lie around and pretend not to care, but hope and fear are all mixed up in their eyes. They haven't given up. Not yet.

Give them another few years, and then they'll be like me. I used to get my hopes up too, thinking that maybe it would be good this time, maybe things would work out, maybe they'd like me. But they were looking for the perfect child, the well-behaved little girl they'd always dreamed of, and I wasn't what they expected.

Adoption only works for the good kids. Not the ones like me.

After an hour or so, the Sisters come in and call out names. Some of the kids who are called come back, looking heartbroken. Some don't.

I won't be called. I'm notorious. Everyone's heard about how I ran away from the families who adopted me, and about the time I tried unsuccessfully to escape the orphanage. The past two years, I was the only girl who wasn't called, and I don't want to ruin my streak this year. And Sister Morgila knows better than to call me. Right?

By late afternoon, almost everyone's been called at least once, and the room's thinning out. I decide to take a nap, but the door opens and Sister Morgila walks in, carrying her clipboard. In the dim light she looks like a ghost with her flowing white robes. A wrinkly old ghost, that is.

She looks right at me.

"Alli Rosco."

I smirk at her. "You need something, Sis?"

She rolls her eyes, a habit she picked up from me. "Come on," she says. "I want you to meet someone."

4

"They don't want to meet me," I mutter, just loud enough that she can hear.

Sister Morgila ignores me and leads the way into the dim, drafty hall. We're halfway to her office when she glances at my face and freezes. "What happened this time?"

She's spotted my black eye, then. "Like it? I think it makes me look lovely."

"Don't tell me you were fighting again."

I scowl. "Sorry to disappoint you, Sis. But I was minding my own business, doing my chores, when stupid Pips decided to mouth off. You know how I can't stand mouthy eleven-year-olds."

"They're almost as bad as mouthy twelve-year-olds."

"Good thing we don't know any of those," I agree, but secretly I'm kind of pleased she remembers how old I am. There are so many kids here, she probably doesn't remember most of their names half the time. But Sister Morgila and I have a special relationship, based primarily on mutual sarcasm and eye rolling.

"And for goodness' sake, could you at least *try* to be civil?" she adds as we resume walking down the hall.

"I am the very essence of civility."

She rolls her eyes again, and I snicker. "You *must* stop doing that," I say, mimicking her voice. "It makes you look hostile." "Hostile" is one of her favorite words to describe me.

To my surprise, she smiles. "Mock me all you want," she says. "Just lose the attitude when we meet this family. By some miracle, they're looking to adopt an older girl and they haven't heard of your, er, reputation yet."

We stop at the end of the hall in front of Sister Morgila's office, which is strictly off-limits except for today. She turns to me, and this time her expression is serious. She puts one hand on my shoulder. If I didn't know better, I'd think this gesture is one of motherly concern. "Remember, Alli, they're looking to adopt you, not torture you. Keep that in mind."

"There's a difference?" I say.

She presses her lips together in a tight line. "Don't look so hostile and aggressive when you meet them."

"But I am hostile and aggressive."

"Yes, but you can pretend, can't you?"

I shrug. She sighs and opens the door.

The room doesn't seem to have changed at all since the last time I was called. But it's hard to tell, since I was only in here for a few minutes last time before I took a walk with the family around the garden. The garden where, on this day, people wander around with their potential adoptees while everyone else is preoccupied inside—including the guards, who are busy letting people in and out of the gates right now.

The realization hits. Today, there won't be any guards in the garden.

The garden that is only steps away from freedom.

My previous plan, up to this point, was to be as rude and sarcastic as possible and wait to be sent back to the playroom. But this is the perfect opportunity for another escape attempt.

After all, who'd expect a kid to run away when she's being adopted, right? And how hard can it be to act civil for a couple of minutes?

I'm about to age out anyway, so I haven't really been planning another escape attempt. I could wait. Let them dump me as soon as legally possible, on the day I turn thirteen.

But why wait when you can run?

I straighten up a little as we walk through the door. Sister Perla stands behind the large desk, and sitting in front of her is a tall, thin woman with a beaklike nose and a sharp face. Beside her is a little girl, probably three or four. The girl's blond curls are tied back with spiraling pink ribbons, and her clothes are drenched in so much lace I'm surprised she hasn't drowned in it. She's annoyingly cute, while the mother is annoyingly stiff. I hate both of them immediately.

My first instinct is to turn to Sister Morgila and say, "Are you *serious*?" But I remember my plan. Okay, it's not much of a plan, but it's better than nothing.

I don't know how to look sweet or docile, and attempting to smile will only make my black eye look worse, so I settle for a neutral expression.

"Here she is," Sister Perla says cheerfully. "Alli, this is Kateline Autsdau and her daughter, Krystallia. Ms. Autsdau, this is Alli Rosco."

It takes all my self-restraint not to say anything. Their names are so delightfully pretentious they *beg* to be made fun of. Sister Morgila looks surprised when I keep quiet. She closes the door and crosses the room, standing beside Sister Perla.

The Autsdaus both stare at me like I'm a creature with two heads. They're not even trying to be subtle about it. My resolve hardens. There's no *way* I'm going anywhere with these snobs.

"Alli is twelve," Sister Perla says. "We celebrate her birthday during Saint Zioni's Month."

Ms. Autsdau, who I have just dubbed Bird Lady, looks at Sister Morgila. "What happened to her eye?"

Anger shoots through me, red-hot and instant. Nothing's worse than the people who talk about me like I'm not even there, like I'm incapable of speaking for myself. I bite down hard on my tongue, and my fingers twitch.

Sister Morgila tries to bridge the awkward silence. "It's a sports injury. Alli is very athletic." Out of the corner of her eye, she's looking at me with suspicion. She's known me long enough to know something's up.

Bird Lady purses her lips. "My Krystallia doesn't play sports. She's more academically inclined."

I choke back a laugh.

"Alli is a highly intelligent child," Sister Perla says, practically beaming at me. "I'm sure she would be quite brilliant if given the proper instruction."

I bite my tongue harder. The best thing Sister Perla's ever said about me before today is, "Alli doesn't tolerate rudeness from anyone." Which, coming from her, may not have been a compliment. Especially since she said it right after I punched a boy in the face for calling me a foul name.

Bird Lady doesn't seem to be buying it either. She purses her lips again, and I swear it looks like she has a beak.

"Why don't the three of you talk in private," Morgila says quickly. "Perhaps you'd like to go into the gardens? We have a refreshment table. . . ."

Bird Lady nods once, her beady eyes fixed on me again. Sister Perla springs to action, ushering us out the door and down the stairs, chattering about the weather in a falsely cheerful voice. Anger still courses through me, and I try to channel it into planning my escape.

There are a few other people milling about in the small garden. Sister Perla points out the refreshments and leads us to a small bench so we can "get to know each other." With one last suspicious glance at me, she leaves.

Bird Lady perches on the edge of the bench with a sour expression, like she's been asked to sit in filth. She pulls her daughter onto her lap, probably so she won't soil her frilly dress by sitting on a garden bench.

I sit next to them and survey the garden. The old gray house, covered in trails of ivy, is far back from here. The whole garden is enclosed by a stone wall, but it's only about ten feet high. If I could find a way over it . . .

"So, dear," says Bird Lady, addressing me for the first time, "why don't you tell us about yourself?"

"Um," I say, looking for a tall tree or something, "what would you like to know?"

Bird Lady looks irritated. "What are your interests? Do you pursue music? Art? Reading?"

"Um," I say again. The orphanage doesn't have the funding for many books or art supplies or musical instruments, so I really wouldn't know. I'm about to make something up when I spot it—a small tree beside the wall, just high enough that I might be able to make the top. It's on the opposite end of the garden, by the table with food on it.

"Are you thirsty?" I say, leaping to my feet. "Let me get us some, um, refreshments." I move before Bird Lady even responds.

I walk to the refreshment table as fast as possible, scanning the garden as I go. There still aren't any guards or Sisters out here. Saint Ailara, the patron of good fortune, must be praying for me today. Good thing, too, since I can use all the luck I can get.

I turn toward the tree, ready to make a break for it, but a door thuds open behind me. Another Sister is coming outside, leading some other family. I spin back to the refreshment table, pretending to be mulling over the pastry selection. I send a quick prayer to Saint Ailara.

But Ailara's never listened to me twice in a row, and today is no exception. The Sister has spotted me and comes hurrying over. It's Sister Romisha, who hates me.

"What are *you* doing out here?" she demands, hands on her hips.

"I'm with my potential adoptive family." I nod toward

Bird Lady and her daughter, who are watching this conversation from their bench.

Romisha looks at them, then back at me. "Then why are you all the way over here?"

"I'm just getting us some refreshments." I pick up the nearest glass, which is filled with a fancy pink-colored liquid that would never in a million years be served to us orphans.

Romisha stares at the glass, probably wondering whether I've poisoned it. "Well, hurry up then." She waits for me to collect my refreshments and return to Bird Lady.

She won't leave until I go back to them, but I'm not about to go live with the snobby bird family. The tree is ten feet away from me. Close enough.

"On second thought," I say, "I have other plans. Send them my regards, won't you?"

I throw the pink liquid in her face and run.

Romisha screams, and everyone's eyes are on me as I grab the lowest branch of the tree. Some of the bark peels off in my hands, making it impossible to get a firm grip. I finally manage to grasp the branch and haul myself up, just as Romisha recovers from the shock and barrels toward me. I find a foothold in the trunk and start climbing.

Romisha's yelling orders at someone, and I hear doors opening across the garden as people come to see what's happening. I look up for the next branch and grab on as Romisha lunges for my foot and catches it. I hang on as tight as I can, wrapping my arms around the branch. I kick blindly with my free foot, seeing nothing but bark and leaves and a sliver of sky. Pain shoots up my leg as Romisha yanks hard on it, but she's not strong enough to pull me down. I twist and kick with all my might, hitting nothing but air and the occasional branch until finally my foot strikes something soft. There's a yelp of pain, and her grip loosens enough that I wrench free.

I swing myself up, throwing my left leg over the branch I'm holding, and wrap myself around it. Something snaps as my full weight lands on the limb, and it quivers so hard that for a second I think it's going to fall. But it holds, thank God it holds. I'm out of Romisha's reach, but someone will start climbing up after me any second, probably.

I straighten up and face the trunk of the tree again. Untangling myself from the branch wastes precious seconds. The tree rustles as someone comes up after me. I climb like my life depends on it, which it probably does since Romisha will kill me if she gets her hands on me. The tree is so much bigger than it looked before. It's an unending tree, and I'll never get to the top; it'll keep going and going and going until I can't hold on anymore.

But now I'm near the top, it's real, and the garden wall is a few feet away. The branches here are thinner, and they snap all over the place, so I only have a few seconds before I plummet to the ground.

Don't look down.

I scan the wall for a handhold, but there's nothing. The

wall is farther than I thought, and I can't reach it from here. I have to jump.

The top of the wall looks narrow, and if I miss it's all over. But I've come this far, and it's too late to turn back.

I jump.

The world spins as I go flying, and my knees hit the wall with a jolt. My hands scrabble desperately against the rough stone. But soon everything stops moving and I've done it, I'm on the wall.

I steady myself and sit up. Sister Romisha is at the bottom of the tree, screaming. One of the younger Sisters, a new one whose name I can't remember, is halfway up the tree. Sister Perla is in the garden now with Sister Morgila, and they're both looking at me like I've lost my mind. And in the corner, right about where I left them, are Bird Lady and her daughter, mouths hanging open, scandalized.

I grin at Sister Morgila. "Thanks for all your help, Sis," I call, "but I can take it from here."

I swing my legs around, grab the opposite edge of the wall with both hands, and lower myself down. It takes a second to find a foothold but I manage it, and I fall the last few feet. Then my shoes hit the pavement.

I'm free. I'm on the other side of the wall.

I take off running. Someone will probably come chasing after me any moment, but I don't care. I can go wherever I want, run as fast as I want. I'm free.

Chapter Two

Unfortunately, being completely free means being completely on your own.

I didn't know this before, but the reality hits me hard after the excitement wears off. I have nowhere to go and no food and no money and no anything.

Azeland is a patchwork city, with buildings of all different types and sizes and materials thrown together, as if scattered haphazardly by a giant hand. Still, there are divisions, some neighborhoods nicer than others. The orphanage sits just outside a round "plaza" that's mostly just rundown secondhand shops. I skirt the edges of the plaza, not wanting to be seen by anyone, but keep to the south side of the city on instinct. That's where the marketplaces and the farms and the poorer shops are. My past experience proved people on the north side will call the protectors if they see me running around. I'm too dirty and orphaned-looking to ever fit in there.

I run as far as I can manage, but before long I'm doubled over in the street, a burning stitch in my side. I'm used to running, but not this much. I can't catch my breath, and my hands burn. They're bleeding, scraped up from the tree and the rock wall, and so are my skinned knees. Great, just one more problem to worry about.

First, I have to get cleaned up. I'm too dirty even for the south side. Besides, word might get out about my escape, and someone will call the protectors on me for sure.

I look around, taking in my surroundings. I'm in the middle of a narrow cobbled street, lined with small, dingy shops. Faded signs advertising clothing stores and furniture repair lean dejectedly above poorly-constructed doors. Judging from the trash piled in the gutter and the boards on the windows, the street is mostly deserted. Footsteps and voices drift from up ahead, so I keep moving, cautiously this time.

Around the corner is a restaurant. A popular one, by the looks of things, in the middle of the lunchtime rush. Perfect.

I follow a family inside, keeping out of sight. The aroma of fresh bread wafts out of the open double doors, churning my stomach. I imagine the softness of the warm, fresh bread, with creamy butter melting on my tongue, and my mouth waters.

The interior is dimly lit and smoky. Dishes clatter, drowning out the low rumble of voices. As the people in front of me head toward the seating area, I spot a sign for the bathroom and head straight toward it. It's empty. I lock the door.

A small mirror is tacked above the sink in the corner. Even though I'm tall for twelve, I still have to stand on tip-toe to see myself in it. A thin, dirty girl stares back at me, a smudgy bruise encircling one of her muddy brown eyes.

I wash off the dirt and blood and tree bark and who-knows-what-else as best I can, which helps my appearance some. But there's nothing I can do about my clothes, which were new a hundred years ago, or my hair, a matted mess of curls which has been in need of a good trim for basically my entire life. A hairbrush would help, maybe. . . . I try to brush it with my fingers, but it's so knotted that I give up.

As I stand there, staring at my reflection in the chipped mirror, the enormity of what I've done finally sinks in. I am alone. Worse than that, I'm a fugitive now. They threatened to throw me in jail when I tried to escape last time, and I'm guessing they'll make good on that threat this time. I'll be locked in a tiny room with no light and no air and the walls closing in on all sides.

My hands shake. I close my eyes and take a few deep breaths to steady myself, but I can't get the picture of a stark prison cell out of my head. Even the walls of the bathroom seem to be shrinking, collapsing on me. My breaths come faster, more shallow, and I can't breathe, can't breathe, can't—

I turn the faucet on again and cup my hands under the stream. The water is freezing. I splash my face, feeling the little pinpricks of cold all over. The jolt to my senses clears my head. I gulp, but the air is so smoky my chest tightens.

A fist pounds on the door, hard and insistent. "Anyone in there?"

"Just—just a minute," I call back, trying to sound older. I turn off the water, wipe my face dry, and glance in the mirror one last time. This will have to do.

I unlock the door and walk out. The woman stares at me, but I don't look at her, trying to act natural. Now, if only I could find a way to get some food—

A protector.

He's just walked in the main doors, right in front of me. He wears a standard red uniform, complete with a silver badge and lots of sharp, pointy weapons. The glint of silver and steel flashes a warning: Run.

The imagined taste of metal chokes me, sharp steel edges pressing against skin. Not again. I run back up the hall, past the bathroom, as far away as I can go.

I hear a shout but don't look back. The hallway forks and I choose a path at random, only to find myself at a dead end in front of a single door. I shove it open, race through, and look for exits. Stairs loom up out of the darkness. I take them three at a time, praying I don't fall.

The family must live above the restaurant, and I'm in their apartment now. There's a small kitchen, a worn sofa, and a hallway lined with doors. Sunlight streams through the window across from me, and I glimpse weathered wood. The roof.

I head for the window, shove aside the thin red curtains,

and examine the pane. It's simple enough to open, like the windows at the Carrians' house. I lift it up, it slides an inch, and then . . . it sticks. It won't open any farther, no matter how hard I shove.

I slam the window back down. In one corner the dirty glass is cracked. It's been hit before, by a ball maybe, and smaller cracks trail out from the corner like a spider's web.

I search for something heavy and find a kitchen chair. I slam it against the window, legs first. The window splinters with a crash, and some glass drops out of the pane, leaving a hole. But it's not big enough.

Behind me, the door to the apartment thuds open. "Freeze!" a deep voice yells.

I don't turn around. I lift the chair and slam the window again, and with another crash the glass shatters into a thousand pieces.

There's a loud crack, and something hot whizzes past my ear. I duck just in time. Oh God, he's using magic.

"Don't move!"

I'm too close to freedom to stop now. I haul myself onto the windowpane, grabbing the frame for balance. Another crack sounds, and something flashes through the air, coming right at me—

Heat engulfs my right hand, and the wall beneath it explodes.

I don't even have time to see what's happening. I climb through the window onto the outer ledge, my burning hand dangling uselessly. Below me, part of the roof juts out from the restaurant, and it's an easy jump from the window. The hard part is getting down from there.

I look around. I'm above the alleyway behind the restaurant. Where I'm standing is too high to jump from, but the roof slants down at a sharp angle. All I have to do is walk to the lower part of the roof and jump from there.

Good thing I'm not afraid of heights.

I should probably be more cautious, take it slow so I don't fall off, but the protector's footsteps sound right behind me, and I doubt he's out of magical ammo. In a few steps I'm across the roof, at the edge of the slant, only a few feet from the ground.

I sit down on the edge, let my legs dangle off, and lower myself as much as I can.

Behind me, what remains of the window bursts apart with a tremendous crash, pieces of glass and wood skidding across the roof. The protector fires again with a crack.

I let go.

The fall hurts, but I land on my feet, and I haven't broken any bones. Success.

I've had quite enough falling for one day, but I still have to run.

Luckily, running is what I do best.

The first time I ran away, I went through a window in the Carrians' house. I didn't have any sort of plan, but it didn't matter. I'd had enough. They seemed all right at first, the Carrians. But it all went wrong so fast, when it became obvious that I wasn't the perfect daughter they were looking for. All I remember of that first night with them is people saying how "adorable" I was and patting my head and bringing me gifts I didn't like—lots of pink and lace and sparkles, which isn't me at all—and asking questions about the orphanage that they didn't really want the answers to. When I tried to be honest, everyone got really uncomfortable and averted their eyes. Mrs. Carrian's smile got more and more manufactured as the night wore on, less teeth and more thinly-pressed lips, and I began to realize that I was not what they were expecting.

I tried to stick it out, honestly. But the neighbor kids kept picking fights with me, and I didn't want to wear the frilly dresses, and the tutor they hired kept pursing her lips and frowning, and all these things made the Carrians upset. Then I overheard Mrs. Carrian crying to Mr. Carrian, and she said my name, and she used the word "mistake." I knew what was coming. They hated me, and they were sending me back. I wasn't about to let that happen.

So, out the window I went.

I'm embarrassed to say how quickly the protectors found me. I was back in the orphanage a few hours later. But, in my defense, I was only six.

The second time, I was eight, and it was the Puceys' house, and I didn't even have to escape, really, since they didn't care if I ran or not. This time, I'd hated them right from the beginning. Having been thoroughly disillusioned with the whole adoption thing, I pitched a fit when the Puceys first showed up. But Sister Morgila gave me this spiel about how they just had to find the right "match" for me, and I believed her. (I was eight, and stupid.) So I went with the Puceys: Mrs., who looked like a dried prune and smelled like dishwater; Mr., who was never actually present long enough for me to determine *what* he was like; and their three kids, who sucked up all Mrs. Pucey's attention. At first I couldn't figure out why they even wanted another kid, but then it dawned on me: I was the charity child. Mrs. Pucey would make us all dress up for church and then parade us around, her perfect family plus the poor little orphan girl who had been so heroically rescued. The rest of the time, they did not particularly care where I was or what I did, except when I got into trouble. And I got into trouble a lot. It was all starting to look so horribly familiar. I packed my bag and walked out. I suspect part of the reason I was able to avoid detection for longer that time is that they didn't even notice I was gone.

I lasted a couple of days, living in the alley behind a sweets shop. I thought the owner was on my side—he was nice, and gave me huge chunks of white chocolate. Then he called the protectors.

I haven't been out on the streets since then. When I tried to escape from the orphanage a few years ago, I never made it that far. So I guess you could say that my street experience is next to nothing. The sweets-shop man taught me an important rule, though: Trust no one.

My first concern now, when I can spare a moment to breathe, is my injured hand. I don't even know what that protector was firing at me, but I know it was magic. Outwardly, there are no signs of injury, but hours later my hand still burns. The black substance that coated it before seems to have seeped through the skin; small black lines trail across the back of my hand like inky veins. I'm not sure if it's permanent, but eventually the pain dies down, so I decide to worry about more pressing concerns.

My second problem is hunger. I start hunting for scraps, but it's not as easy as I thought it would be. Any leftover food is picked off quick by stray animals roaming the streets. The few outdoor trash bins behind shops have been ransacked and picked clean already. All the shops keep their doors locked.

The orphanage taught me not to be picky about what I eat, so I take food when I can get it. But the lack of food at the orphanage was nothing compared to this. I can't ignore the hunger anymore.

So I set out on a mission.

The marketplace teems with people, and I'm afraid someone will spot me if I try to steal there. So I pick the most rundown shop I can find, which has paint so faded I can't tell what color it used to be, thinking I won't look out of place inside. That much is true. The shop is as dirty as I am, which is saying something. But there's food.

Inside, the walls and floor are gray, streaked with dirt and dust. There's only one other customer in the shop. Ignoring the knot of fear in my stomach, I head over to the food shelves.

I wait, pretending to examine some of the items for sale. The customer heads to the register, distracting the shopkeeper. It's now or never. I take a deep breath, my hand shaking, and reach for the shelves. I start slipping little packages into my pockets. I'm not even sure what I'm taking, just that it's food and it's here. When my pockets are full, I turn and head for the door.

Only to bump right into a protector, who has chosen this exact moment to walk in.

I must have seriously offended Saint Ailara at some point in my life.

The protector takes one look at my guilty expression and slightly bulging pockets and stops. His hand moves toward the knives in his weapons belt. "Miss, I'm going to have to ask you to empty your pockets."

I try to look innocent. "Sir, I really don't think that's necessary."

His jaw tightens. "I'll be deciding what's necessary. Now please, empty your pockets. There's no need for any trouble here."

"You're the one causing the trouble." The words are out of my mouth before I think about it. Idiot. Why couldn't I keep my mouth shut for once in my life?

His eyes narrow. "Miss," he says through clenched teeth, "I'm going to have to arrest you for uncooperation if you don't—"

"*Un*cooperation?" I repeat. I can't help it. I may not have paid any attention in language class, but Sister Romisha accused me of noncooperation enough times that I have to laugh. "I think you mean *non*cooperation. *Non*, not *un*. Even I know that. Apparently they're letting any idiot become a protector these days."

Apparently I'm an idiot too.

His face reddens, and he pulls a weapon out of its sheath. Just seeing it makes me think of the first time I ran away, of being six and cold and scared and having the hard edge of a knife pressed against my skin, but my fear is mixed with anger, too. I'm so tired of running. I've spent my whole life running, but the protectors and their knives always find me.

"Sorry," I say quickly, reaching into my pockets, "I didn't mean that. See, I'm emptying my pockets now. . . ." My fingers close around one of the packages.

I pull it out, throw it at his face, and run.

He's not as slow as Sister Romisha, though. He's on me before I get out the door. His hand grabs the back of my shirt and it's over—

A scream pierces the air. The guard whirls around, taking me with him, still not loosening his grip. The customer now has a knife to the shopkeeper's throat.

"Let go of the girl," the customer says, real calm. He's a

boy, not much older than me, but there isn't any fear in his voice or expression. He's totally in control.

The protector's hand starts shaking. "Put away your weapon!"

Right, like he's just going to listen.

The boy smirks. "Nobody needs to get hurt. Release the girl, and we'll be on our way. Otherwise . . ." He moves the knife a little. The shopkeeper makes a sort of strangled whimper.

The protector lets go of me, and I stagger backward. The boy mutters to the shopkeeper, and they both start moving. Slowly, they shuffle past me and the protector toward the door. I bolt for the exit.

I'm out. I should keep running, but I turn back to the door of the shop.

The boy walks backward through the door, holding the shopkeeper between himself and the protector like a shield. Abruptly, he lets go, spins around, and races toward me.

"Run!" he yells.

I don't need to be told twice.

Instinct tells me to get away from the boy. He's dangerous. But he seems to know where he's going; he runs purposefully, not randomly like me. Following him seems like a good idea. Anyway, he just saved me.

So I follow him through the twists and turns of the streets and the crowds of a marketplace, whizzing past food stands until the cobbles turn to dirt under my feet. The streets grow narrower, the stalls and crowds disappearing, until we're in a tight alleyway, wedged between two small shops. I've never been in this part of the city before, but it looks the same as the rest of the south side: dim, dirty, and mostly neglected.

Finally we both stop, leaning against an alley wall and gasping. We don't say anything for a minute, just try to catch our breath. The dust we've kicked up from the street clogs my nose. The stone of the wall behind me scrapes against my skin, but I'm glad to have something solid to lean against.

I look at him closely for the first time. Like me, he has unruly black hair that's been poorly cut and possibly never combed. But his skin is an even darker tan than mine, and his eyes are a warmer brown. His limbs are skeletally thin, his knees and elbows bony and sharp. He's probably about thirteen.

He's staring at me, too, and we just look at each other for a couple of minutes until I can't take the silence anymore. "What did you do that for?" I ask. It sounds more accusatory than I mean.

He raises his eyebrows. "Is this your way of thanking me for saving you?"

"I had everything under control," I say, even though I didn't and we both know it. Softer, I add, "Why did you help me?"

"You needed help. And I'm no fan of the protectors myself." He hesitates. "And thieves help each other."

I guess it should've been obvious by now, but this still surprises me. "You're a thief?" I take another look at his clothes. Long pants, a plain cotton shirt, sturdy shoes. They're not nearly as bad as mine—a little grungy, maybe, but not patched or frayed or faded.

He hesitates again, like he's about to say something else. "I'm Beck," he says finally, extending his hand. "Beck Reigler."

I shake it. "Alli Rosco." In that brief second before our hands drop, it occurs to me that I should be scared of him. I just saw him hold a knife to a man's throat. But I'm not scared. It's something about the way he did it—like it was easy. He's tough, and unafraid.

There's another long silence as he looks like he wants to say something but never does. Then, "That was your first time stealing from a shop, wasn't it?"

I start to deny it, but there's no point. "How did you know?"

The corner of his mouth quirks up. Heat floods my face, and I glare at him. "Glad you find it amusing." I turn away.

"Wait." The trace of a smile is gone. "I'm sorry. It's not funny."

I want to just walk away, but . . . I need to know. I need to know what I'm doing wrong. So I turn around, hands on my hips, and scowl at him. "What? What do you want?"

"Look," he says, "I can help you. I know . . . well, I know how hard it is to live on the streets. And—"

"Why are you so interested in me?" I don't trust him. He's like the man in the sweets shop, all nice and friendly until he betrays you. He starts to speak again, but I cut him off. "Look, I appreciate your help back there, all right? But I can take it from here."

He shakes his head. "No offense, but you won't last five minutes. The streets will eat you alive if you don't know what you're doing. I've seen it happen. But I can teach you—"

"For your information," I say furiously, "I don't want your help. Save your concerns for someone who cares." I turn away again. I can figure out what I'm doing wrong by myself.

"Do you have anywhere to stay tonight, Alli?" he says quietly. "I know of a place, if you want."

I don't speak. He waits for a minute, then shrugs and turns around. "I'll just go, then."

He walks away, toward the other end of the alley.

It's stupid. I shouldn't do it. I don't trust him. There must be a catch.

But I'm curious, and I don't know what to do on my own. I don't have anything to lose.

"Wait," I say. He stops. "I changed my mind. I'm coming."

Chapter Three

B eck leads me to a street that looks totally abandoned, just like the one outside the orphanage. All the buildings have peeling paint and broken windows, and the grass grows up around them like a snare. The street is unpaved and strewn with garbage and mud. It's like the whole world's forgotten about this place.

It's perfect.

Beck's hideout is an old clothing shop. The paint on the front sign has faded so much that I can't tell what it used to say. The front door and windows are heavily boarded and stained with graffiti. A lone shingle dangles precipitously from the roof, probably knocked loose during a storm.

Beck and I trip over the uneven ground in the narrow, dark alleyway between buildings to reach the back of the shop, where Beck shows me how the old door pops off its broken hinges. Just like that we're inside, but no one can tell we've ever been here. Beck's reasons for choosing this place become obvious as I look around. The back room we're standing in is full of cardboard boxes, and those boxes are piled high with a seemingly random variety of clothing. Up front, there's a table with a cash register in the corner. Another corner houses two dressing rooms, and the rest of the space is racks and racks of clothing, in all sizes. Almost everything is coated in a fine layer of dust, and some of the clothes look moth-eaten, but otherwise it's all still wearable.

Seeing my jaw drop, Beck smiles. "Take whatever you want."

I find some bags in the corner and grab a particularly large pack to throw extra clothes in. I wander among the racks, looking for things in my size. I seize a sturdy-looking pair of pants, a cotton shirt, and a dark red jacket with plenty of pockets. I change clothes in one of the dressing rooms, leaving my old patched things on the floor. I remove the few packages of food I managed to steal from the shop and put them in my bag. Unfortunately, this shop doesn't have any shoes, so I'll make do with my old ones.

I find Beck in the back room. He's using one of the boxes like a table and laying food out on it: bread, a strip of meat, an apple. "Help yourself," he says.

This is a suspiciously generous offer, but I'm too hungry to refuse. The fresh bread tastes like heaven and I devour it all in one breath. Beck eats more slowly, but meticulously—he doesn't waste a single crumb. He's used to being hungry too.

"You never answered my question," I say after several

minutes of silent eating. "How did you know I'd never done that before?"

"You picked the wrong kind of shop," he says. "There are a lot of thieves in this part of town. Shopkeepers over here know what signs to look for. And there are more protectors on patrol, as you discovered."

I frown. "So what's the right kind of shop?"

"This kind," he says. "The abandoned kind. There are lots of places like these, if you know where to look. And for food, the marketplaces are the best. There are so many people around that no one will notice you."

"But more people means more chances you'll be spotted," I argue.

He shakes his head. "Everyone in the marketplace is too distracted by what they're doing to pay attention to anyone else. There're so many people that no one will see you if you blend in right. Don't take too much from one place. Take a little bread here, an apple there, and no one will notice."

There's something funny about the way he says the word "bread" that distracts me. "You're not from Azeland," I say, almost to myself.

His jaw tightens. "How did you know that?"

"You have an accent," I say. "You try to hide it, but it's there."

For a long moment he doesn't say anything. In seconds he's closed something off, hiding it from me. Then he says, "I knew I was right about you."

"Right about what?"

"I thought you were like most of the other kids out here, at first. Stupid, clueless. But then . . . the way you talked back to the protector. You weren't scared. You were defiant. And I thought, maybe there's hope for you yet."

I don't know what to say to that. What I said to the protector was stupid, not defiant. I'd never admit it out loud, but he's the one who got us out of there.

He's definitely hiding something from me. Maybe I can keep him talking. "So where *are* you from? And what are you doing here?"

"Arat," he says. Which is weird. Arat is the name of the mountain, not the city where everyone lives. The orphans I knew who'd been born there would say they were from Ruhia. Which makes me think he's not from Ruhia. But there is definitely something northern about his accent, like the Ruhian orphans. And if not there, where?

He adds, "I'm here because I was . . . looking for someone."

"I see," I say curtly, making it clear I'm not buying it.

"What about you? You're an Azeland native?"

"Yeah." For the sake of full disclosure, I add, "I think so. I mean, I don't know exactly where I was born, but I've lived here as long as I can remember."

He nods and doesn't question it. "So. Alli. What are you running from?"

"What makes you think I'm running?"

He raises his eyebrows. "You're out on the streets alone.

You don't know how to steal, so you've never done this before. You don't have anything with you, not even a change of clothes, and the ones you've got haven't been new in a while. You're running from *something*."

I scowl. "What makes you think you know me? You've talked to me for five seconds and you think you know everything?"

"Tell me I'm wrong."

"If you're so smart, tell me where I'm running from," I taunt.

He seems to think about it for a minute, surveying me like I'm a puzzle he's piecing together. His eyes widen. "You're that girl. The one who jumped the wall at Sisters of Harona this morning." He sounds impressed.

There's no point in denying it now. I can't think of a reason to lie. "Yeah, that was me."

"Everyone was talking about it. No one's ever escaped from Harona's before. How'd you do it?"

"Easy. The guards were all busy on Adoption Day, not in the garden like usual. I walked right out, climbed a tree, jumped the wall. Oh, and I threw a drink in Sister Romisha's face."

He smiles slightly. "Bet they never saw that one coming. But . . ." He trails off, looking confused. "If you were about to be adopted and get out of there, why run?"

I sigh. "Adoption isn't what everyone thinks it is. It's not some paradise. What nobody tells you about adoption is that when you hate the family, or when they hate you, you're stuck with them and there's nothing you can do about it except run away, which I did. Twice."

There's silence for a second as he takes this in. "You were adopted *twice*?"

"Yeah. Both times it was awful and I tried to run, but the protectors caught me. And then the families didn't want me anymore and I didn't want them, so they put me back in the orphanage. I knew it would happen again. So I thought, why not skip the awful part and run now?"

He nods. "Yeah, I get that. How long were you there?"

"Total? Nine years. Before now, I hadn't been out since I was eight."

He looks suitably impressed. "What are you going to do, now that you're out?"

"I haven't thought that far ahead," I admit. "But I'm twelve now, so I thought maybe I could pass for thirteen and get a job somewhere."

"But, if you're almost thirteen, you were about to leave the orphanage anyway. Why'd you run *now*?"

"What, you think I should've waited around so they could just dump me somewhere? No thank you. Being abandoned once was enough."

"Ah."

"Besides, I still have, like, half a year to go before my birthday, and who wants to wait that long?"

The corners of his mouth curl into a smile. "Practically

an eternity," he says, with all the smugness of someone who doesn't have to wait for *his* thirteenth anymore. But it occurs to me that if he's thirteen, the labor laws no longer apply to him. He should have a job and not be living in an abandoned clothing shop.

"How old are *you*, anyway?" I say.

"I'll be thirteen in eight days. My birthday's the first of Mirati's Month."

My eyes widen. He shares his birthday with Saint Samyra, the patron of intelligence and cunning. To be born on a saint's day is supposed to be a sign of their favor, and Samyra is definitely one you want to have on your side. "So, what are you planning to do for the big birthday?"

"I'm going back to Arat."

I wait, but he doesn't elaborate. "Did you find the person you were looking for, then?"

"Yeah," he says. "Yeah, I did."

"And?"

"And . . . well, I was looking for this, uh, friend because he was supposed to be back home weeks ago. I thought maybe something bad had happened. Turns out he was arrested. For theft."

"Oh." The way he says it makes me think he's telling the truth, but he's also leaving something out. "So, if your friend lives in Ruhia with you, why'd he come here?"

"I don't know. He didn't tell me."

It's obvious he's holding something back, but I still think

35

he's being honest. I don't know why I believe him, but I do. Maybe it's because he saved me from that protector, or because he took me here when he didn't have to, but I like Beck. I don't know if it's right to trust him, but I like him.

By now we've finished all the food, but I'm still not full. Beck sees me looking wistfully at the empty box-turned-table and guesses what I'm thinking. "Still hungry?"

"Yeah," I admit. "But it's fine. I don't want to eat everything—"

"Don't worry about it. I'll get more in the morning. I can show you how, if you want."

"Okay," I say, standing. As I turn, I notice for the first time a small pallet of blankets and clothing heaped in the corner. A makeshift bed.

Beck follows my gaze. "We'll have to get you one too. I don't know how many more blankets there are, but there are some big winter coats that should work. . . ." He trails off, already heading into the main room, hunting among the racks.

I follow him and stand in the doorway, watching him comb through the racks for a suitable blanket. He's done so much for me just in the last few hours. I hate to get all mushy and everything, but it seems wrong to let him do all this without at least thanking him.

"Beck."

He looks up.

"Thanks. I mean, for letting me stay here and giving me

your food and—and for helping me with the protector. I really—"

He looks down, his mouth twisting into a pained frown.

"What's wrong?" I ask. "Beck?"

"Don't thank me," he says, not looking up.

"Why not?"

"Just . . . don't."

He looks guilty.

"What aren't you telling me?" I say. "What did you do?"

He still doesn't look up. "It—it was my fault. Back at the shop. It was my fault you almost got caught in the first place."

Too late, the explanation occurs to me. How odd it was that another thief happened to be in the same shop I was, and then a protector walked in at the exact same moment.

Beck already told me that shop wasn't the kind he would steal from, and there wasn't anything in there worth buying that he couldn't have stolen in the marketplace.

He wasn't there to buy, or to steal. He was there to hide.

The truth is all over his face.

He looks at me and knows that I know, but I say it anyway. "That protector was following you."

He takes a step toward me. "I'm sorry. It's not like I knew you'd be in there, and I was hoping I'd lost him in the crowd—"

For some reason, his apology just makes me furious. A wave of anger washes over me, blurry and red like it always is before I lose control. I step back, away from him. "This whole time you've been acting like you saved me because you're a good person, you just wanted to help, you know what it's like, you felt sorry for me, whatever. Because you *liked* me. But it's because you felt guilty."

"That's not—"

"It was your fault he was there. If I'd been caught, it would've been your fault."

"Well," he says, "all right, yeah, but that's not—that's not the only reason I—"

"You lied to me." I clench my fist, feeling the anger boiling up inside. "This whole time you wanted me to believe that I don't know what I'm doing, I'm a bad thief, I need your help or the protectors will get me! None of it was true, was it? I was doing just fine on my own. I would've gotten away if you hadn't been there. But you wanted me to think I needed you." My voice comes out a bit strangled at the end. I had believed him. I'd thought I needed him. Thought he'd been honest with me. "I don't need you. I don't. I don't need anybody."

He looks at my clenched fist and backs away slowly. "You don't," he agrees. He doesn't really mean it.

"But Alli, that's not—that's not how it is, okay? I just wanted to help, that's all. I never lied to you. Everything I said before about wanting to help you was true." I open my mouth to say something, but he keeps going. "Yes, it was my fault the protector was there, and yeah, I felt guilty about that. But honestly, Alli, everything else I said was true too.

And even if—even if you don't need my help, I *can* help. I want to help."

I wish I could believe him. I really, really want to. And I hate myself for that. The sweets-shop owner who turned me in all those years ago taught me not to trust anyone, but I forgot so easily. I'm not even all that angry at *him*. He still saved me, regardless of what his reasons were. I was so stupid, so naive, when I knew not to believe anything anyone says.

"I don't even *know* you," I say, more to myself than to him. "Why do I believe you when I don't even know—" I remember the funny way he talked about being from Arat, and how vague he was about the "friend" he came to find here. "Where are you really from, anyway?"

"What?" He's still looking at me like I'm going to punch him at any moment. Maybe I am. But the anger is fading as quickly as it came. I still want an explanation, but my hand unclenches.

"You said you're from Arat, but nobody says that. People from Ruhia just say they're from Ruhia. Why didn't you?"

Realization spreads across his face. "You're right. That was stupid." He smiles hesitantly. "I didn't lie, I'm from Arat. I live—I live on the mountain. Not in the valley, where Ruhia is."

I consider this. "But I thought nobody lived on the mountain. It's uninhabitable, right? Except—oh." Now I'm the stupid one. "So you live in Hesmea? On the peak?"

He looks slightly confused for a second, but then his

smile returns. "Right. From Hesmea. The peak."

He's lying. This still doesn't add up. "But then, why didn't you say so?"

He looks sheepish. "Well, I don't know how it is here, but in Ruhia there's a stigma about people who live on the peak. Most people think of Hesmeans as lonely old hermits in igloos . . . they think it's weird to live there, you know? Because the weather at the peak is so extreme."

I could push him on this, but the anger is gone, and now doesn't seem like the right time. "Oh, here in Azeland we think that about everyone living anywhere near Arat," I say, smiling to let him know I've calmed down. "Ruhians included. I mean, doesn't it snow, like, every day there?"

He smiles back. "In Hesmea, yes. But not in Ruhia. Ruhian winters are bad, though. During the heavy snows you can be trapped inside for weeks."

"And I thought *our* winters are bad."

"Your winters are nothing. Our winters mock your winters."

"Yeah, but our summers are brutal. You wouldn't survive a single day of our summers." I grin as another thought occurs to me. "That's why you're going back to Arat by the first of Mirati's! You can't handle even the first day of our summer!"

He scowls, but I know he's faking it. "Well, I'd like to see you last one day during a Hesmean winter."

"I bet you five majas I could do it. Or I would if I had five majas."

"Majas?" he scoffs. "Please. Hesmeans only bet in jamars."

"Whatever. Our currency is *so* superior to your currency."

We both laugh then, and we both pretend that the tension of a few minutes earlier didn't happen.

I know he lied to me, but I don't say anything. Yet.

Chapter Four

I catch the sounds of the marketplace before we reach it—voices chattering and shouting, footsteps pounding, canvas tents flapping, coins clinking. The smells drift after the sounds. Spices swirl through the air, making my stomach grumble. Bright splotches of red and green and yellow appear as we draw closer, painted tents glimmering in the sunshine, and soon we're in the center of it, a whirl of colors and sounds and smells that bursts around us. Today the crowd adds to the heat as the sun beats down, but the air tastes of another late-spring rain.

The bustle and noise of the crowd masks us, so we don't have to worry about being overheard. As we walk, Beck gives me some advice. Thieving advice. He has an arrogant way of talking about thieving strategies, like he knows everything there is to know about it. It grates on my nerves, but I keep my mouth shut.

"Rule number two: Don't draw attention to yourself, and you won't get caught."

"What's rule number one?" I think of my own rule: Trust no one.

"You already know it," he says. "Rule number one: Stealing is necessary to survive."

Yeah, I learned that one pretty fast.

The first time Beck takes something from a marketplace stall, I don't even notice he's done it until, a few feet away, he passes me the piece of fruit he swiped.

"How'd you do that?"

"Practice." He grins, and although it's annoying, it's also sort of infectious. I grin back without meaning to, but hide it by biting into the fruit. The juice bursts into my mouth, tarter than I expected, but still sugary. The mix of sour and sweet lingers on my tongue as we wind through the crowd.

The second time Beck steals, I pay more attention. With every furtive glance around, he's surveying the crowd, looking for protectors or observant shopkeepers, waiting for the right moment. His movements are subtle, seeming to shift with the flow of the people around us, never out of synch. "Rule number three," he says softly. "Always scan the crowd for anyone who looks suspicious. Protectors aren't always in uniform."

He might as well be talking about the weather. He's totally casual, totally calm, like he was when he saved me from that protector. He's patient.

If patience is a requirement for being a good thief, I might as well give up now.

I say as much to Beck, and he laughs. "You might be a bit too hasty," he agrees, "but that comes from being new at it. At first you want to grab everything fast. The trick is not to be too rushed."

Rule number four: Be quick, but not reckless.

"So what should I look for?" I ask. "If protectors aren't in uniform?"

"Concealed weapons," Beck says. "They sometimes try to hide them at the shoulder or ankle or waist, and that's the most obvious sign. They'll also be wearing heavier clothing, even in summer, in order to hide their weapons underneath, so look for that, too. But more importantly, look at their eyes."

"Their eyes?"

"An ordinary person in the market will be focused on the stalls, seeing what's for sale, or talking to the people beside them. But protectors? They won't be looking at the stalls or the goods. They'll be scanning the crowd."

"Like us," I say.

Beck nods. "If you see someone scanning the crowd, it's most likely either a protector or a thief. Either way, someone you want to avoid."

Weapons, clothes, eyes. "Got it."

"Okay, now it's your turn," he says.

I nod. "No problem."

I watch the crowd, looking for a warning flash of red or an overly attentive shopkeeper. Beck's rule number five is to choose a mark who's distracted, so I find a busy stall where the owner is preoccupied. Fresh produce sits out in neat little rows, glistening in the sun.

The prickling feeling on my back hints that Beck's watching me as I slip closer to the stall. The owner is a middle-aged man with dirt stains on his shirt. He's haggling with a woman over the cost of some leafy plant thing. *Now, move now—*

"Daddy?"

I freeze. From the tent behind the stall, a little girl emerges. She tugs insistently on the man's hand. "Daddy . . ."

"Not now," the man murmurs, his attention not wavering from the customer in front of him. "As you can see, my produce is among the finest in Azeland. I'm sure you'll agree that this price is more than fair. . . ."

This is the thing I never liked about stealing. The people who are easy to steal from are the ones who don't have much. Will this girl be fed if I take food from her father?

One little piece of fruit couldn't hurt, right?

Besides, we all need to eat, me and Beck and this girl, and right now there's plenty of food laid out in front of her, and nothing for us.

Rule number one: Stealing is necessary to survive.

I can't look at the girl anymore. I pick a target from among the fruit, bright red and gleaming and fresh. I wait, and wait, until I'm sure I will crack with the waiting. . . .

No one's looking my way.

My hand darts forward, grabs the fruit—

"What is it, Lyll?" The man turns to look at his daughter. And sees me.

I'm frozen, one hand still wrapped around the fruit. Caught.

The man is in front of me in a half second, his eyes hard. "What are you doing?"

I think fast. "How much for this?" I ask, holding up the fruit.

The suspicion doesn't leave his gaze. "Two majas each."

I pretend to examine the fruit critically. "Really? Looks a little too ripe to me."

That distracts him. Vendors love to bargain. "You won't find better anywhere in Azeland, I guarantee it. Picked them myself."

The back of my neck prickles. No doubt Beck is watching me. And even though it would be so much easier to just walk away, I can't bear to fail. I can only imagine the arrogant remarks Beck will make when I walk back empty-handed. And the little girl has wandered back inside the tent, so now I only have this guy to worry about. . . .

"Two majas for three," the man is saying. "Final offer."

"On second thought," I say, "I'm not interested." I set the fruit in my hand down—and bump into the stand as I do. Several pieces of produce roll to the ground.

"Oh, I'm so sorry," I say. The man grunts and ducks

down to pick up the fallen fruit. Now's my chance, but I only have a few seconds.

I reach for a different, smaller piece, one he won't notice is missing.

My fingers circle around the soft spot of red, then my hand slips inside my jacket pocket and deposits it safely inside.

I've only just pulled my now-empty hand back out when the man stands up again. He's looking *very* suspicious. "Can I interest you in anything else?" he asks gruffly.

I linger for a moment, as though considering buying something. "No thanks," I say. "Have a nice day." I turn and melt into the crowd.

The little girl's voice still haunts me as I walk away, but I don't look back.

"Nice," Beck says dryly, appearing out of nowhere at my side.

"Hey, it worked," I say.

"You almost got caught."

"But I didn't."

He sighs. "Only because you talked your way out of it, which won't always be an option. You were way too hesitant in the beginning. Why'd you wait so long?"

I don't dare tell him about the little girl and my moment of weakness. "You told me not to be reckless."

"I also told you to be quick."

"Okay, okay. I get it. I'll be quicker."

This time I offer him the fruit. He smiles and reaches for

it. Even after it leaves my hand, the red stain from its juice remains on my fingertips. It reminds me of the weird black lines that still linger from the protector's attack yesterday, and I shove my hand back into my pocket.

Beck doesn't want to risk swiping from a market stall again, so he shows me how to pick pockets. As always, first he demonstrates for me. Every time, his targets—or "marks," as he keeps calling them—never even notice him, and it happens so fast that I almost miss it.

There are so many rules to remember. Be patient and wait for the right moment. Move fast. Never underestimate a mark, but wait until their guard is down and their attention is focused somewhere else.

There's one rule Beck doesn't say, but I add it to the list: Don't think too much about who the marks are. Looking at what they carry, not who they are, makes it easier to ignore the lurch in my stomach that might, maybe, be guilt.

Maybe that should be a rule too: There's no place for guilt in thieving.

At last, when Beck's convinced that I can do it on my own, I select a few marks. I'm not nearly as smooth as Beck, but in the chaos of the crowd no one seems to notice me. By the time the sun sets, we're fifty majas richer.

With my stomach finally satisfied, we head back to the clothing shop. I glance down at my right hand again. It's been aching all day. I expected the black lines of the protector's magic to fade over time, but if anything they've thickened.

They're longer now too—one reaches all the way up to my index finger, while another crawls across my wrist. I yank my shirtsleeve down farther and pretend the lines don't exist.

We walk in silent contentment, enjoying the feeling of the gold coins weighing down our pockets.

"I told you I'd be good at this," I say smugly.

"You were *okay*," he says, "but only because you had such a good teacher."

I roll my eyes. "That's ridiculous. I got more money than you did!"

Beck starts to reply but catches sight of something behind me. I turn and spot a merchant who's packing up her tent for the day at the edge of the marketplace. A rich, sweet scent floats over to us, even from twenty feet away. Chocolate.

Before I say anything, Beck races up to the woman. I run after him. "What are you doing?"

"We're celebrating. What do you want?" He gestures to the array of sweets laid out.

"We shouldn't spend any money on—" I stop speaking as something catches my eye and I can't resist. Anyway, the gold is clinking in my pockets like it's begging to be spent. "The white." I point. "I like white chocolate."

Beck gets a piece too and hands the woman some majas. As Beck and I walk down the street, eating our tiny pieces of candy as slowly as possible, I'm reminded of the last person who bought me this—the sweets-shop man.

And then there's that other thing, the hazy memory from

before the orphanage. It feels sweet in a way that reminds me of white chocolate. I think *he* might have been the one to give me chocolate for the first time. The older boy I can't quite remember, whose picture in my mind is fuzzy. His name is half-forgotten, on the tip of my tongue. But I know who he was.

My brother.

Beck catches sight of my frown. "What's wrong?"

"Nothing. It's just, it's been a really long time since I had this."

"Me too," he says quietly. "I haven't had chocolate since—I don't even know. Not since my mother died."

This is the first time he's said anything to me about his family, but I already figured he's an orphan. "I'm sorry. When did she . . . ?"

"Two years ago." He looks away from me, gazing into space.

"I'm sorry." I repeat it because I don't know what else to say.

Beck opens his mouth, but before the words come he stiffens, stopping in the middle of the street.

I freeze, instantly on alert for protectors, but there are no telltale signs of red. "What?" I whisper.

"Look."

I follow his gaze. Tacked below a nearby street sign is a black paper—a warning from the protectors.

Bright red letters scroll magically across the top. The

headline says, "Wanted: Orphanage Escapee."

And after the phrase "description of fugitive" is a description of *me*. And below the physical description is this:

Name: Alli Rosco. Age: 12.

Caution is advised. Fugitive is dangerous.

Reward for information. Report suspicious activity to the nearest protector.

"Well," I say, trying for flippancy but sounding squeaky, "that's a new development."

"Come on." Beck's voice is tight. "You need to get off the street."

We practically run until we reach the clothing shop. We start to turn into the alleyway, heading for the back door, but Beck freezes and grabs my arm. I stop too, instantly on alert.

"Something's in the alley," Beck whispers.

Now I hear it: a rough scratching sound.

Beck leans forward and peers around the corner. His whole body relaxes. "It's okay," he says, stepping forward.

I follow him, looking to see who the intruder is. "It's a cat?" Its eyes glow in the dark before it turns away from us. Claws skid through the dirt as it runs away.

"Yeah, it's just an alley cat." He smiles. "It's an *Alli*cat, get it?"

"Ha-ha," I say dryly. "You should be a comedian."

We eat our dinner—some more fruits from the market and day-old bread—on one of the boxes in the back room, like yesterday. During the meal, Beck calls me Allicat about a hundred times, just to annoy me. I pretend not to be amused.

We both make excuses about being tired and go to bed early, but I can't sleep at all, not with the words from that flyer floating around in my head.

Wanted.

Fugitive.

Dangerous.

Reward.

They're words that sound like they belong to someone else. Someone who actually knew what she was doing when she jumped that orphanage wall. If only I really *were* dangerous. Then I wouldn't have to worry about the protectors and their words and their weapons. Then I could sleep and not have to care about anything.

Apparently Beck can't sleep either; I can hear the rustling as he tosses and turns in the next room. It's just like in the orphanage, when a dozen of us would share a room. Everybody knew who had nightmares and who cried in their sleep, and everybody pretended not to know.

But this time it's going to be different. I'm not going to stick around here for long. Beck's nice and everything, but this can't last. I'll be better off on my own. That's something I learned early at the orphanage: Stick with people who are useful to you, and be prepared to ditch them when necessary. No point in making friends, especially with the littler kids—they're not useful, and they'll be gone quick anyway. But there were always groups of older kids who took charge, who became the unofficial leaders, and *those* were the kids you wanted to get in with. But even then, you have to be prepared for them to turn on you.

It's like when I spent ages hanging around with Striker and his little gang of stragglers. Striker established himself as the guy in charge pretty early on after he arrived at the orphanage, mainly because he was bigger than everybody else. I tried to make myself useful to him whenever possible, relaying insider information about the Sisters I'd gained over the years. In turn, Striker and the guys left me alone most of the time, which suited me perfectly. Plus they could always be counted on to cover for me when I skipped grammar lessons, or to help carry a jar of spiders into Sister Romisha's room.

Except then I got a little too trusting. As I planned my first escape attempt, I let Striker and the gang in on it. I asked them to play decoy for me and promised that once I was out I'd open the gates so they could escape too. That last part was a lie, and Striker knew it.

The next day Sister Morgila marched me down to her office and gave me the worst lecture of my life, followed by four months of extra chores. Turns out Striker had gone straight to Morgila after our little planning session and told her everything, hoping it would endear him to her and keep me in check. He wasn't wrong. From then on the Sisters all glared at me whenever I so much as spoke to one of the other kids, like I was inciting rebellion or something. Striker got promoted to prefect duty, which meant he only had to "supervise" while the rest of us did all the hard chores.

Of course, I wasn't going to let that stand for long. Striker had as good as declared all-out war, and I was ready. One day he woke to find himself stuck to the bed, covered in a sticky mixture of syrup, honey, glue, and whatever else I could sneak out of the storage closet. None of his homework assignments ever got turned in on time, having been mysteriously destroyed. His shampoo somehow dyed his hair blue. The walls of the front entryway got covered in bright red graffiti overnight, and incriminating evidence was found under his bed, resulting in his spending an entire week scrubbing the paint off the walls and floors.

He broke easily, in the end. Shortly after the graffiti incident, he asked me for a truce. I told him to do whatever I said and to stay out of my way, or things would only get worse.

From then on, *I* was in charge. I was careful not to abuse my power and push him too far, but he was there when I needed him. And once I became the girl in charge of Striker, nobody messed with me.

I was almost sorry when Striker left. Almost.

But I'd learned my lesson, again. *Trust no one.*

Not even nice boys who save you from protectors and show you their secret hideouts and teach you how to survive. I'll stick with Beck only for as long as he's going to be useful, and then I'm gone. It'll be better that way.

I roll over, trying to close my eyes, only to hear footsteps in the other room. A second later Beck comes in, holding a lit candle. "Did you hear something?"

"Yeah," I say, "it started raining." The raindrops beat a steady rhythm against the roof.

"Not that."

I start to say "Probably the cat," but the loudest bang I've ever heard shatters the silence like a cannon, and the front door of the shop falls to the floor.

People in red uniforms stand in the doorway.

I'm on my feet and running before I decide to move. I scramble after Beck, toward the back room. A deep voice yells at us, but I don't waste time listening.

Beck's at the door with me on his heels. A blinding flash fills the room, and Beck leaps to the side. Something bright and magical-looking flies past him, grazing his arm, and explodes against the far corner. With a burst of heat, flames flare up, licking the walls.

I just have time to see that Beck's shirt is burned where he was grazed before he grabs my hand and yanks me forward. The protectors are right behind us as we dart across the room, out the door, and into the rain.

I run harder than I've ever run, harder even than when I ran from the orphanage. The rain pounds against me, louder than everything except the rapid, panicked gasps of my own breath and the unsteady beat of my footsteps.

The streets widen and turn to cobbles again as Beck leads me north, but we make so many turns I soon lose all sense of direction. I don't know if the protectors are behind us. I don't even know where we are, or if Beck knows where he's going, or how they found us, or what we're going to do now that everything is ruined, or what *I'm* going to do now that Beck is going to ditch me to save himself. I don't know anything except how to run.

Until I'm done. I can't keep going. My footsteps falter as I wheeze out another breath.

"Almost there." Beck is still in front of me, still guiding me. I keep running.

He makes an abrupt left turn, squeezing between two buildings. I follow, my arms scraping against the stone of the narrow passageway until we emerge on the other side. Suddenly, the skyline is filled with shadowy, rustling shapes. Trees.

We run into the park. A low fence encircles it, but we vault over easily and keep going. Mud squelches under our feet as we cut across the sodden grass, darting for the cover of a cluster of trees.

Only when we're out of sight behind the trees does Beck stop.

"I think we lost them," he pants.

"Right," I gasp. At the moment I don't really care, I just want to stop running. "Now what?"

"Just give me a minute. Make sure they're not still following us."

"Okay." I turn around and gaze through the branches

of the nearest tree, scanning the park. "I don't see anyone. I don't know if they made it this far—"

I turn back to him, and a flash of blue catches my eye. I blink, and the flash is gone, just like that. I whirl in a circle, scanning the trees.

"What's wrong?"

"I thought I saw magic. I thought a protector was here."

Beck doesn't answer at first. "Come on," he says, "it's around here somewhere."

"What—" My eyes lock onto Beck's arm. "I thought you were hurt?"

His sleeve is still burned, but beneath the burned sleeve is—nothing. His arm looks fine.

"Nah, it just caught my sleeve."

He's lying, but I don't have time to argue. He's already weaving through the trees.

"Wait," I say, trudging after him. My feet tangle in the underbrush. "Beck—"

There's a wooden door in the ground.

Beck kneels down beside it, one hand digging in his pocket.

"What *is* this?" This is too much. Too many weird things are happening. The protectors shouldn't have been there and there shouldn't have been blue light and Beck's arm should be injured and there most definitely should not be doors in the ground.

"It's an old storage cellar," Beck says. His hand emerges

from his pocket, and something gold glimmers in his palm. I blink, but I'm not imagining it. I have no idea what he's holding, but it must be valuable. If I didn't know better, I'd say it was solid gold.

"Park maintenance used to store things in here," he continues, seemingly oblivious to the fact that anything unusual is happening. From this angle, I can't see exactly what he's doing, but the hand holding the gold object is pressed against the wood, and with a thud the door drops open, revealing a yawning hole in the ground.

Without a second of hesitation, Beck descends into the earth.

Chapter Five

After following Beck down a few rickety wooden steps, I find myself in a little earthen room. Somewhere there must have been a lantern and a match, and somehow Beck knows instantly where they are. In seconds there's a flickering light to see by, and Beck lowers the cellar door closed above us.

"Okay, now that we're hidden," I say, "you want to tell me what in Saint Ailara's name is going on?"

"Huh?" He looks genuinely confused, but it could be an act. "I don't know how the protectors found us, if that's what you mean, but I'm guessing someone saw you in the marketplace today and followed us to the shop."

"Not that." I shake my head, trying to clear it. *"This."* I wave my hand to indicate the space around us. "What is this place, and how did we get in, and how did you even know it was here?"

ALEXANDRA OTT

"I told you, old park cellar," he says with an unconvincing shrug. "I just did some exploring and—"

"And what's with your arm?" I interrupt. "I swear it was injured back at the shop, and now it looks fine. How did *that* happen? I know I'm not seeing things, and there really *was* a magic blue light in the woods. . . ."

He can't meet my eyes anymore. "I don't know what you're talking about."

"Do you really think I'm stupid? I know you're lying. And I know you lied to me last night. About being from Hesmea."

In a second his face goes tight, sealing something off. "What makes you say that?"

"I'm the one who suggested Hesmea, and you hesitated before you answered. You're not a very good liar, you know."

"I'm not," he agrees. "And I didn't want to lie to you. But—I don't know how to tell you the truth. And I don't know if I should."

Even though I know he lied to me, it hurts to hear him admit it. I curse myself for being so stupid. For liking him too much.

"I just asked you where you're from. It's not a complicated question."

"It is for me," he says. "I'm sorry. But it's not—it's not my secret to tell."

"What's so secret about where you live?" The anger surges up again, always hot and fast and uninvited, pulsing under my skin. I don't even know why I'm angry.

"I can't, Alli, I can't—"

"What? You can't trust me? Even though I trusted you?"

I'm not being fair. We barely know each other, and we *shouldn't* trust each other. But I don't care. I trusted him anyway, despite everything, despite common sense, and he lied to me. Again.

"I *can't*." There's an edge in his voice, but it's not anger.

"I've had it with you." I stand up. My hands shake, and I ball them into fists to hide it. "I don't even know why I'm still here. I don't know why I went with you in the first place."

I stomp over to the stairs. Beck doesn't move. I shove open the cellar door, storm out, let it bang closed behind me. And I run.

Trees leer out of the darkness like skeletons, limbs waving in the breeze. My feet skid and slip across the soggy ground, mud seeping into the cracks in my shoes.

I'm halfway across the park before I remember I have nowhere else to go.

But I won't go back. I won't.

The nearby street is completely dark. There are little noises all around me, animals scurrying. Probably rats.

"Alli." His voice is quiet.

"Go away," I say, but my voice catches and it comes out wrong. The rain is so cold. Why did I leave my jacket in the shop?

"I'm sorry," he says.

I don't turn around. "You keep saying that."

"It's always true."

"Whatever." But he did seem sincere. For some reason, I really want to trust him. I want him to give me a reason to trust him.

"Please, Alli, come back inside. I'll—" Abruptly his voice cuts off, sounding almost strangled.

Now I turn around. "Beck?"

He's staring at me, and horror is all over his face. He opens his mouth, but nothing comes out.

"What? What are you staring at?"

I follow his gaze, looking at my right side. A flickering light from his lantern is playing across my right hand. The black lines are barely visible in the lantern's glow, but it's clear that they're deeper than they were before.

Beck finally speaks, his voice a whisper. "What happened?"

"Why?" I'm not easily scared by anything, but his reaction is sending chills up and down my spine. "Do you know what this is?"

"You don't?" He's slowly regaining composure, but it's too late—I've already seen the fear. "You really don't know?"

"Do enlighten me," I say. "I have no idea what you're even talking about."

"What happened?" he says again, ignoring me. "Did you . . . did a protector do that? Hit you with magic?"

"Yeah. It was before I met you, right after I got out of the orphanage."

He mutters something, so fast I can't catch it.

"Why does it matter?"

He pauses. "We need to talk about this inside," he says quietly. "I think you need to sit down."

"Why should I go anywhere with you? How do I know you're not making all this up?"

"You'll just have to trust me. And honestly, if that is what I think it is, you don't have a choice. Please, come back inside and let me explain."

He might lie to me again, but I'm pretty good at spotting lies.

I sigh. "This had better be good."

Inside the cellar, we huddle against one wall, as if we're more secluded that way. Beck holds my hand under the light, examining it. The dark lines wrap around my fingers, crisscross the back of my hand, and trail off just past my wrist. They run under my skin alongside the blue lines of my veins—but the dark lines are thicker than the veins now.

"This is . . ." Beck seems to be unable to speak as he studies my hand. "This is not good."

The sight of the darkness crawling against my skin like an infection makes my stomach churn. "What *is* it? I thought it would just wear off, but it's been—"

"It's been getting worse," Beck finishes for me. He drops my hand and runs his own through his hair absently. "It's called Xeroth's Blood. It's a kind of magic, but it doesn't fade like an ordinary spell. It's a curse."

"Xeroth's Blood?" I repeat. I think I've heard of this before, or maybe just whispers of it. I don't know what it means, but anything named after the patron of death can't be good.

"It's like slow-acting poison. It starts at the source, where the magic touched you, and travels under the skin. It spreads everywhere, until . . ."

"Until what?"

"Until it reaches your heart," he says, so quietly I can barely hear him. "And then you die."

He's joking. He can't be serious.

For a second I can't breathe. "Wait a minute. And then you *die*? That doesn't make any sense! If a protector wanted to kill me, why not use a quick death spell or something? Why have a slow-acting curse as a weapon?"

"It's a marker," Beck explains. "Because it's visible under the skin, protectors sometimes use it to mark someone they're pursuing. They usually aim for the hands. The idea is that even if you escape, other citizens will see the mark and turn you in. Plus, you'll eventually have to get medical help, and then you'll be turned over to the authorities. If that protector had no proof of your guilt but suspected you of something, he wouldn't want to kill you, but he'd mark you so you couldn't escape for long."

Well, that explains why that protector was such a bad shot.

"Wait, you said something about seeking medical help. So there's a cure, right? Or a healer could . . . ?"

"Um." Beck picks at a thumbnail, not looking me in the eye. "That's the other bad news. Healers can't cure it. There's only one way to get rid of Xeroth's Blood."

"And that is?" I say, even though I'm pretty sure I know the answer.

"The Healing Springs."

My guess was right, but I wish it wasn't. The Springs may contain the most powerful healing magic in the world, used to treat only the worst illnesses, but there's no way I have enough money to get in. I don't even have to know how much it costs to know I can't afford it. Not to mention the fact that it's all the way in Cerda, and I have no way of getting there.

Now I'm as speechless as Beck. "That's . . . that's not good." I try to stay casual, but my voice comes out in a squeak.

"That's one way of putting it."

"So, basically you're telling me that unless I can come up with the money to go to the Healing Springs, I'm going to die?"

"Basically, yeah."

"How much time to I have? Before the curse reaches my heart?"

"I don't know exactly. I'm not an expert. But I know someone who died from it after about ten days. And since you've already had it for a day . . ."

"I've got, like, eight or nine days?" Even as I say it, the

words don't feel real. None of it's really sinking in. "Unless . . . unless I could somehow sneak into the Springs and—"

Beck shakes his head. "They're heavily guarded, and enchanted. Believe me, you wouldn't be the first to try it."

"Well thanks for your optimism," I say sharply. "I guess I should just resign myself to dying and not even try, is that what you're saying?"

"No. I'm saying there's another way. All you need to enter the Springs is ten thousand majas. And I know how you can get it."

I snort. "Oh, is that all? Just ten *thousand*? No problem, let me just check with the bank—"

"Do you want to hear what I have to say or not?"

I glare at him. "Go ahead."

"You wanted to know where I'm from," he says quietly.

"Yeah, although suddenly it doesn't seem so important. Funny how being told you're going to die puts everything in perspective."

"Okay, here it goes." Beck takes a deep breath.

"Sometime today would be good."

"Patience, Allicat," he says. "I don't—I'm not sure where to begin."

"The beginning," I suggest.

"Okay, um, I'm not sure how to say this, but . . ." He won't look at me. "I'm in the Thieves Guild."

I expected him to say a lot of things, especially after everything I've heard already tonight, but this wasn't one of them. I'm pretty sure my mouth fell open. "You're joking."

"I'm not." He's still not looking at me. "That's how I knew about this cellar. The Guild's been using it as a hideout for a long time."

The Thieves Guild. No way. It's not possible. It's even more ridiculous than the idea of my imminent death.

"It's not real. The Thieves Guild isn't real, it's . . . I thought it was only a legend. A *myth*."

Beck shakes his head. "It's real. But some of the things you've heard probably aren't true."

"Is it true that the Guild stole the signet ring from the king of Cerda? And the queen's jewels? And aren't you all magicians or spies or something?"

"I don't know if those stories are true." He still won't look at me. "We don't talk about what we steal, in case someone gets caught. And a lot of us have magic, or magic objects, but we're not all magicians. And not all of us choose to live in the guildhall, but I do. It's on Mount Arat, but not in Ruhia or Hesmea. It's hidden."

Finally he looks up at me, staring like he's trying to gauge my reaction. "I was born there. In the Guild. My mother was a healer who worked for the Guild. I have—I have a little bit of her healing magic. She left me a few enchanted objects, and I can heal cuts and bruises, but that's about all. That's how my arm is healed now. I used magic in the woods to treat the burn, and that was the blue light you saw. Anyway, I've lived in the Guild my whole life."

"Oh." My voice comes out small. "Well, thanks for clearing that up."

"I'm sorry I didn't tell you. But I didn't know you, and I can't just go around telling everyone I meet about it, you know?"

"Stop apologizing already. I get it."

Thoughts swirl around in my head, and I can't decide what to think about this. I don't know what it means. The Guild exists. Beck's in it. He has magic. I'm cursed and I'm going to die.

I repeat these statements over and over like they'll make more sense somehow, but the words don't feel real.

Beck's look is pleading. I'm not sure what he's asking of me.

"I just always thought . . ." I pause, putting my thoughts into the right order. "I just always thought a Guild member would be, you know, dangerous."

He raises an eyebrow at me. "What makes you think I'm not dangerous?"

I can't tell if he's offended or joking. I decide to take it as a joke and tease him back. "Just look at yourself. You're a scrawny kid who needs a haircut. You're not exactly tough looking."

"I'm not a kid," he says. "I'll be thirteen in seven days."

"Then you're still a kid for seven days."

His teeth flash white in the dark as he smiles. "Maybe so, but you're one for—wait, when's your birthday, anyway?"

"Dunno. The Sisters always celebrate it on the sixteenth of Zioni's Month, because that's when I arrived at the orphanage. I don't know the real day." Personally, I never thought the day I was abandoned was a day worth celebrating, but the Sisters never seemed to understand that point.

He's quiet for a moment. "You never told me how that happened. How you went to the orphanage, I mean."

"There's not anything to tell. I was abandoned. Left on the doorstep."

We're both quiet for a minute. It's one of those moments when there's nothing you can say.

For half a second, I'm tempted to tell him the rest of it. The important bit of it.

About my brother.

When I was little, I used to say it all the time, like a badge of pride—"I have a brother." But then I got older and realized what that meant and why the Sisters always looked so pitying when I said it. Because *he* wasn't dropped off on the orphanage doorstep.

I had a brother, and she chose him over me.

I don't tell people that anymore.

"So," I say finally, "what does any of this have to do with me? How am I going to get ten thousand majas?"

"I'm on my way back to the Guild," Beck says. "The reason I came to Azeland was to find another member of the Guild. I don't know why he was sent here, but he was supposed to be back weeks ago and never showed. So I was sent to find out what happened to him. Turns out he was caught. Nothing we can do about that. So I'll be heading back to the Guild now. I sent a message to my—my transportation, and he'll be here tomorrow."

"Oh." He told me he was going back to Arat for his birthday, but somehow I'd forgotten. "You're leaving tomorrow."

"Yeah." He hesitates. "And you can come with me."

"What?" He can't possibly mean what I think he means. "Can I—can I do that? Go to the Guild?"

"There are certain . . . precautions we take. There are enchantments protecting the hall. If you pass through the enchantments, then yes, you can come in. But you can only stay for a few days unless . . . unless you join. And joining the Guild is a little more complicated. If you choose to leave instead, you'll have to take a potion that makes you forget everything about the Guild. But, yeah, you can come if you want. And when you join the Guild, you're paid. Usually it's around twenty thousand jamars, but on a good year it's more."

Twenty thousand jamars! That's . . . that's like fifteen thousand majas. If I only need ten thousand to get into the Springs . . . "Do you think I should? Join the Guild, I mean."

"That's up to you," he says slowly. "I mean, it's not a decision to make on a whim. But it's the fastest way I know of to get the kind of money you need for the Springs. Plus, the Guild can give you food and clothing and shelter. Whatever you need. There won't be any protectors looking for you. And there are healers that can help with minor illnesses, though nothing like Xeroth's Blood. But you'll have to work for the Guild in return. The Guild leader will send you on assignments. It can be dangerous, too. Guild members *are* dangerous."

But even as he warns me, his eyes shine with excitement. He wants me to go. To join.

"Well . . . if I have to steal anyway, and the Guild can help me . . . If the Guild gives me the money I need for the Springs . . ."

"Exactly." He smiles. "And you'll be far from the orphanage, far from anyone who might recognize you. And while you're in the guildhall, there aren't any protectors to worry about."

This is probably reckless. It sounds dangerous. But mostly it sounds exciting, and there's something to be said for the promise of food every day and a warm place to sleep.

Plus, I don't have any better ideas for getting ten thousand majas.

"Okay," I say.

And just like that, I agree to go to the Thieves Guild.

Chapter Six

I lie awake for most of the night, trying to stop looking at my right hand and failing.

I wait for it to sink in, but it doesn't. Everything feels like a bad dream I'm going to wake up from, or some kind of practical joke. What Beck said made sense, but . . . I can't be dying. It can't be real.

I'd feel it if I were dying, right?

But the next morning, the black lines are still there. Some of them have spread onto my palm, and two others are creeping up my arm.

Guess I'll have to start wearing long sleeves and gloves or something. Maybe Beck and I can steal some today.

Right after I wake up, Beck comes in and tells me we're supposed to meet our transportation to the Guild at noon outside of Centre Cathedral.

"Do you really think it's a good idea to meet in the middle

of the city in broad daylight?" I ask. "Isn't it a . . . I don't know, prominent location?"

"Believe me," Beck says, "it's the best place for us to meet."

After breakfast, Beck and I steal some provisions for our trip, since we both left our bags back at the raided clothing shop. Among the things we take are some cloth bandages that I wrap around my hand to cover up the black marks.

Beck and I follow a crowd of tourists into the cathedral. The doors open into a wide circular room of white stone and colored glass. Tiers of benches are arranged in a half circle, facing the raised platform at the back. Dramatic arches curve around the room, making it feel immense and echoing. The sound of my own footsteps on the stone makes me jumpy; it's impossible to hide in this room, to go unheard.

The tour guide is explaining the meaning of all the runes carved around the room, which apparently spell out lines of prayer. Massive gilded windows of sparkling colored glass line the stone walls, letting the sunlight stream in. Statues of saints sit in niches, encircled by candles. The central statue is one of Saint Ailara that's elaborately decorated. Ailara is always a popular saint. Everybody wants to improve their luck.

Beck and I lurk at the back of the tour, trying to look inconspicuous. Beck darts glances out the windows.

"Shouldn't we go outside where he can see us?" I whisper.

He shakes his head. "We'll see him first."

"Why? Is he, like, a magician in a fancy cape? Or—"

"No, he's a—"

Beck doesn't have to finish his sentence. At that moment, the sunlight flooding the eastern windows vanishes as the shadow of something massive descends outside, literally dropping from the sky. As everyone in the tour turns to look out the windows, Beck takes my arm and tugs me out the door.

A large carriage sits in the street on the east side of the church.

It's being pulled by a thilastri.

So much for being inconspicuous.

"Try not to look so surprised," Beck whispers. "People are going to notice us, so act like you're nobility and you do this every day."

No one's going to buy that we're nobility. We look—and probably smell—like the homeless orphans we are, but the carriage certainly fits the part. It's fancy, embellished with gold spirals that are repeated intricately in the spokes of the wheels. A massive blue crest is painted on the side of each door and the roof, but I don't recognize it as an Azelandian noble house. It's probably Ruhian.

The carriage is nothing compared to the creature pulling it. I've never actually seen a thilastri in person, just drawings. He's even bigger than I imagined, twice the width of a horse, and his head rises several feet above the top of the carriage. Almost every inch of his body is covered in thick plumage that is the deepest blue I've ever seen. His head is feathered too, and he has a beak like an eagle or something. He sort of reminds me of the parakeet in the Puceys' house, except a thousand times bigger, more blue, and with four legs that end in paws.

"Alli, this is Serenier, but we call him Ser. Ser, this is Alli Rosco." Beck keeps his voice low, since everyone in the vicinity is staring at us.

The thilastri looks at Beck, then at me, then sternly back at Beck. "You didn't say you were bringing someone." His voice is a deep rumble that reminds me of mountains.

"Long story," Beck says. He pulls on the carriage door and holds it open for me. With one last disbelieving look at Ser, I climb in. The seats are velvety plush and soft, like nothing I've ever felt before, and I run my fingers over the fabric. In front of me is a little window, and through it I can see Ser's back and parts of his wings and head. He's even bluer close up.

Beck slides in after me. As soon as the carriage door closes, Ser moves, and the carriage picks up speed. With the flapping of Ser's wings, the carriage *lifts*, shoving me back against the seat. My stomach churns, and even though I'm not scared I grip the edge of the seat tightly. I've never actually flown before, and it feels different than I imagined. Full of bumps and jolts.

I try to keep my voice steady despite the sickening rolling of my stomach. "So why exactly are we leaving Azeland in the most conspicuous way possible?"

"The guildhall can't be reached on foot. We've figured out the best way to travel is by thilastri. In other cities, like Cerda, thilastri are more common, so it's not a conspicuous way to travel. That's why we had to wait at the chapel—it would seem too strange to have thilastri falling out of the sky in other parts of the city, but the center square is where most nobility have their carriages pick them up."

It's annoying that Beck knows this and I don't. "I know," I say. "I've lived in Azeland my entire life, remember?"

"Right. Sorry."

"So what's the story?" Ser's deep voice is so loud in the carriage that I flinch. I can't see his face from back here, so I can't try to read his expression.

"What?" Beck calls, a little too innocently.

"Why are you bringing an outsider to the Guild?" The way he says "outsider" makes me cringe.

Beck starts to say something, but I interrupt him. "Excuse me, but I'm capable of speaking for myself, outsider or not," I say, loudly so that Ser can hear.

Ser chuckles, and it's like the sound of a rockslide. "My apologies, miss."

"What I was *going* to say," Beck cuts in, glaring at me, "is that she decided for herself that she wanted to come, and I think she's capable of passing the trial. So she's here."

"But you told her about the Guild." I'm not sure if I'm imagining the accusatory note in Ser's voice.

Beck keeps his tone light. "Like Mead always says, it's on

a need-to-know basis. And she needed to know."

"You may have Mead's approval," Ser says, "but will you have Kerick's?"

"Why are you so concerned about it?"

There's a pause. "Sorry, Reigler. I just don't think it's a good idea to challenge Kerick on this. Especially with your trial coming up. You know how he is."

"What trial?" I say. "Who are Mead and Kerick? What's going on?"

Beck doesn't say anything. His mouth is a hard line. This is a first. I've seen him look defensive, and apologetic, but never angry.

"Didn't he tell you?" Ser says conversationally. "He'll be thirteen soon, and then he's got to pass his trial, same as everyone else. You will too, if you want to join."

I narrow my eyes. "I thought you were already in the Guild."

"I am. But I was born into it. People who are raised in the Guild still have to pass a test—they call it a trial—like everyone else, just to make things fair. Prove we can handle it and we're ready to be an adult member, even if we've already been on assignments before. It's like a rite of passage. That's why I'm going back today—it's almost my birthday, so it's time for my trial."

"What happens if you don't pass?"

"I have to leave the Guild."

"Same as you will," Ser says, "if you don't pass."

Beck glares in Ser's direction. "That won't happen. We're both going to pass."

"*If* I take the test," I remind him. "I haven't decided for sure yet."

Beck shrugs. "Whatever."

"So what exactly are the rules here?" I say. "They just hand out all this money to anybody who passes the test, and that's it?"

"Er, not exactly," Beck says.

"Not at all," Ser says.

Beck taps his index finger against the seat. "Basically, all Guild members are given certain . . . assignments. The king chooses specific targets, and determines whether a group or an individual should go after them."

"So, he tells people what to steal?"

"Yeah." Beck's finger taps faster against the seat. "And some assignments aren't stealing at all, like me being sent to Azeland to find out what happened to a missing member. But if you do steal something on assignment, the Guild keeps it, and you get a cut of the profit. You get paid up front when you join, plus the Guild can take care of clothes and food and whatever else you need."

"As an incentive for thieves to join? And give part of their profits to the Guild?"

"Right. And there are other advantages too, like being able to team up with others to get items you couldn't steal on your own. And when you're not on assignment, you can pretty much do whatever you want."

I'm tempted to ask what exactly he means by "pretty much," but there are too many other, more pressing questions at the moment. "So once you join, are you a member forever? For the rest of your life?"

He hesitates. "Yes, for the most part. To leave the Guild is considered a sign of disloyalty. Rumor has it that the king has allowed certain members to leave under rare circumstances, but I've never known anyone who left."

"Does anyone ever, like, get kicked out? If they do something bad? Like betray the Guild?"

Beck's jaw tightens. "People can get kicked out, yes. But if you betray the Guild, they'll do a lot worse than kick you out."

I'm pretty sure I know exactly what he means by "a lot worse." I gulp. "Good to know. So what's with this whole trial thing? When are we supposed to do this?"

"People born in the Guild, like me, have to pass their trial when they turn thirteen. But for outsiders, they have to go through some basic training before their trial, to help them prepare. Then they'll go see the king, and he'll assign their trial."

"Um," I say. I hold up my right hand. "I don't exactly have time for a whole lot of training, Beck."

"I know. We'll go see the steward right away when we get there, and I'll make sure he sends you to see the king immediately."

I frown. "And why exactly didn't you tell me about any

of this training or trial or lifetime commitment stuff before now?"

He doesn't say anything.

"What, you thought I'd just be *totally fine* with all this?"

"Like you said, you don't know for sure you're joining," he mumbles, his gaze falling to the floor. "But I thought you should at least see it for yourself. Besides . . ." He lowers his voice. "You don't exactly have many options, Alli."

"That's for me to decide," I say. "You don't get to withhold information, or decide what I do and don't need to know."

We sit in silence for the rest of the flight.

Beck keeps looking at me, like he's waiting for me to say something. I ignore him and stare out the window. The view is much more interesting than whatever he has to say.

I've seen the blue-gray shadows of the Elkany Mountains from a distance for my entire life, but I never knew they were so *big*. Their points stab at the sky, reaching higher than our flying carriage, higher even than the clouds. Up here, it's like the sky is an illusion: not a solid, not a ceiling, but something you can pass through, like an ocean. The sturdiness of the mountains, on the other hand, makes even the storm clouds seem delicate in comparison.

The largest mountain is in the center of the range, and I don't need Beck to tell me which it is: Mount Arat. It gets bigger and bigger out the window. This is the first time I've ever seen it so close, the first time I've ever been outside of Azeland.

I try to remember what little the Sisters said about Ruhia in history class, but I wasn't paying much attention at the time. Sister Perla always made a big deal out of Azeland's Independence Day during Raumna's Month, having us draw pictures of the national crest and decorate everything in Azelandian colors—red and gold. (Although the so-called gold was always just yellow.) According to her, Azeland declared its independence from Ruhia, who used to own it. I never really understood why anybody would *want* to own Azeland, but Sister Perla said Ruhia needed the land. Apparently the problem with building your city in a valley surrounded by mountains is that you can't actually expand much when you need, say, farms. So Ruhia started using the farmland south of the mountains, which became Azeland.

But Azeland kept growing bigger and bigger, until it became its own city. Eventually we realized that we didn't really want the Ruhians telling us what to do, so we set up a government council with our own nobility instead of theirs, and now we have a holiday where we decorate in our colors to celebrate the time we told Ruhia to go away. Or something like that.

Except we couldn't actually tell Ruhia to go away, because they still have all the money. Ruhians became filthy rich ages ago when they started mining rare gems and stuff in the mountains, but Azeland has always been farmland and factories. We still sell lots of crops and things to Ruhia, and they still look down on us for being poor or whatever, so as far as I can tell not much has changed. (Sister Perla didn't tell us the part about Ruhians looking down on us, but I met enough Ruhian kids at the orphanage to figure it out myself.)

The problem is that the Sisters never told me anything useful about what Ruhia is actually *like*. I know it snows all the time, and they speak with an accent, and a lot of Ruhians are wealthier than most Azelanders and that's why they don't like us very much. But that's all. I guess I never really cared, because I never thought I'd actually be *going* there. I could ask Beck, but I'm pretending to ignore him at the moment.

I keep my eyes glued to the window.

The carriage doesn't head straight for Mount Arat. Instead, Ser flies between Arat and the closest mountain to the right, whose name I don't know. Lights come into view below, shining from the valley formed by Arat and its neighbor. The lights can only belong to Ruhia, cradled in the midst of the mountains. The clouds here are so heavy that I can't make out any of the city itself, just light bouncing around in the air.

From what I can see out Beck's window, it looks like the carriage is hugging the side of Arat. We're probably about to land. Beck's head blocks most of the view, and I almost tell him to move, but I don't want to be the first to break the silence.

The carriage jolts, and I bang against the side door. We've arrived. Beck, of course, is totally unfazed by the rough landing. As the carriage skids to a stop, he opens the door and a blast of cold air hits me. Beck leaps out first.

I'm not totally sure how the door on my side actually opens, so I slide across the seat and follow him out. I jump down like it's no big deal, but I stumble as I hit the ground, my feet skidding in . . . snow. I guess I should've figured there'd be snow here year round, but I wasn't prepared to land in it.

Beck looks like he's about to catch my arm and help me up, but I glare at him and he backs off. I straighten up without his help and look around. The carriage is sitting, a bit too precariously for my liking, on some kind of ledge. There's nothing much to see but gray rocks and the blinding whiteness of snow in every direction. I avoid looking past the ledge to see how far up we are. Not that I'm afraid of heights or anything.

"This way," Beck says, breaking the silence. He walks along the ledge, and I follow after him, careful not to skid again. I'm not wearing the most practical shoes for mountain climbing in the snow. They're not practical shoes for anything, actually, since they've been falling apart for two years now, and the snow seeps in, freezing against my skin. The wind, whipping in our faces and stinging my eyes, is no better. I hate the cold.

"I can't believe you live here voluntarily," I say. "It's like winter *all the time.*"

"Some people like winter." I wish I could see his face so I'd know if he's teasing, but he doesn't turn around.

"Yeah, and those people are wrong."

"Careful," he says. "You might offend your own patron."

Now I know he's teasing. But how did he even remember that my birth month is Zioni's?

"Sorry, Saint Zioni," I say, not very reverently. "I know you're the patron of winter and all, but I'm not real fond of this whole snow thing."

I glance behind me at Ser, who's still pulling the carriage, steering it along the ledge after us. I don't envy him that job. But I guess the height doesn't seem so bad if you can fly.

Beck stops, and I do too. In front of us is a wall of rock, and to the left is more rock. To the right is the ledge, and I don't even want to know what's beyond that.

"Um, Beck, we appear to have reached a dead end," I say. "Shouldn't there be, you know, a secret Guild around here somewhere?"

Another gust of wind hits me in the face, biting at my skin, but Beck's not shivering so I try not to either. Despite my best efforts, I can't keep my teeth from chattering.

"There *is* a Guild here." Beck turns back to me. "There's a lot of magic protecting it," he adds. "The entrance is spelled so that only someone who has been in the Guild before can open it. You have to be with someone from the Guild to get in."

Beck runs his hands over the wall in front of us. I'm starting to think Saint Zioni is his patron, not mine, since he doesn't seem affected by the cold of the snow on his bare hands. He clears the powder away, revealing a rock wall with some kind of indentation carved in it.

He pulls something from his pocket and holds it up so I can see. It's a gold pendant, shaped like a coiled snake, and in the center is what looks like a real gem, sparkling green even in the dim sunlight. It must be the object I saw him holding last night in the rain, when he opened the cellar door.

"Everyone who lives in the guildhall or is an official Guild member has one of these," Beck explains. "It's enchanted to look like an ordinary object until you need it. Once you're officially a member of the Guild, you'll get one too."

He places the pendant up against the indentation in the rock and presses it in. Then he gives it a twist. The pendant rotates once in a circle and starts *glowing*. Before I can even process this, the whole rock wall trembles.

"Step back," Beck says, but I don't need the warning. I back up so far I almost run into Ser, who's standing silently behind us.

The rock wall shakes for a minute, and then part of it *moves*, sliding up, leaving a cavernous doorway in the vacant space. The rock stops moving, and Beck strides forward and plucks the pendant from the wall. He slips it into his pocket and glances back at me.

"Come on," he says, and he ducks inside, disappearing into the blackness behind the rock.

Chapter Seven

I hesitate for a split second. The door is so big and I can't really see what's inside. But there's no turning back now, so I run after Beck.

It's dark for a long time. We're in some kind of tunnel, maybe? A light flickers up ahead, so I can just make out Beck's movements, and the heavy pad of Ser's steps sounds behind me along with the squeak of the carriage's wheels. But there's nothing else to break up the silent blackness. The air is damp and chilly against my skin.

The light gradually gets closer and closer, and finally the arched doorway at the end of the tunnel stands before us, framed by two flickering torches bracketed to the wall. Beck stops in the doorway and turns, looking at me. For a second I think he's going to take my hand, but he doesn't. He walks through the door, and I follow right behind.

As I step through the doorway, Beck turns back to look at me again, then sighs . . . in relief?

"What?" I say.

"I told you, there's magic protecting the Guild. The enchantments might not have let you in if you were untrustworthy."

"What would've happened if I was?"

Beck shrugs. "Who knows? I've never had to find out."

I shiver and follow him, stepping out of the doorway.

The room that opens up before us isn't exactly what I expected. There's no sign of sorcery, no bubbling black cauldrons or runes carved into walls or anything cool. It's a bare, low-ceilinged room, with the dark rock of the mountain forming the walls and floor. Some wooden tables and chairs are spread around, and doors line the walls. People are everywhere: in chairs, walking around the room, disappearing into some doors and emerging from others. Most of them are people I would pass on the street without a second glance. Some are unkempt, like Beck, but nothing out of the ordinary. Lanterns illuminate the doorways and candles flicker from tables, but the spaces between are shadowed. The air is dense and smells of smoke.

There are a few people in long robes like magicians, but I can't really get a good look since Beck moves quickly, making his way across the room, and I have to hurry to keep up. I glance over my shoulder, looking for Ser, but he's gone.

Beck leads me down a narrow hall with plain stone walls and floor and a low ceiling. After passing four or five doors, we stop. The entryway in front of us is adorned with a wooden nameplate, carved with a single name: Durban. Below the name is some kind of symbol that looks like a spiral.

"What's that symbol mean?" I ask. "Is it some other language?" Maybe they use some kind of cool rune system to communicate. . . .

"Everyone uses a different symbol on their door in addition to their name, 'cause some Guild members can't read."

"Oh." It's a helpful system, actually. My own reading skills aren't the best. But a secret language would've been cooler. "So who's Durban?"

"He's called the steward," Beck says softly. "We report to him after finishing assignments. He handles day-to-day business that the king can't be bothered with. Providing resources and prep for assignments, that kind of thing."

Before I can respond, he knocks sharply on the door.

"You may enter," says a voice from inside.

The room is small, dim, and chilly, with hardly any furniture. Across from us, a man hunches over a tiny desk, scribbling furiously on some parchment.

The man looks up, revealing a pointed chin, long nose, and sharp eyes that fasten on us critically. He's like one of the guards at the orphanage, who were always looking at us with suspicion, always accusing, always a little too eager to draw a weapon.

"Who's this, Reigler?" His voice is as sharp as his eyes, cutting into us like a blade.

Beck ducks his head. "New recruit," he says to the floor.

The steel in Durban's gaze could pierce skin. "Is that so? Step forward, girl."

I don't like being told what to do, but Beck's sudden nervousness makes it clear that this man isn't someone I want to offend. I take a small step forward.

Durban examines me in silence before looking back at Beck. "Pick up a stray in Azeland, did we?"

"Excuse me," I snap, "but I'm perfectly capable of speaking for myself. I'm not a stray dog." I'm also tired of explaining this to everyone.

Beck winces, but Durban's eyes are fixed on me again. "Well," he says, like he's contemplating something. "Well."

We wait for Durban to form an actual sentence. His expression is hard, his lips pressed into a tight line.

"Your name?" he says at last.

"Alli Rosco."

Durban's gaze flicks back to Beck. "And what makes you think that Rosco is qualified to be brought into our midst, Reigler? Or did you confuse the Guild with a shelter for wayward orphans?"

I open my mouth to use some very foul language, but Beck comes to my defense. "She escaped protectors in Azeland. And before that, she managed to break out of a guarded orphanage. I've seen her steal; she's good."

Heat floods my face. I didn't know Beck thinks I'm a good thief. Although everything sounds much more impressive when he says it like that.

Durban sighs in resignation. "And what of Grent? Did you remember to look for him, when you weren't rescuing orphans?"

"Grent's in prison," Beck says, "serving five years."

Durban gives an unconcerned shrug. Almost as an afterthought, he jots something down on a piece of parchment. I can only guess what it says. *Reminder: Bust fellow thief out of prison in Azeland?*

"Well," Durban says. I'm starting to think it's the only word in his vocabulary. "Your trial is coming up, isn't it?" Beck nods. "You'll need to visit the king tomorrow, then. Come by here at lunchtime and I'll see what I can do. Rosco, if you want to join the Guild, you can accompany Reigler to visit the king and see if he will assign you a trial. If you come to your senses and decide to leave . . . Well, we can't have you blabbing about the Guild to everyone you meet; your memory will be modified, and a thilastri will take you down to Ruhia."

He turns back to his papers and resumes scribbling. We're dismissed.

In the hallway, I can't contain myself any longer. "He's a piece of work, isn't he?"

The corners of Beck's lips quirk. "Yeah, maybe a little." He leads me back down the hall, toward where we came in. "But he's really important here, so could you maybe not mouth off to him?"

"I would never," I say in my best fake-innocence voice.

Beck smiles. "Come on, it's time for dinner."

We return to the first room, which is even more crowded than before. A few people are grouped around a long serving table on one wall that holds the food.

Beck and I join the end of the line. As we wait, I examine the Guild members. Most of them are big and rough-looking, the kinds of people you'd expect to be bodyguards or protectors or something. Many of them have weapons prominently displayed. There are lots of knives and sharp pointy objects attached to their belts.

We finally reach the table, grab plates, and serve ourselves. Beck takes a slice of bread, and I imitate him. We reach the main dish and . . . I have no idea what it is. The tray is full of a gooey green substance that can't seem to decide if it's a liquid or a solid. Beck doesn't seem alarmed by the appearance of our dinner and scoops up a large helping. Seeing no alternative meals on the table, I do the same. Maybe it tastes better than it looks?

I sit down across from Beck at a nearby table, eyeing the gooey mass on my plate with suspicion. Is anything inside it alive? I poke it with the tip of my fork. Lifting the fork from the glop, I stare in disgust at the sickly goo congealing on the prongs.

"Beck, are you completely sure this is edible?"

"What?" He looks up from his own plate, which is already half empty.

"What is this, exactly?" I take a cautious sniff and grimace at the scent of burned rubber.

He shrugs. "It's better not to ask."

"I've had some questionable meals in my time," I say, "and I'm not exactly a picky eater. But I'm not totally convinced that this is actually *food*."

Beck looks confused, but before he can respond, we're interrupted by a boy shouting "Reigler!" and striding over to Beck.

Beck jumps up, and he and the new boy do some kind of funny hand-slapping thing that must be a greeting. "When'd you get in?" the boy asks.

"Just now," Beck says, grinning. "How're things here?"

"The usual," the boy says. "A few fistfights, small assignments, steward nearly killing everyone . . ." He trails off. He's noticed me.

"Mead, this is Alli Rosco," Beck says quickly. "Alli, this is Koby Mead."

The boy offers me his hand, and we shake. He's pale as a ghost, with a shock of light hair and gray eyes. He looks to be a little older than us, but his goofy grin makes him seem even younger.

"Pleased to meet you, Rosco," he says. His Ruhian accent is even more pronounced than Beck's. "You an Azelander, then?"

"Yeah," I say.

Beck sits back down, and Mead pulls up a chair beside me. "Spill, Reigler," Mead says. "I want every gory detail of your trip."

"Sorry to disappoint," Beck says dryly, "but there wasn't much gore involved."

"Yeah? So ol' Grent's not dead, then?"

"Nah. Doing a fiver."

"Too bad," Mead mutters, "I had money down on him losing a fight and going to Xeroth. Y'know how he is, always picking a fight with the wrong guy."

"How inconvenient for you that he's alive," Beck mutters around a mouthful of green goo.

Mead turns to me. "So, Rosco, you joining the Guild?"

"I don't know," I say. "Maybe."

"Haven't gotten Kerick to agree?" he asks. I have no idea what he means and look at Beck for help.

"We haven't exactly gotten that far," he says. "Durban was . . . well, Durban."

Mead laughs. "Less than enthusiastic, was he?"

"You could say that. Anyway, we're both meeting with Kerick tomorrow to see about trials. That is, if she decides to stay."

"Better hope he approves then," Mead says. "Don't want him to be in a bad mood when he assigns your trial."

Seeing Beck's expression, he adds, "But no worries. You had good reason for bringing her, right? Kerick's fair." Beck doesn't look reassured, so he keeps going. "My trial was so easy anyone could pass. Nothing you can't handle."

"Right," Beck says. "You passed with only half a brain, so how hard can it be?"

"Considering your stressful situation, I won't take offense at that comment." Mead rises from his seat. "I'm gonna get some food before it's all gone." He strolls off, greeting people cheerily as he goes, joining the food line.

"What's everyone talking about?" I demand as soon as he's gone. "First Ser, and now—"

"It's nothing," Beck says, but he lowers his voice. "It's just, we're supposed to be selective about who we bring into the Guild, and not everyone welcomes outsiders. The Guild's not a charity. Only the best thieves are supposed to be allowed in. That's why you have to pass a trial before you're officially a member. Kerick is the king of the Guild, so he decides what the trials will be. He can make them easy, or hard. And you don't want to get on his bad side."

"So Mead thinks Kerick won't approve of you bringing me here." I try to figure it out. "But why?"

Beck shrugs. "Like Mead said, Kerick's fair. It'll be fine."

"You're a terrible liar."

Beck opens his mouth to say something, but Mead returns with a plate full of green goo, and the conversation is dropped.

Through the rest of the meal, Beck and Mead talk about people I don't know. Mead fills Beck in on what he's missed and who's gone where. It seems like they know everybody here. While they talk, I stab at the green goop with my fork and try to choke it down. Not thinking about the taste is the only thing that makes it bearable. It's worse than the cough medicine Sister Perla made me take, maybe worse even than the time Sister Romisha tried to wash my mouth out with soap. . . .

"So, Rosco, has Reigler given you the tour?" Mead asks suddenly.

I swallow my mouthful of glop, trying not to gag as it goes down. "No," I say when my mouth is empty, "I haven't seen much of anything."

Mead shoves back from the table and stands in one quick motion. "This is an outrage!" he says, but he can't keep from grinning. "This is no way to treat a guest, Reigler! You should be ashamed of yourself." He doesn't bother to keep his voice down, and I have a feeling half the Guild is staring at us now.

Beck just smiles. "How inhospitable of me."

"This is no laughing matter!" Mead cries. He looks at me and winks. "If you're finished eating, Rosco, allow me to give you a tour."

"All right." The three of us pick up our plates and add them to a large stack of dirty dishes on one of the tables. Who has to clean those up?

"This way," Mead says. Beck and I follow him as he sets off briskly down a hallway.

"Here're the kitchens," Mead says, gesturing to a wide set of doors on my left. "Otherwise known as my favorite place in the Guild. The cooks are especially fond of me."

From behind me, Beck snorts.

"And to the right is the laundry," Mead continues,

ignoring Beck. "Everybody does their own clothes, or pays someone else to do it for them, so you'd best learn where it is now."

I try to take his advice and memorize where we are, but the black rock walls of the hallways and the bare wooden doors all look the same to me. There's no time to ask, though. Mead's already moved on.

The hallway branches into two corridors. "The main living quarters are that way," Mead says, pointing to the left fork. He then takes the right. "Down this way are the offices for some of the officials—you've already met the steward. There're also some others who manage little stuff—housing arrangements, food delivery and preparation, transportation, all that. The steward oversees most everything, but he delegates the grunge work to others."

We pass all the closed office doors without stopping. The hall forks again, this time into three passages.

"We can't go to the left," Mead says. "That's where the vaults are—the place where all the Guild's wealth is stored. It's magicked and guarded, so nobody can get in 'less the king lets 'em. Supply rooms are down there too. The supply clerk'll take you to get a year's worth of supplies once you join, and every year after that you'll get to go again. And this here's the magicians' wing. Magicians like their quarters separate from everybody else, so they can practice their secret spells or potions or whatever. It's magicked too, of course, so we can't go there."

Mead turns down the last hall, the one farthest to our right, and, to my disbelief, the hall immediately branches off in different directions. How big *is* this place?

"This'll take you back to the dining hall," Mead explains, "and the healing quarters and training room are off that way."

"Training room?" I ask, remembering what Beck said before about needing training before a trial.

"Yeah, everybody in the Guild needs to have the same basic skills, so everybody gets trained. Don't worry, you'll see more than enough of that room before you're done. And here's the second set of living quarters. The first set is only one person to a room, but these are bigger, designed for two or three, sometimes four. I lived down here with my father and sister till I passed my trial and got a room of my own on the other side. Reigler here still lives in this hall till he passes his trial. This is his room."

We stop in front of one of the doors. A plain wooden nameplate hangs on it, carved with a single name, and below it, a symbol. Thanks to my poor reading skills, it takes me a second to make out what it says: LIANICE GRIMSTEAD.

Beck unlocks the door and ushers us inside. It's so dark I can't see anything, but then somebody lights a match, fumbles with something, lights a candle. Now I can see Beck, holding the candle. He sets it down and tosses another candle to Mead. After a minute, they've lit enough that we can see a bit better.

The room is cramped. A small bed, clearly designed for

a child, is shoved into one corner. The opposite corner has some kind of stove-looking contraption that I saw in both the dining hall and Durban's office, probably for putting out heat.

Against one wall is a small sofa, which Mead now reclines on, and in the center of the room is a table cluttered with papers, stubs of candles, dirty dishes, and God-knows-what-else. The walls are studded with little brackets holding candles, and more candles sit atop a dresser. Right beside the dresser is another tiny doorway, and I can just make out the shape of a larger bed tucked inside the space beyond. In the far corner is yet another doorway, which leads to the bathroom. I ask Beck how they can possibly have plumbing in hidden caves in the middle of a mountain, and he says some magicians spelled it so it actually works.

"So, Rosco, whaddya think?" Mead says, propping his feet up on the table.

I look at Beck, who's been awfully quiet during the tour. In the shadowy room, I can't make out his expression. "About what?"

"The Guild, of course," Mead says impatiently. "Think you'll join?"

"I dunno," I say, trying to keep my tone light. Beck's avoided mentioning my near-death condition to anyone, so I figure it should be kept secret. "I was promised food, but if tonight's meal is any indication, I think I'll risk starvation."

Mead barks out a laugh. "I forgot, you orphans practically get five-star meals compared to us."

"How is it that everyone knows I'm from an orphanage?" I say in exasperation.

"Well, just look at your shoes," Mead says, nodding at my feet. "Even street rats wouldn't be caught dead in those rags. No offense."

"Right," I say. "But was this, like, an average meal here, or just a fluke? Because that seriously might be a deal breaker."

"No, the food's always bad," Mead says, "but don't let that be the deciding factor. Just think, you can go out into the streets and dodge protectors every day, or you can stay here, with the reliability of our terrible meals served fresh daily in the dining hall, not to mention you'd have me to keep you company."

"In that case, I think I'll take my chances with the protectors."

Beck laughs, and Mead grins. "Just as well," he says. "Everyone knows I'm the comedian around here, and you might give me some competition."

I laugh. "Oh, there's no competition. You'd need more than half a brain to compete with my wit."

"She's got you there, Mead," Beck says. "There's a reason they say Saint Samyra cursed you."

Mead pretends to be offended. "That's ridiculous," he says. "Though, now that you mention it, she's been a bit miffed at me ever since I helped myself to a few jamars from her church."

I have to admit, I'm impressed. "You stole from Saint Samyra's Church?"

"Not her *high* church," Mead says flippantly. "That's in Astia, and who wants to go there? It was just some little church named after her in Ruhia. She's got a few dozen of them down there."

I'm about to reply, when Mead's gaze falls on my right hand, and his eyes widen. A black streak is curling out from the edges of the bandage I've been using to hide it. Mead looks at Beck.

"We didn't want anyone to know she's marked," Beck says softly. "They might think she's just going to take the money and run."

Mead nods. "How are you going to hide it from Kerick? He won't even give her a trial if he sees it."

"She'll just have to keep her hands in her pockets."

"When were you planning on telling *me* any of this?" I hiss at him.

"Sorry," Beck says. "I figured you had enough to worry about."

Mead starts to say something, but suddenly the door flies open and a high voice shrieks, "Koby Mead!"

Chapter Eight

I jump a little, but nobody else does. I'm starting to wonder if Beck and Mead have some kind of master-thief superpowers. They don't even look surprised.

"Yes, Rosalia?" Mead drawls, not moving from the sofa.

A tall girl, probably older than Mead, enters the room. She's pretty, with long dark hair and soft features, but her eyes flash with anger. "How dare you," she says. "How *dare* you—"

"I'm afraid I've no idea what you're talking about," Mead says without looking at her, "but there're an awful lot of shocking things I'd dare to do."

The girl glances over at Beck and me. "Reigler," she says, nodding at him.

"Rosalia," Beck responds.

Her eyes flick dismissively over me before she turns her attention back to Mead, who hasn't moved from his sprawling position on Beck's sofa.

"How many times do I have to tell you to stop involving my brother in your hair-brained, foolish, idiotic schemes?"

"That's the third time tonight my intelligence has been insulted," Mead observes to no one in particular. "Just out of curiosity, which scheme are you referring to?"

Rosalia continues like she hasn't heard him. "The cooks are in an uproar, the whole kitchen nearly burned down, the cook's cat's running around with a singed tail, and my brother is the one who got caught with the firecrackers in his pocket—"

"Oh, *that* foolish scheme," Mead says. "Well, Peakes does have a talent for being in the wrong place at the wrong time. It's no wonder he was caught, really—"

Rosalia lets out another shriek, picks up the nearest object—a candle stub—and hurls it at Mead's head. It narrowly misses, landing on the sofa.

"Fix it," she says, "or I'll tell the steward." Then, with an overly dramatic huff, she storms out as quickly as she stormed in.

There's a second of silence. Then Mead sighs, real slow, and stands. "Guess I'd better go see to Peakes—"

"Wait," Beck says, moving toward the door. "I doubt the cooks will be very happy to see you. You'll just make it worse."

Mead seems to consider this for a second, then nods slowly. "Perhaps."

"I'll go smooth things over," Beck says. "You stay here

and try not to get into any more trouble while I'm gone. And look after Rosco."

"I do *not* need looking after," I say, but he's already gone.

"Well, that was exciting." Mead settles back down on the couch. "Close the door, will you? Don't want anyone else to find me in here."

"Why don't you get up and do it?" I say, but I go ahead and pull the door closed anyway. It swings shut, and the wooden nameplate thunks against it. Which reminds me.

"Who's Lianice Grimstead?" I ask.

Mead looks surprised. "She was Beck's mother. This room was issued to her, that's why her name's on the door."

"Oh."

Mead hesitates for a second. The humor has vanished from his face. "Did Beck tell you anything about her?"

"Not much. Just that she died two years ago."

Again, Mead is hesitant. He leans forward, staring down at the floor. "I'm only telling you this," he says, "because if you hang with Beck long enough you'll hear rumors about it, and Beck might not want to explain." He takes a breath. "His mom was sick for a long time before she died. But it was the mental kind of sick."

He stops, waiting for my reaction. When I don't say anything, he keeps going. "Most of the time she seemed okay," he continues. "And she was a great healer, nobody could deny that. Not to mention that she was one of the smartest people here. But sometimes she'd see things that weren't there. She'd mutter things to herself like she was having a conversation. And then sometimes she had these sort of breakdowns, where she'd start screaming in the middle of the dining hall or the healing room and nobody'd be sure what set it off."

Mead looks down at the floor, tracing circles on it with one foot. I still don't say anything, so he keeps going. "There at the end, some people in the Guild were downright scared of her. Thought she'd been cursed. She wasn't allowed to heal anymore, and the steward almost threw her and Beck out of the Guild. But Beck went to the king and begged him to let them stay, promised he'd go on assignments even though he was too young, swore he'd earn his keep. The king let him stay, probably because he knew Beck's a good thief. Or maybe because he knew Beck and his mom were being treated unfairly. Anyway, Beck's been trying to keep that promise ever since, even though some people in the Guild don't like him. Think he might be cursed too."

"Why's the Guild so important to him?" I say. "If people are cruel, and if he has to work so hard, why would he stay?"

"Partly because he knows how hard it would be to survive without the Guild." His foot circles a little faster. "But also because . . . well, it's different when you're born here. You can't understand. Beck and I, we've spent our whole lives here. Everyone and everything we know comes from here. We've been outside plenty of times, we've been taught what we need to know to survive . . . but it's different. The Guild is a lot of things, but it's also our home, the only place we know, the only place our families have been. And once you join, it's hard to leave."

"I need to join," I say. "But I just . . . I don't know if I want to."

Mead looks up. "It's a big decision," he says. "And not everyone can survive here. But you can."

"How do you know? You just met me."

He meets my eyes for the first time. "I don't know you, but I know Beck. And to tell you the truth, Beck's scared to death about his trial. Being in the Guild is all he wants. He knows there's a good chance the king will be hard on him, since he did Beck a favor by letting him stay this long. And he knows bringing you here is risky, because the king might not approve. But despite all that, he brought you here anyway. What does that say about you?"

"Nothing. I'm just an orphan from Azeland. I ran into Beck on the street, that's all, and he offered to help."

Mead doesn't argue the point, but he doesn't look convinced. "I just thought you should know what he's risking for you."

"So you think I should leave? And not let him take the risk?"

"I never said that." He looks down at the cluttered table. "I think you must be pretty important to him, if he'd rather risk failing his trial than leave you in Azeland. He's always had a kindhearted streak, but this is extreme even for him."

"That's ridiculous. In fact, when he told me about the Guild, he practically tried to convince me not to come."

"But he did tell you about it," he says quietly. "Just think about it, that's all I'm saying."

We sit in silence for a moment, and I watch the flickering flame of the candle on the table. I try to imagine what it would've been like living here, in this room, with a mother. What it would be like to *know* that you'll have three meals tomorrow, to have the stability of this room, of this place. The certainty of it. And the uncertainty of his mother's health. And how empty it would feel after she was gone.

But better than not having had a mother at all.

Mead stands abruptly. "So, Rosco, let's kill some time while we wait for Reigler."

"Beck will probably be back soon—"

He waves one hand dismissively. "You'll have plenty of time. This'll only take a minute."

"What will?" I say, but Mead's already out the door. Reluctantly, I follow.

Mead leads me down one of the passageways, moving so fast that I don't have time to read the labels on the doors to try and figure out where we are.

"Since you're staying," Mead says, not even glancing over his shoulder to see if I'm following, "you'll want to learn a few useful skills."

I stop. "What's in it for you?"

Mead spins around theatrically, wearing a pained expression.

"What makes you think I'd ask for anything in return? Maybe I'm just a compassionate person, helping the poor and the downtrodden—"

"Do you really think I'm stupid?"

Mead grins, dropping the pretense. "Okay, okay. So, I really need to retrieve something of mine from one of these rooms. I'll teach you how to pick the lock, and if you'll just open the door for me, I'll do the rest. And in exchange, you learn how to pick locks from a master."

"Why not just pick the lock yourself?"

"There are enchantments on the inner doors of the Guild to prevent people from picking the locks, but they only work on Guild members. You're not one," Mead says with a grin. "And no one else needs to learn how to pick locks. It's a win-win situation."

"Except for whoever it is you're stealing from. And don't tell me that's not what you're doing. I'm not as brainless as you are."

"It's not stealing, really," he says, "'cause it was mine to begin with, and it was stolen from me. I'm just stealing it *back*. Anyway, you're at the Thieves Guild, Rosco, so you'd best get used to it."

Fair point. I don't want to make an enemy of whoever it is Mead's stealing from, but I don't want to make an enemy of Mead, either. Hopefully no one will know it was me.

So why do I feel unsure about this?

"All right. Show me what to do."

"First we must practice," Mead protests. "Lock picking is an artistic skill that takes years to properly master."

"I haven't got years."

"True, but you've got me for a teacher, which counts for something. I'll give you the crash course."

Mead turns around and keeps walking, forcing me to run after him or risk being lost in these tunnels forever.

We finally stop outside a door that looks identical to all the others, but with the name Koby Mead on the nameplate. Mead unlocks the door and ushers me inside with a dramatic flourish.

Again we go through the process of lighting candles in the darkened room, and I'm starting to think there's got to be a way to carve windows or something because I seriously don't have time for this candle thing every day. Once everything's lit, I see the room is much like Beck's, except even messier, with clothes and stuff scattered all over. The basic furniture is the same—bed, sofa, table, heating unit thingy, dresser, and another bathroom with magic plumbing. Mead doesn't have a second bedroom, though.

I sit on the sofa. Meanwhile Mead rummages under the bed, pulling out some kind of box. In one quick movement he flips the box over the bed, and dozens of metal things fall out with a clatter. They're *locks*.

"Okay, Rosco, these are the basics." Mead shoves a bunch of objects off the table and sits down on it, right across from me. "Locks aren't difficult to open, really. They're all pretty much the same. There are little pins inside that keep the lock closed. Picking a lock just means forcing the pins out of position so that it can open, the way a key does. Now, I personally prefer to use more sophisticated tools when possible, but I'm going to keep things simple for you, so we'll go the basic pick-and-wrench method instead."

He holds up a small, thin stick-looking thing. "This is the easiest pick to use," he continues. "I can teach you the more advanced stuff some other time."

Now he holds up an L-shaped metal object, barely larger than the pick. "And this is your tension wrench. You'll need both the wrench and the pick to open a lock. Here, make yourself useful and hold the candle."

He hands me a candle so I can see as he selects one of the locks, inserts the end of the wrench into the bottom of the keyhole, and demonstrates how the pick works, talking as he does so, explaining what he's doing. "See," he says, "you're just applying pressure and lifting the pins up, one at a time, until . . ." There's a series of soft clicks, then he uses the wrench to turn the lock, and the bolt slides away.

Then he resets the lock and hands it to me. "Your turn."

He made it look way easier than it actually is. I try to mimic what he did, but I'm just jabbing uselessly at the inside of the lock and probably making it worse. Mead gives me instructions, then corrections, in an increasingly irritated voice, and I snap back at him with equal irritation.

"God help me," he says after I throw a lock in frustration.

"It's a *lock*, Rosco. You don't have to stab it to death. Stabbing things is a lesson for another day. Now, look, it's very simple—" He takes the lock from me and demonstrates again, more slowly this time. But no matter what he says, it isn't simple. It requires tiny, delicate, precise motions with the pick. None of which I am good at.

Eventually I get the stupid thing to click open, but that's not good enough for Mead. He picks up the next lock, which is more complicated, and we start the whole process over again.

It takes a very, very long time, and I still haven't mastered lock picking to Mead's satisfaction, but eventually I can open a few of the locks without much help. "Well," he says, "you'll have to do. Come on, we've gotta go."

Taking the tools with me, I follow Mead out of his room and down the maze of hallways. This time I'm pretty sure we're back in the second set of quarters, where Beck lives, but I don't have any idea how close his room is.

"Here we are," Mead whispers. "Now, like I said, the lock's been magicked so I can't touch it, but it should be fine for you."

"*Should* be?"

"Well, yeah, but if you feel any burning or stinging you might want to, you know, finish picking the lock and then go see a healer. Anyway, this lock's like the last one we practiced on, so it will open the same way."

I sigh and step in front of the door. I glance up at the

nameplate. TADDEO JARVIN. And right below that, TREYA MEAD JARVIN. Below the names are more funny symbols.

I look at Mead and gesture to the nameplate questioningly.

"My sister," he says flippantly. "And her extremely obnoxious husband who stole from me. Now hurry up before they get back."

I roll my eyes at him but don't press the issue. Someone really might show up at any moment. I turn my attention back to the lock and say a quick prayer to Saint Ailara, just in case.

For a second, my stomach clenches. It's like I'm crossing some kind of invisible line, committing a crime that isn't totally necessary for my survival, and it doesn't feel right. The hair on the back of my neck stands up. I try to wave the feeling away and reach for the door.

Mead was right about the lock. It's just like the last one I practiced with. I take a deep breath, apply tension to the lock with the wrench thing, and start poking at it with the pick, listening to Mead's impatient foot tapping behind me the whole time.

Slowly, slowly I lift the pins up, hearing a telltale little click each time. Just one left. I take another breath and slide the pick into place—

"Almost done?" Mead calls, and I jump in surprise. The pick falls from my hand and clinks to the floor.

"What'd you do that for?" I say, whirling to face him. "I almost had it, until you startled me."

"Er, Rosco," Mead says.

"And you're making it hard to concentrate with all your *tapping*—"

"Ros—"

"If you'd just stop interrupting me—"

"Rosco! The pick!"

I turn back to the door to see what he's pointing at. The pick has been slowly rolling across the stone floor . . . right toward the gap under the door.

"Grab it!" Mead yells. "Before you lose it."

I drop to my knees and reach for the pick, grabbing it just as it rolls under the crack beneath the door. "Got it," I say triumphantly. I turn back to the lock.

"Wait," Mead says. "If there are any extra spells against intruders on the door, that may have set them off."

I back away from the door, and we both stare at it. Waiting. Nothing happens.

"I guess it's okay," I say. "Shouldn't something have happened by now, if it's magicked?"

"Guess so," Mead says. "I think you're safe."

I approach the door again and pick up where I left off. Only one pin left to go . . .

The lock clicks.

"I got it!" I whisper, turning the lock and retracting the bolt.

"Great." Before I can react Mead rushes forward, flings the door open, and sweeps inside. "Stay there and warn me if anyone's coming."

"But—" I start to protest that no one said anything about being a lookout, but he's already disappeared into the darkness of the room.

I wait outside for several minutes, peering anxiously down the hall, but no one comes. Maybe I should just leave. Maybe I can find the way back to Beck's room by myself—

Something rattles behind me, and I spin around. The entire doorframe is shaking, and the rattling is coming from furniture inside the door.

"Mead?" I call hesitantly.

The doorway is *glowing*. I blink, and it's changed from brown to violent green in an instant.

"Mead!"

From somewhere inside the room, he curses. "Run!"

A second later he flies out the door, knocking me into the wall. He doesn't stop, racing down the hall and around the corner.

And the doorway explodes.

Chapter Nine

The stone floor underneath my cheek is cool, but my back burns and my stomach aches like someone punched me in the gut. I open my eyes. The rock floor in front of me is streaked with black. Slowly, I sit up.

The doorway itself didn't explode, but green flames are still licking its edges. The wooden door is charred. I've never seen magical fire before, but it's not hard to guess that this is it, since it's green and all. The damage extends directly in front of the doorway, about where I was standing, and all the way across the hall to the opposite wall. It's like a fireball appeared from nowhere and blew me off my feet.

A bit of debris is scattered around that must've come from inside the room, but I can't tell what it is. Some of it must've hit me in the stomach, though. It hurts. My head hurts too, but that's probably from the part where I hit the floor.

Somewhere, a door opens. I stumble to my feet and run from

the scene, moving as fast as the ache in my stomach will allow.

After turning the corner, I'm halfway down the hall when Mead jumps out of a doorway right in front of me. He's holding a small silvery box in his hands.

"You." I spit the word at him. "You *left me*—"

He looks unconcerned. "This is the Thieves Guild, Rosco. It's every man for himself around here. Don't like it, don't join."

His flippancy is infuriating, especially since he knows I don't have a choice about joining. "That could've *killed me*, and you just left me there, you coward—"

"Calm down," he interrupts. "I didn't know that would happen, now did I? Jarvin must've added extra protection spells to the door, to shoot magic at anyone who breaks in. Your pick probably set it off when it rolled under the door. Course, it wasn't a very good spell. Took it a couple of minutes to work. And it probably wouldn't have killed you. Jarvin isn't a good magician, just bluff and shiny lights."

"Well, his shiny lights *hurt*," I mutter, but my anger ebbs a bit. He's right about one thing: I need to get used to how things are around here. I feel betrayed, but I shouldn't expect anything else from a thief. "And how do I know his magic isn't some kind of death curse too? My last encounter with magic didn't go so well."

"Trust me, he's not powerful enough for anything like that. The other magic users don't even consider him a real magician; that's why he doesn't live in their special quarters.

Besides, look at it this way. Given your current condition, how could it possibly be worse?"

My hand clenches into a fist, sending little stabs of pain up my cursed arm as if to punctuate his point. "I'm so glad the fact that I'm dying is funny to you."

I've never said the words out loud before—*I'm dying*—and even now it still doesn't feel real.

"We're all dying," Mead says. "Some of us are going about it more quickly than others, that's all. Now if you'll excuse me, I have other matters to attend to."

"What was so important, anyway?" I say, looking at the tiny box in Mead's hands.

"None of your business."

I scowl. "I almost died for that thing, so tell me what it is."

"Fine." Mead yanks the lid open just enough that I can see a ring glinting dully before he snaps it shut again. "That's it. Now run along to Reigler. You can keep the tools as a thank you." He turns and strides down the hall.

"Um, Mead?" I call after him. "How do I get there?"

"Just keep going straight down this hall. Second door to the end, on the right."

"You're welcome," I yell.

Only a minute after I find Beck's room, the door flies open, and Mead walks in again, this time without the package. "Wouldn't want Reigler to think I ditched you," he says by way of explanation, plopping back down on the couch.

We sit in silence until Beck walks in, looking flushed and

out of breath, swinging the door shut behind him.

"You owe me one, Mead," he says. "One of the cooks tried to kill me with a rolling pin."

Then he takes in the expressions on our faces, the guilty way we're looking down at the floor. "What were you two talking about?"

Mead and I exchange glances. At the same time, we both say, "Nothing."

Mead stands. "Well, it's been fun, but it's late, and Reigler needs his beauty sleep."

Beck scowls at him. "Go ahead. You won't be missed."

Mead puts one hand over his heart. "You've wounded my sensitive ego," he moans, opening the door.

"You'll get over it," Beck says. "Close the door behind you."

I can't make out Mead's reply, but I get the gist.

"Sorry about him," Beck says with a grin. "He's . . ."

"He's great, even if he is a little—" I bite my tongue. I was going to say "crazy," but now that I know about Beck's mother it seems like a poor choice of words. "Well, you know," I finish awkwardly, unable to think of a word. "Untrustworthy" would be accurate, but I don't really want to tell Beck about what happened.

If he knows what I was about to say, his expression gives no indication of it. "Yeah. But he was right about needing sleep. I don't know when the king will send us out on trial." He produces a blanket from a dresser drawer and throws it to me. It's worn, but still soft.

"You can take the big bed," he says, nodding toward the doorway to the second bedroom even as he moves across the room, putting out candles.

I start to protest that I'll take the small one, but he cuts me off. "I always sleep out here anyway," he says. I know he's not just trying to be chivalrous; the tangled heap of blankets on the smaller bed proves it's been slept in more regularly.

"All right." I grab a candle and move toward the doorway. I look back over my shoulder. "Thanks, Beck."

"No problem, Allicat." His back is to me, so I can't see his face. "'Night."

"'Night."

Inside the room, I hold the candle up. The space is barely large enough for the bed. A dresser identical to the one outside is stuffed in a corner, but otherwise it's empty. The clutter that filled the other room is totally absent here. The bed is made up neatly with sheets and a single pillow, but there's a fine layer of dust over everything. No one's been in here for a while. It's not hard to guess why Beck still sleeps in the other room, in a bed that he's outgrown. This was his mother's room.

I set the candle down on top of the dresser. It's chilly, so I wrap the blanket tight around me and slide under the sheets. I'm so tired, but my mind's racing too fast for sleep.

Mostly I think about tomorrow. I have no idea how this trial thing works, or why everyone's so worried that the king might not approve of Beck bringing me, or what his disapproval will mean for me, exactly, though Mead was pretty clear about what it will mean for Beck. . . .

I have to push those thoughts away. I don't know if I want to join, but I don't have a choice.

Instinctively, I look down at my arm. I can't see the lines very well in the candlelight, but a few of them are halfway to my elbow. How many days do I have left? Eight, maybe? Will I even make it in time? How long will the trial take? What will happen if I don't pass?

What will happen if I do?

Mead's words come back to me. *It's our home.*

I've never had a place that felt like home. I get the general idea, but I don't know what it's like. I don't remember enough about my life before the orphanage to know anything. The orphanage never felt like a home, not the way kids arrived one day and were gone the next, the way nobody noticed or cared about anything I did, except when I was getting into trouble. The only other places I've lived were with the Carrians and the Puceys when they adopted me. I thought they were real homes at first. I was deceived by their fancy houses and nice clothes. But it didn't take long to realize I was wrong about that. No matter how hard I tried, I couldn't be part of either family.

I don't know what this place has that makes Beck want to live here so badly, but I want it too.

Maybe home is just the place where you're wanted.

Maybe the Guild can be that place for me.

I take a long, deep breath, trying to relax so I can fall asleep.

I whisper the words out loud, like saying it makes it real.

"I'm going to join the Guild."

The next morning, Beck wakes me up to get breakfast. The main hall isn't as crowded as it was at dinner. The line is short, and before long I'm holding a bowl full of a mysteriously thick, pasty substance. Beck claims it's oatmeal but he's not fooling anyone. The only other option is some kind of mud-brown soup with unidentifiable substances floating in it, though, so I take my chances with the oatmeal.

Beck makes his way over to a table where Mead is sitting with a few other young guys and Rosalia, the girl who yelled at Mead last night.

As Beck and I sit down, everyone except Mead looks at me curiously.

"Guys, this is Rosco," Mead says, like he's the one who brought me over to the table. "She's joining the Guild."

I never actually told Mead I'm definitely joining, but he seems to take my silence for a confirmation. "Rosco, this is Peakes, Flint, and Bray. And you've already met Rosalia, Peakes's sister."

I nod politely at Rosalia, but she barely seems to notice. She's sitting as far away from Mead as possible and glaring at him, but Mead ignores her.

The largest of them, a guy with big, bulging muscles,

who I think is Bray, looks up at me. "Rosco?" he says, like he recognizes the name. "You wouldn't happen to be related to a lawyer's apprentice in Ruhia, would you?" He says it a little suspiciously.

"A lawyer in Ruhia?" I laugh. "Not a chance."

"Where you from?" one of the other guys asks me.

"Azeland."

"Really?" The scrawniest and youngest-looking of the bunch, who Mead called Peakes, looks excited. "I've never been there."

"You've never been anywhere," Bray scoffs. "You haven't even passed your trial yet."

The one across from Mead, who I think he called Flint, scrapes the bottom of his bowl clean, which makes my stomach churn in disgust. "Speaking of trials," he says, "when do you find out about yours, Reigler?"

"Today," Beck says, swallowing a mouthful of the so-called oatmeal. "At lunch."

"Ailara be with you," Peakes says politely.

"Yeah," Bray says with a snort, "'cause you're gonna need it."

Mead elbows him. "Don't be such a downer. You said your trial was easy, and so was mine. It's no big deal."

"Yeah," says Flint, "stop scaring the newbie."

I look up from my bowl of sludge. "I'm not scared."

Flint laughs. "That's what they all say. You're gonna fit in just fine here, Rosco."

"She's funny, too," Mead says, beaming like he's a proud

parent on my first day of school. I'd like to kick him under the table, but Beck's sitting between us so I can't reach. "Thanks to me, of course. I taught her everything I know."

I roll my eyes. "Which didn't take long."

All the guys roar with laughter. As it dies down, Mead says, "*And* she catches on faster than Peakes." The guys laugh again as Peakes turns scarlet.

"Oh, lay off him," Beck says, but he can't stop grinning.

"Yeah, he can't help being a wimp." Mead shoves a spoonful of paste into his mouth.

"That's enough," Rosalia says sharply. I expect them to turn on her, but they actually quiet down. Why does Rosalia seem to have so much power over them? I should've asked Beck more questions about the Guild's hierarchy and how it operates.

I drift in and out of the conversation as the guys make jokes, mostly at each other's expense. Even though Beck is quieter than he was last night at dinner with just me and Mead, he seems comfortable here. I've figured out that Peakes must have been born in the Guild too, if he hasn't had his trial yet, but I don't know about the others. Am I the only outsider? Have they known each other their entire lives?

Bray and Flint stand up from the table, and with a quick good-bye they carry their dishes away. Peakes leaps up after them like he doesn't want to be left behind. Rosalia manages to fit in one more angry glare at Mead before shoving away from the table and going after her brother. And Sister Morgila thought *I* was hostile.

Mead lingers for a few more minutes before he, too, leaves the table. Beck and I finish our meals mostly in silence, though he keeps glancing at me like he's going to say something and then looking away again.

Finally I give up on him and speak first. "Were all of you born in the Guild?"

"Not Rosalia," he says, swallowing a mouthful of paste, "or Bray. But Rosalia came here with her parents, and Bray with his father, a long time ago, so they've basically grown up with us."

"Oh." I frown. "How come all of you listen to Rosalia? Is she, like, in charge of something?"

He's surprised. "What do you mean?"

"All of you do whatever Rosalia tells you to."

Beck considers this for a long moment and laughs. "Because we're all secretly terrified of her."

"But Peakes is her brother, and everyone teases him . . . ?"

Beck shrugs. "Peakes is the youngest, and aside from me he's the only one who hasn't passed his trial yet, so he's an easy target. But Rosalia never lets it go too far."

"Okay, new question. You call everyone by their last names except her . . . why?"

Beck shrugs again, finishing his mouthful of nonfood. "It'd be too confusing to call both of them Peakes, and it suits him better than her." He looks at my untouched oatmeal, which has taken on a sickly green hue in this light. "Are you going to eat that?"

After Beck finishes my breakfast, he picks up both empty bowls and carries them over to the dirty-dishes stack. We head back through the maze of tunnels to Beck's room. With nothing much to do and hours to go before our meeting with the king, we lie around the room, bored, until someone slams open the door.

"Beck Reigler," Mead announces, standing in the doorway, "I've been instructed to fetch you. By force, if necessary."

"For?" Beck says, not looking up.

"Tunnels. Racing. The usual crew."

"I don't think so."

"Reigler. This is not optional."

"I—"

"You don't need to spend all your time moping around and worrying about the trial. Besides, we need you for the team. Bray's recruiting Dryn."

Beck finally looks up, but his gaze rests on me, not Mead. "I don't think so," he repeats.

"What are we talking about?" I ask.

"You can join us, Rosco," Mead says jovially, though I suspect I'm an afterthought. "If you want. But it's starting now, so let's go."

"What's starting now?" I ask.

Beck sighs. "All right."

Mead grins. "You might want to dress warm, Rosco. The ice tunnels can be drafty."

Chapter Ten

I ce tunnels?" I ask Beck as we rush down the hallway. Mead left a minute ago, with a warning that we'd better be there in five minutes or he'd track us down. Beck threw me an overlarge coat and gloves from his dresser, put on similar ones himself, and then grabbed, of all things, a small wooden sled, which he's now dragging behind him. He's also refusing to answer any of my questions.

"You'll see when you get there," he says for the tenth time.

"Okay, but how about you give me a preview?"

"It's just a game," Beck says. "A race. This part of the mountain is full of caves and tunnels. The Guild converted the larger ones into our headquarters, but there a lot more that are covered in enough ice."

Enough ice. A race.

I look at the sled trailing behind us.

"Are you serious?" I say.

Beck grins. "Did I mention that Guild games can be somewhat reckless?"

"Somewhat?" I object, but the idea does sound sort of fun. There's never enough snow in Azeland to sled properly, and I've always wanted to try it. . . .

Beck leads me back to the front entry. Like before, the door-disguised-as-rock slides open with the press of pendant to stone. Abruptly we're outside, the icy wind whipping into my face. I should've taken the time to button this coat.

"Come on," Beck says, jogging toward the ledge where Ser landed our carriage before. "This way."

I am not fond of how quickly he's taking this really very narrow strip of rock, but I'm not about to be a coward. I run after him.

Thankfully, after a minute or so the ledge begins to widen. A couple of turns later, we duck under an overhanging icicle, squeeze between two rocks, and emerge victorious on a wide expanse of snow. We're in a cavern, surrounded on three sides by the same gray rock, but directly across from us the rock drops sharply away. The snow here is hard-packed and thin, barely providing traction as we walk. My feet skid over slick spots where the snow doesn't completely cover the ice that lies beneath it. The rocky walls stretch so far above our heads I can't see how high they reach, but shafts of sunlight filter in from above.

Several other people are gathered on the far side of the expanse. I spot Mead, with his height and paleness, right away. Next to him is Flint, the wiry boy from breakfast. I recognize Bray and Peakes too, the latter looking even scrawnier in contrast to Bray's bulk. There are also a couple of people I don't recognize: a girl, probably several years older than me, with short-cropped dark hair, and another boy, probably Mead's age, with some kind of twisty tattoo wrapping around one arm.

"About time," Mead says. "Dryn, Kierr, this is Rosco, by the way. New recruit."

The girl—Dryn?—looks at me, frowns, and turns to Mead. "New girl's on your team," she says to him. "We've already got Peakes."

Peakes's scarlet blush reflects my own embarrassment, but Mead shrugs indifferently. "All right, but I get Reigler and Flint."

"Deal," Bray says. "Have we got enough sleds for the Fall?"

Mead glances around, doing a quick count. "Nope. Let's do the Pass."

"No way," Bray says. "You know Flint's fastest on the Pass."

Mead gives another lazy shrug. "Got any better routes for eight players with four sleds?"

Bray frowns but seems to concede the point. "All right. Five minutes for strategy, and then we start."

Bray, Peakes, Dryn, and Tattoo Guy form a huddle, and the rest of us—Mead, Beck, Flint, and me—move to the other end of the cavern, as far from them as possible.

"Okay," Mead says, clapping his hands together. "Rosco's

going to be our first, and she'll hand off to Flint. Reigler's second, hand off to me. Got it?" Everyone nods except me. Mead approaches a wooden sled and pushes it across the snow toward me. "Flint and I will go get in position. Reigler, explain the rules to Rosco." Mead and Flint race off, passing between two large rocks and out of sight.

"Explain," I say to Beck.

"Okay, each team has four players, but only two sleds," Beck says. "So we've chosen two tunnels that we call the Pass. The first tunnel ends on a ledge, and then the second tunnel starts. The finish line is the bottom of the second tunnel. Each team will send two players down the first tunnel, then they'll hand off their sleds to their teammates, who will take the second tunnel. That way everyone gets a go. First team to have two sledders reach the finish line wins. So Mead and Flint are climbing down to the ledge to wait for us. You'll go down first and give your sled to Flint, and I'll be right behind you to give mine to Mead."

"So how do you and I get to the finish line?"

"We run."

Before I can respond, someone shouts over at us. "You guys ready?"

"Ready," Beck yells back, grabbing his sled. "Come on!"

Beck and I follow Bray and Peakes, who are both tugging sleds behind them. And now I finally realize what we're doing.

The rocky platform we're standing on drops off abruptly.

The only thing between us and a very long fall to the ground is a wide, ice-encrusted tunnel so steep that I can't see how far down it goes. The walls of the tunnel are slick, tight curves that twist and turn. Every inch of it is covered in thick, jagged layers of ice, gleaming blue and white in the dim light.

This won't be like sledding down a hill, or sledding on snow. This will be a fast drop, full of rocks and other obstacles, with the tunnel itself twisting and curving around.

I gulp.

Peakes has set his sled down on the left side of the tunnel, with Bray just behind him. Beck leads me to the other side. "You're up," he says gently.

"We're going at the same time?" I ask, looking at Peakes. "What if we crash into each other?"

Beck's mouth twitches. "Avoid that," he says.

Shouts filter up to us, echoing and distorted, from our other team members, waiting on the ledge somewhere many, many feet down.

I position my sled at the edge of the drop, in imitation of Peakes.

Jumping over the wall at the orphanage suddenly seems laughably easy. "This," I say, "is the most ridiculous thing I've ever done." I climb onto the sled.

Beck positions himself behind me, to give me a push.

"One," Bray calls.

"Two," Beck shouts back.

Then, in unison: "Three!"

Beck pushes the sled, and everything drops out from under me.

The sled shoots down the tunnel, runners skidding and carving on the ice. My stomach has dropped somewhere near my feet. I'm dying, I'm dying, *this* is how I'm going to die—

Across the tunnel, Peakes shoots ahead of me. He's riding his sled along the left wall, letting the curve push him forward. He doesn't appear to be dead, so . . .

I steer as best I can, throwing my weight to the right, tucking my arms in tight for more speed—

I've overdone it. The sled arcs up the wall, careening forward, runners gliding across the unbroken ice at the top—

The wall curves away, and I'm gliding on nothing but air. I'm flying.

I let out a scream of equal parts delight, adrenaline, and fear as I shoot through the air, overtaking Peakes. The sled lands back on the ice with a jolt, runners skidding. I hear shouts, but the frigid air whips against my face so hard I don't dare look up to see how far away they are. There's nothing but me and the sled and the ice as I speed toward the finish.

My feet hit the hard-packed snow first, and I tumble out of the tunnel, landing on the ledge on my knees. As Flint whoops in triumph and runs toward me, I roll away from the sled, letting him grab it. In a blink, he's gone, leaping gracefully onto the sled like it's an extension of his body. He goes down the second tunnel headfirst.

"All right, Rosco?" Mead asks. All the breath has been

knocked out of me; it's all I can do to smile. Mead smiles back.

From the tunnel above me come shouts. "I hate to rush you," Mead says, "but you might want to move."

I lurch to my feet and stumble away from the tunnel exit just as Peakes slides into view. He's winded and staggering, but he manages to land on his feet, at least. Dryn grabs the sled from him and races away, shooting down the second tunnel almost as fast as Flint did.

"Wow, Rosco," Peakes says when he catches his breath. "That was some stunt you pulled back there."

Mead gives me an affectionate pat on the back, so I decide this must be a compliment.

I glance down at my right hand. The snow has dampened the bandage covering it and seeped through, threatening to expose the black markings. The cold is making it ache even worse, too. I quickly shove my hand into my coat pocket.

Peakes and I back against the rock wall, out of the way of both tunnels, as first Beck and then Bray arrive and hand off their sleds, and Mead and Tattoo Guy disappear into the second tunnel.

"How was it, Alli?" Beck asks me, still gasping for breath.

"I think I almost died," I say. "Can I do it again?"

Everyone laughs. "Flint was right," Bray says with a chuckle, "you're going to fit right in here. Come on, if we hurry we can see the finish."

A snow-packed pathway curves away from the ledge.

The four of us remaining—Beck, Bray, Peakes, and me—run across the path, the ice tunnel shooting somewhere below us. At the end of the path there's a three-foot jump to another, larger ledge, where the second tunnel ends. Since the tunnel curves around a bit before ending here, we've beaten the second set of sledders to the bottom; only Flint and Dryn are waiting.

"I would've been first," Dryn is grumbling. "You got the better sled."

"Excuses, excuses," Flint says. As Beck and I approach, he grins at me. "Nice work up there, Rosco."

I can't seem to stop smiling.

A moment later the scrape of runners against ice echoes down the tunnel, and we all glance at the exit. Something barrels down, a blur of brown and black and pale hair—

Beck, Flint, and I erupt into cheers. Mead staggers to his feet and barely manages to dive out of the way as the second sled shoots forward, pitching its rider into the snow in a heap. At least I'm not the only one who landed that way.

Flint and Mead are already taunting our defeated opponents, but the teasing is good-natured. Beck and I burst into laughter as Peakes tries and fails to pick the ice out of his hair. Bray, not at all sore about losing, gives Peakes a high five. Shouts and laughter echo through the caves and bounce back to us. We are euphoric with adrenaline and recklessness.

I can't remember ever feeling this way before.

Kids at the orphanage were never like this. We didn't

have running jokes about previous exploits and victories, with designated positions in a group. No one ever stayed at the orphanage long enough for that. Kids came and went, in and out, even me. There was never a shared history to connect us.

It feels like a family.

This must be what it's like. To have brothers and sisters that you actually know, to grow up with the same group of people, to bond over shared lives. These are people who don't leave.

I've never wanted anything more in my life than to be a part of this family.

By the time we all head back inside, we're soaked head to toe, shivering, and laughing so loudly that half the Guild stares at us as we reenter the hall. Shouting boisterous good-byes, everyone heads off down separate hallways to their respective rooms in search of dry clothing.

I don't have anything dry to wear—I'm in the same clothes I stole from that shop in Azeland and have been wearing ever since. But Beck offers to let me look through his dresser to find something that fits.

"I'm just *borrowing* these," I say firmly, opening the bottom drawer. Beck's been way too generous already, and I don't want to owe him anything else.

"Of course," Beck says. "You'll get plenty of your own clothes once you join. But you're welcome to anything in there in the meantime."

I'm too wet and cold to argue the point any further. I find a nice warm sweater that actually fits me pretty well, and some worn but sturdy trousers that bunch a little at the ankles but aren't too bad otherwise. The only thing I don't have is a dry pair of shoes, but oh well.

After changing in the back bedroom and bandaging my aching hand again, I rejoin Beck in the main room, only to abruptly notice what he looks like for the first time this morning. The shirt and pants he's changed into are not only dry but also very clean and barely wrinkled, and it looks like he's actually attempted to tame his hair. The bagginess of my sweater and pants suddenly seems offensive in comparison. "Oh," I say, "am I supposed to be dressed up for this whole meeting-the-king thing?"

Beck barely glances at what I'm wearing. "It's considered a sign of respect to wear your best clothing, but for most of us here that just means anything that's clean. And you're new, so he'll know you don't have anything to wear yet."

"Are you sure?" My stomach is churning, though whether from nerves or magical injury I can't tell. The whole ice-sledding escapade helped me forget about meeting with the king today.

God help me, I'm about to meet the king of the Thieves Guild.

"Don't worry, Allicat," Beck says. "It's no big deal. Although, it might be helpful if you try not to insult him or mouth off."

"Who, me?" I say, too innocently. "When would I ever do such a thing?"

"You did with Durban, but this will go a lot smoother if you don't. Even if he says something awful and makes you angry, which he probably won't, don't say anything."

I'm about to make another joke, but I can tell from the look on Beck's face he's seriously worried, so I nod. "No problem. I can be quiet and respectful and whatever."

Beck makes a startled choking sound. "Somehow I doubt that," he says when he's finished sputtering.

"No really. How do you think I got out of the orphanage? I just played nice for a while."

"And here I thought you killed all the Sisters, set off a large explosion, and burned the orphanage to the ground."

"Oh, that happened too. But before all that, I had to play nice for a couple of minutes. And it nearly killed me, but I totally did it."

"Guess we have nothing to worry about, then." He scrubs one hand across the back of his neck. "I guess it's time," he says.

"Guess so," I say back, but he doesn't move for a second, just takes a deep breath. "You okay?"

"Sure. It's just, I've been waiting for my trial for a long time."

I smile, trying not to show that I'm feeling nervous too. One of us has to be the strong one. "What are we waiting for, then? Let's go."

Chapter Eleven

We stop outside Durban's door. Beck takes a shaky, deep breath and knocks. There's silence for a long moment. Too long. Is he even here?

"You may enter."

I sigh in relief. At the last minute, I remember to shove my hands into my jacket pockets before we go in. The black lines are much more noticeable now than they were the first time I was here, and there's a chance they'll peek through the bandage.

Durban takes us both in, his gaze as intense as before. "You've decided to stay," he says to me. He doesn't sound happy about it.

"Yeah." I can think of plenty of other things I could say in reply, but Beck was probably right about not mouthing off. I hold my tongue and try to think calm thoughts.

Durban sighs like we're the most dreadful inconvenience he's ever had to deal with. From his desk, he picks up a massive brass lantern. "Follow me," he says, brushing past us and sweeping out the door.

"See?" I whisper to Beck. "I was totally civil."

Beck rolls his eyes and follows Durban out the door.

Down one hall, then another, until we reach the spot where the hall branches into three—this much, at least, I remember from Mead's tour. Durban doesn't hesitate, taking us down the hallway Mead said we couldn't enter, lighting the way with his lantern. I expect to feel magic or something that would show the hall's spelled, but nothing happens. Maybe Durban did something to take the spell off, so we can walk down here?

The doors in this hallway aren't wood, like in the rest of the guildhall. They're silvery metal, with heavy locks bolting them. Protected by magic too, probably. I almost laugh out loud at the thought of thieves having to protect against thieves.

Durban stops in front of one of the doors. This one's not as large as some of the others and doesn't have a fancy lock on it. Durban knocks once, twice, three times. He pauses for a second, taps again, and again. There's some kind of pattern to his knocks like a secret code, but before I can figure out what it is the door swings open by itself.

Durban steps over the threshold. Beck and I look at each other and follow him, side by side. Durban blocks my view of the room. It's dimly lit, with only a few candles in sconces like everywhere else.

"Beck Reigler to see you about his trial, sir," Durban says. For once he actually sounds *meek*. His voice is still cold and clipped, but it's lost its edge. "And he's brought a . . . new recruit. From Azeland, where he was last assigned. Name's Rosco."

"I see," says a man's voice softly. "Thank you, Durban." There's nothing commanding in the man's tone, but that's clearly Durban's cue to leave. He bows his head stiffly and exits.

A desk sits in the corner of the room, lit by a single candle. It's cluttered with papers and strange objects and—my eyes widen—a small bag overflowing with gold coins. They're majas, without a doubt. More than I've ever seen at once in my entire life.

I finally wrench my eyes away from the coins and take in the king himself, who's sitting behind the desk. He's younger than I imagined, no older than thirty. His brown hair is combed and trimmed neatly around an angular face, framing blue-gray eyes. He's dressed in all black, from what I can see.

Even as I stare at him, he examines us. I feel like an orphan on Adoption Day all over again.

"Have a seat." He gestures to the two chairs opposite the desk. We sit quickly, both trying to keep from staring at the coins piled in front of him and both failing.

"So," he says softly, "you wish the join the Guild, Rosco?"

"Yes, sir."

He looks at Beck now. "And you think she can do it?"

Beck doesn't hesitate. "Yes, sir."

Well, at least one of us is confident in my abilities.

Kerick nods slowly. "I don't have to remind you that we usually do not accept new members younger than thirteen, do I?"

Nobody told me that. I look at Beck, who's staring at the floor. "No, sir."

"I am willing to make an exception," Kerick says. Beck looks up. "But only if you're confident that Rosco will be an asset to this Guild. We are not a charity."

"I understand, sir," Beck says quietly.

"And you vouch for her?"

"Yes."

"Very well." Kerick steeples his fingers, revealing a deep, rough scar slashed across the back of his hand. "In that case, you may take Rosco with you on your trial. Since you vouch for her, you can train her. The two of you will work together to complete this task."

I have no idea how this typically works, but this seems like a relief to me. I won't have to do it alone. I'll have Beck with me.

I glance at Beck's face. He's trying to mask his expression, but a muscle twitches in his jaw. Obviously he's not as happy with this idea as I am.

"Now," Kerick continues, "since there are two of you, I expect you can handle a challenging task."

From within the desk he pulls out a small scrap of

parchment. He lays it flat in front of us so we can see. It's a sketch of a necklace, with a gray chain that's probably silver, and some kind of blue stone in the middle.

"This necklace," Kerick explains, "was recently purchased by Lord Atherton of the Shoringham estate in Ruhia, as a gift for his wife, Lady Atherton. The Guild needs to acquire it. Take the necklace and bring it here, and you will pass your trial. You may use any of the Guild's resources if necessary, although you cannot ask anyone else to steal it for you. Tell Durban if you need anything, and he will assist you. However, you may not share the specifics of your trial with anyone, even Guild members; when asking for Guild resources or making preparations, you must provide as little information as possible. Otherwise, you may do whatever you feel is necessary to complete this task, as long as you tell no one about the Guild. If caught, you will say you were working alone."

Kerick stops, letting all this sink in. I have a bad feeling in the pit of my stomach. The task seems straightforward enough—steal the necklace, bring it back—but stealing from a noble will probably be even harder and more risky than it sounds. Judging from the tightness of Beck's jaw, he's reached the same conclusion.

"If I may offer some advice," Kerick continues, "there will be a ball held for Ruhian nobility at the Dearborn barony tomorrow evening. The Athertons attend every year, and I have heard from a reliable source that Lady Atherton plans to wear the necklace at the event. The crowds at a ball may make sneaking in easier."

Beck perks up a bit at this. He nods slowly, and I can practically see him formulating a plan. I'm glad to be doing this with him. Making plans isn't really in my skill set.

"You have until the first day of Mirati's Month to report back here," Kerick says. "If you do not return by then, it will be assumed that you have been captured or chosen not to continue. Understood?"

We both nod vigorously and say, almost in unison, "Yes, sir."

"Reigler, you're dismissed. Rosco, stay a moment."

My stomach lurches. What does he want to say to me that he won't say in front of Beck?

Beck casts a worried glance at me, but he leaves.

I'm alone with the king of the Thieves Guild.

Kerick meets my eyes and holds me there. "I don't know how much you have been told about the way the Thieves Guild operates. But before you undertake this trial, there are some things you should know."

He leans back in his chair, his gaze still locked on me. "I've known Beck Reigler for many years, and I trust his judgment. If he thinks you can pass the trial, I have no doubt you can. Your ability to complete the task is not what concerns me."

Well, there's an unexpected vote of confidence. It seems everyone thinks I'm a good thief except me.

"What concerns me," Kerick says, "is not whether you are able to do what is necessary, but whether you are willing."

Now he's totally lost me. Didn't I just say I want to join?

His gaze is uncomfortably intense as he continues. "You must be willing to do anything and everything the Guild asks of you. Being a member means doing whatever is necessary to ensure its survival. Being a thief means doing whatever is necessary to ensure yours. If you want something, if you need something, you must take it. But taking something for yourself, for your Guild, means you will always be taking away from someone else. You must be willing to take from anyone. From everyone. That's the first rule of survival. Someone's loss is another's gain. Someone's death is another's life. If you can't accept this, then I can't rely on you. So I will ask you only once. Are you sure that you want to become a member of the Thieves Guild?"

The answer should be easy, since I don't have a choice in the matter. I have to join the Guild to get the money. And I have nothing to lose, right?

So why do I feel like I'm giving something up?

The first rule of survival. Just like Beck's first rule: Stealing is necessary to survive.

Who knew being a thief had so many rules. I guess even freedom has limits.

"I'm sure."

Kerick nods once, looking satisfied. "Very well. You may go."

"Thank you, sir," I say, because it seems like the thing to say.

On my way out, I glance back. He's already looking at the papers on his desk, sparing no more of his attention on me.

Beck waits for me at the end of the hall, holding Durban's large lantern. His face is ashen.

"So, that went well," I say.

Beck gives me a withering look.

"What? What's wrong?"

"I've never heard of anyone being given a trial this hard before," he moans. "Only some of the older thieves are sent to steal from nobility. This is bad. This is really, really bad."

"Don't be so whiny. We get to work together on it. How hard can it be to sneak into a crowded ballroom and take one little necklace?"

"You don't get it," Beck insists. "He wants us to fail. He thinks you're too young to join and that I shouldn't have brought you. He thinks we're going to mess this up."

"Well, that's not what he just told me."

Beck's eyes widen. "Really? What did he say?"

"He said he trusts your judgment about me. He said he's not concerned about my 'ability' or something."

"Seriously? He said that?"

"Yeah, he said that."

Beck frowns. "What else did he say? Why'd he keep you so long?"

"He just wanted to give me some overly dramatic speech

about making sacrifices for the Guild or whatever. I get the gist."

"Oh." He sounds relieved. "Well. Guess we need to go see Durban then." Without another word he sets off down the hall, waving the lantern in front of him. I practically have to jog to keep up.

"Wait, we do? Why?"

"To get everything we need," Beck says, not slowing down. "We'll need transportation. And clothes. And a forger, probably. . . . How are we supposed to get all this ready for tomorrow?"

"I really have no idea what your plan is," I say.

"Isn't it obvious? We'll need to disguise ourselves. Servants disguises would be less conspicuous, but we'll be traveling by thilastri anyway, and we'll need an excuse to get close to Lady Atherton . . . unless we have one of each costume?"

"Huh?"

"But it'll probably be harder to get the right clothing for us on such short notice. Olleen probably won't have anything to fit you. . . ."

"Slow down and explain what you're talking about."

"But a servant could hardly walk up to Lady Atherton and just grab the necklace off her neck—"

"Beck Reigler, if you don't tell me what the plan is right this minute, I will beat you over the head with that lantern."

Beck glances at me, figures out I'm serious, and slows a little but still doesn't stop. "We're going to have to disguise ourselves as nobility to sneak into the ball."

Chapter Twelve

Um, Beck?" I say. "That is a bad plan. A really, really bad plan."

"Why? How else can we get up close to Atherton?"

"I don't know, maybe because neither of us could pass for nobility even if a million majas suddenly landed in our laps?"

"Nobles don't notice anything unless it's obvious. If we have the right clothes and arrive by thilastri they'll never know the difference. It's the clothes that count."

"Who are we going to pretend to be? The heirs of Lord and Lady Thief of the estate of Delusion?"

"All right, genius, do you have a better plan?"

"Your disguise-ourselves-as-servants plan wasn't totally ridiculous," I say, to distract from the fact that I have no plan.

"Won't work. We have to arrive by thilastri, for one thing, since we don't have any other transportation, and how're we going to explain that? And somehow we're going to have to get close enough to Atherton to get the necklace from her, and servants won't be able to do that. Besides, people suspect servants to be thieves. They won't suspect fellow nobility."

Fair points. "But even if we dress up as nobility, which may be impossible, and come up with a good story about who we are, which is even more unlikely, we'd still have to try and fit in. We don't have noble manners, we don't know who anyone is, we can't dance—"

"Speak for yourself," Beck says lightly. "I, for one, am a terrific dancer."

"Oh, now you decide to make jokes."

Beck takes a deep breath. "I'm just trying to figure this out, okay?"

I open my mouth to respond, but Beck stops paying attention. We've stopped outside Durban's door again. Again we wait, and again Durban's voice says, "You may enter."

I've seen way more of this man and his office than anyone ought to in one day.

Durban doesn't ask for the details of our trial, and Beck doesn't share them. Beck starts listing off things we need, and Durban alternates between jotting things down on his parchment or protesting that he can't get something Beck's asked for. They go back and forth, Beck asking for things and Durban arguing about it. Within a few minutes, I've totally lost track of what they're talking about, but I notice the pattern of their conversation, the way Beck keeps his voice calm yet firm during the arguing, while Durban's voice sharpens with every back-and-forth. I can't tell who's winning.

Finally they seem to be wrapping things up. "The invitations will be difficult, with so little time," Durban says, "but we have people in Ruhia. I'll see what they can do. As far as the disguises, we should have the clothing available, but it may not be in the right size. You'll need to see Olleen Mighan about the clothes and alterations."

"Thank you." Beck's not totally sincere but very polite. He and Durban look at me like I'm supposed to say something.

I manage a curt, "We appreciate your help." Looking relieved, Beck ushers me out the door.

"See, I don't mouth off to people if I try," I say smugly.

Beck snorts. "Come on, we've got to go see Olleen."

Great, more running around through hallways. "So who's Olleen?" I ask as Beck takes off at a brisk pace. "Is she, like, the clothing and disguise person?"

"Yeah. She's head seamstress."

"Oh. Will she have time to make us disguises by tomorrow?"

"Hopefully there will be some already made that can be altered to fit us," Beck explains. "But yeah, it will be hard to get the clothes ready by tomorrow."

We haven't gone very far, but Beck leads me over to a big wooden door near the kitchens. This one doesn't even have a nameplate.

Beck knocks once, then opens the door without waiting

for a response. We step into one of the largest rooms I've seen here. Yet somehow the room isn't large enough for all the furniture and material crammed into it—wardrobes, dressers, boxes, tables, cupboards. Clothes are scattered everywhere: piled on tables and tumbling out of drawers and falling off boxes and draped over chairs.

The room's only occupant is an older woman with graying hair and crooked eyeglasses, sitting at one of the tables. She holds a piece of fabric with one hand and needle and thread with the other. She's the most motherly-looking figure I've ever seen in my life.

She sees Beck, and a huge smile lights her face. "Beck! So good to see you, I hadn't heard you were back!" In a flash she's across the room, giving him a quick hug.

Then she spots me. "Who's this?" she asks warmly. For a second I'm afraid she's going to hug me too, and I have no idea how to respond to that. But something in my face must warn her off, because she doesn't come any closer.

"This is Alli Rosco," Beck says. "We're doing our trial together."

Olleen looks vaguely surprised. "Is it time for your trial already? You've grown so quickly, I'd forgotten. . . ."

Beck nods. "Yeah, and we've got a big favor to ask."

In an instant, Olleen's expression grows serious, and she's all business. "What do you need?"

"We'll be attending a ball," Beck explains, "at a barony. And we'll need disguises to get inside."

"You'll need noble's wear, then," Olleen says instantly, already looking around the room, surveying the clothing that's been thrown around. "Unless you were thinking of servant disguises . . . ?"

"We're considering both," Beck says. "We're trying to get a forger to get us an invitation as nobility, but if that fails we'll need the servant disguises."

Olleen nods. "When?"

"Tomorrow evening."

"It'll be difficult," Olleen says. She looks sharply at me. "This one'll be hard to fit. We don't have many girls her age or size. But I have some gowns we can reuse, if I get them tailored right. . . . And as for the servant disguises, there's usually a uniform for an event. I'll need to know what it is."

Beck frowns. "We don't know. And we don't have time to find out."

Olleen nods again. "In that case, I'll just make you something generic. You won't be able to pass as one of the servers in the ballroom, but you could pass as a stable boy or even a carriage driver, and Alli could be a maid. . . ." Her expression is distant as she looks at both of us, apparently imagining how we'll look.

"Whatever you can do," Beck says. "But there's one more thing." He looks at my hand, which is still hidden in my pocket. Olleen follows his gaze, looking quizzical.

"Alli needs something with long sleeves," Beck says, "and gloves."

"I'll do my best. But I'll need some help." Abruptly she strides toward the door. "I'll need to call in all my seamstresses, and then we'll take your measurements. . . . Alli, do you know how to sew?"

"Um, yes," I say, "but only for mending and little things."

She waves a hand dismissively. "We can find a use for you. Wait here while I round everyone up."

Before I even know what's happening I'm being poked, prodded, and jabbed by Olleen and three of her assistants. They stick me with pins, wrap measuring strips all around me, hold cloth against my skin, and shove all sorts of frilly fabric over my head. Just when I think there can't possibly be another layer to this costume, they throw something else on. I'm doing the best I can to hold my temper, but it flares up under my skin, and I'm suffocating in all these folds until I'm about to burst. It doesn't help that my poisoned arm is aching even worse, with extra little shooting pains from my fingertips to my elbow.

One of the girls stabs me again with a sharp needle. "Could you *please* watch where you're poking that thing?" I ask, my voice straining. It kills me to add the "please." But I got the sense that Beck likes Olleen, so I'm trying to be on my very best behavior. It's just so *hard*.

"Almost done with the underskirts," Olleen says briskly, like that's supposed to make me feel better. It just means there's still the outer layer to go. "Anik, bring me that red dress with the lace—no, not the brocade, the red silk—in the cabinet on your left. . . ."

One of the girls, whose hair is elaborately coiled into a braid that reminds me of a snake, eyes me critically. "Will we have to cut the longer layers out?" She says it like the very idea of cutting the dress makes her want to cry.

"How am I supposed to walk in this?" I say, looking down at the many layers of skirts ballooning out below me. "I can't even see my feet."

"Oh, her shoes," Olleen gasps. "I forgot the shoes. We'll never find a pair small enough—"

"Doesn't anyone around here have small feet?" Snake Braid says.

"Rosalia does," says the girl who stabbed me with a needle.

Another girl scoffs. "Rosalia doesn't have any shoes decent enough."

"Um," I say, "if no one can even see my feet, why don't I just go barefoot?"

Every girl in the room stares at me like I've just said Saint Zioni is the patron of spring and Saint Samyra is for fools. There's a minute of total silence, then Needle Stabber says, "Maybe if we stuff something in the toe of the shoes, they'll fit her?"

"I've got some newspaper around here somewhere," Olleen says in agreement.

I sigh. "Now would probably be a bad time to mention I hate heels, right?"

But then a girl carries over the red dress, and we all stare at it. Even I can't come up with anything sarcastic to say. It's beautiful, a deep red silk that shimmers even in the dim candlelight, with layers of fabric falling gracefully into folds at the bottom, and a trim of delicate white lace all around the edges. It's the kind of thing the queen of Ruhia or duchess of Azeland would wear. But it's not something Alli Rosco, the abandoned orphan-turned-thief, would ever be given.

This time I don't protest as Olleen and the girls help me into the dress. I'm afraid to move, as if it might burst into flames if I touch it. The delicate lace is smooth against my skin, and for a second I imagine it falling to pieces.

After fiddling with the layers of fabric, Olleen and the girls step back and look at me.

There's another long silence, finally broken by Olleen. "Well," she says. "Aren't you something."

I look down, and the reason for all the layers of underskirts is revealed. The gown was made for someone larger than me, and would've swallowed me without all the extra skirts filling it out. As it is, I feel like all the fabrics are suffocating me, but at least the gown seems to fit, though it's maybe a bit too long.

"Shoes will help with that," Olleen says, looking at the bottom of the gown. "They'll give her the extra inch or two she needs."

Oh. That's the reason for the shoes.

Snake Braid squints up at me. "And her hair. It'll need to be styled—"

"And trimmed," Needle Stabber adds. I glare at her.

"Someone else can handle that tomorrow morning," Olleen says firmly. "Right now we need to get her alterations done. Some of the underskirts don't hang right—"

"And the pleated skirt is bunched up a bit on the left," someone adds.

"Olleen, do you think some of the lace on the sleeves needs to be trimmed? They look too long otherwise."

"Do you think it's laying across her shoulders right? Do we need to—"

"—and maybe a bit off the very edge—"

"—says there might be some more shoes in that cupboard, but I doubt they'll fit—"

I sigh and surrender myself to the torture, wondering why I ever agreed to this.

As it turns out, the fitting was the easy part. It's followed by the alterations, which involve hours and hours of sewing by candlelight while Olleen's assistants talk about other people in the Guild I've never heard of. And sewing is even more difficult when you have thick bandages wrapped around your hand and fingers and it hurts to even move your arm.

What's Beck doing right now, while I'm pricking myself in the finger for the hundredth time and ripping out incorrect stitches? Whatever it is, it can't be as bad as this. If only he were here to suffer with me. Not because I want to see him, or anything. Just because I think he should have to suffer through this too. Maybe this would be more entertaining if he were here. But it's not like I need him around all the time. I can do things by myself.

I stab the fabric with the needle a little harder than necessary.

Finally, Olleen notices I can't keep my eyes open anymore. "Go to bed, Alli. We'll take it from here."

Some of the other girls glare at me as I leave. Judging from the amount of work left to do, they'll be up all night sewing. I'd feel bad about it, except I'm still sore where they pricked me with pins.

This time I manage to find my way back to the living quarters without help, but I'm not totally sure where Beck's room is. I wander the halls, glancing at every door, struggling to read the nameplates. It takes me a while to read some of them, but I spot names I recognize along the way: Peakes, Bray, Flint. . . .

Finally. Lianice Grimstead. The familiar door. It's sure to be locked, but I've still got that lock pick and tension wrench in my pocket and I'd like to try it again. . . .

It's unlocked. Beck's inside, sitting on his bed in the corner, sketching on a piece of paper.

"Hey," I say.

He looks up. "Hey. You missed dinner, so I brought some back for you." He gestures toward the table, where a plateful of food is sitting.

As soon as he says it, my stomach rumbles. I didn't even realize how hungry I was. "Thanks."

I sit on the couch and shovel food into my mouth. The taste's still awful, but I'm getting better at ignoring it.

"How'd it go?" Beck asks.

I swallow. "Fine. Olleen seems nice."

He nods, his eyes still on the paper in front of him.

"It seemed like you know her really well," I say hesitantly. I've tried not to pry into his life—I'd hate it if he did that to me—but I'm really curious. And I have a feeling he'll tell me if I ask. Aside from the times when he lied to avoid telling me about the Guild, Beck's been honest with me.

He looks up. "Mead told you about my mother." He doesn't say it questioningly. How long has he known?

No point in denying it now. "Yeah, a little."

"It's okay," he says. "I don't care if you know. I'm not ashamed of her." He takes a breath. "Olleen really helped her. They were friends. And whenever I had to go on assignments, Olleen would look after her, make sure she was doing okay. . . . Nobody else would."

"Oh," I say. "How did . . . how did she . . . ?"

"There was a flu epidemic," he says quietly. "Before, she would've healed herself, but by then she wasn't able to heal anymore. Magically, I mean. The other healers did what they could when it got bad, but . . . sometimes there's nothing they can do."

I nod. "I'm sorry." When he doesn't say anything, I ask, "How many healers does the Guild have?"

"Right now? Three or four. It's hard to find good ones

to join the Guild. The ones that pass certification can make tons of money without the Guild, and the ones that don't pass aren't very good healers. Most of the ones we have are people who couldn't afford the instruction and never got to take the test, but have been healing their whole lives anyway. Like my mother."

"So she came to the Guild 'cause she couldn't get certified?"

"Right."

"And . . . was your father a Guild member too? Did you know him?"

Beck fiddles with the pen in his hand, picking at the quill's feathers. "I don't know who he was," he says matter-of-factly. "All I know is . . . my mother's last name was Grimstead. But everyone's always called me Reigler. No one ever told me who he was, and I never asked."

It's not hard to guess why. No one here is exactly the fatherly type.

"Sorry," I say, "I didn't mean to pry."

Beck smiles. "Yes you did. But I don't mind. It's not like it's a secret."

Now would be the time to volunteer information about myself. To tell him about my brother. But it's one thing to tell him that my mother abandoned me. How could I tell the full truth—that she abandoned *only* me, that I was the child she loved the least? No one needs to know that part. I wish *I* didn't know it.

I ignore the memories that are flashing through my head and change the subject. "So," I say, "what are you scribbling over there? Battle plans?"

"I'm trying to memorize the layout of the ballroom. The Guild has blueprints to almost every building in Ruhia, apparently, including the Dearborn barony, so Durban lent these to me. I'm trying to draw them. Helps me memorize them."

"Okay," I say, "so what *is* the battle plan, at this point? And what else don't I know, besides the fact that we suddenly have access to *blueprints*?"

Beck launches into a long explanation of every detail and change I missed while in the sewing room. He passes me the blueprints to memorize while we discuss strategy, trying to figure out where we'll be entering and how best to get the necklace. It'll be impossible to get it from her in the middle of the ballroom without someone noticing, but I might be able to follow her to a better location, maybe a bathroom or something.

After what feels like hours of planning, my eyelids droop. I fight to keep them open at first, but then my mind gives in too and I fall into sleep, Beck's voice echoing in my ears.

Chapter Thirteen

I wake to a papery crinkling sound. Something sharp digs into my thigh. I open my eyes, unfamiliar shapes blurring in front of me. I'm on Beck's couch. I've rolled over onto one of the papers, a drawing of the ballroom we were scribbling on. I must have fallen asleep right here, without making it to the bed in the other room.

Instinctively, I look down at my right arm. As usual, the curse has spread during the night. It's more than halfway up my arm now, past my elbow. The lines on my hand have grown so thick that they bleed together; only hints of my tan skin peek through. Worse, my hand aches dully, and pain shoots up my arm whenever I move.

I sit up. Mead's lock pick is beneath me. Must've fallen out of my pocket when I rolled over last night. I stuff it back into place and look around for Beck. He's not here. But there's a bowl of food on the table in front of me, in addition to the dirty dinner dishes from last night. Did I sleep through breakfast?

Oh well. I'm starving.

I've nearly emptied the bowl when the door swings open and Beck walks in. "Good, you're up."

"Why didn't you wake me?" I say. "I didn't mean to sleep so late."

"You needed to be well-rested for today," he says, striding across the room. He's full of energy, but dark circles sit under his eyes.

"Why didn't *you* sleep late, then?" I say.

"I couldn't sleep," he admits. "There's a lot to do, anyway."

"Okay." I jump up. "Tell me what needs to be done."

"I've got to go see Durban to make sure the forger's finished our invitations. You need to go to training."

"Training?" I ask skeptically. "What kind of training?"

"Just the basics," he says, waving one hand dismissively. "Most people have time to do more training before their trials, but . . . well, you'll have to make do. I've already arranged it for you. Just head to the training center that Mead showed you on the tour."

"Okay," I say, but I hesitate. "Couldn't *you* just show me whatever it is I need to know?"

The corner of his mouth quirks up. "Please, Allicat, could you do this one thing without arguing?"

"Of course I could," I huff. "If I wanted to."

He waits.

"Fine," I say, realizing I've been tricked. "I'll go to this stupid training thing. But I expect to find lunch waiting for me when I get back."

"Sure, sure," Beck says. Already his gaze is wandering to the piles of notes and blueprints spread out on the table, still planning things out in his head.

I sigh and head for the door.

I enter the room and gasp.

It's the largest open space I've seen here, larger even than the entry hall. Where the Guild's other rooms are like little caves, narrow and low, this one is a cavern. The ceiling arcs dozens of feet above, shrouded in shadow. And the room below it is so big that calling it a room seems like an understatement. It's divided up into a bunch of different sections, and dozens of people are walking and running and leaping and doing who-knows-what else. To my immediate left, there's a guy armed with some kind of shiny metal weapon that I think might be a mace. To my right, an arrow whizzes through the air and strikes a sandbag all the way across the room. Nearby, I recognize one of Olleen's seamstresses from last night, who clearly has talents other than sewing— she's hurling daggers at distant targets.

"Rosco!" someone yells, and I turn. It's Dryn, the girl from the ice sledding, running up to me. "There you are," she says, in a tone that lets me know both that I'm late and that she disapproves.

"Here I am," I repeat. "Beck said I'm supposed to report for basic training?"

"Right, he told me you were coming," she says. "I'm one of the basic trainers here. I get all the newbies."

I take a second, more critical look at her. She's slight but sharp, like her bones are both lighter and more pointed than other people's. Her hair only reinforces this impression, cut short in a way that's all edges. And there's something very jagged about her smile. Still, I find it hard to imagine that these scary Guild guys, like the mace-wielding giant over there, take instruction from this tiny girl.

I must look skeptical, because she grins and says, "I'm even tougher than I look."

"I believe you," I say sincerely.

She eyes my right hand. "What's with the bandages?"

"Um, I had a little accident while escaping an orphanage in Azeland. There was jumping from rooftops involved." I shrug as if it's no big deal. And it's not technically a lie. "So, what exactly am I going to be learning?"

She touches a finger to the corner of her lip and looks me up and down, considering. "Since we don't have time for the full training," she says, "let's stick with the things that are absolutely necessary to your assignment, okay? I know you can't tell me any details, but I'll just ask you some very general questions and we'll go from there."

"Okay," I say, already feeling nervous. How much will we have to skip?

Dryn must be asking the same question, because she says, "So is there anything you already know how to do? Any particular skills you've picked up?"

I don't know what she considers to be a skill. "Beck taught me how to pickpocket, and steal from markets," I say, rather pathetically. "And Mead taught me how to pick locks."

Dryn doesn't say anything, but her stony expression suggests that this is not good. "Is your task going to involve a lot of direct combat? Hand-to-hand fighting or boxing, swordplay, anything like that?"

I am completely thrown off by this question. I thought the Guild was all about *thievery*, not combat. "I . . . don't . . . think so?" I manage. "Is that *normal*?"

Dryn ignores the question. "Any specialty weapons? Bows? Explosives?"

"*Explosives?* You have those?"

"Focus," Dryn says, stern but not impatient. "If we don't have to worry about any of that, then we'll skip it for now. I *would* like you to have some basic fighting skills so you can defend yourself, but we'll see if we can work it in later. Okay. Theft-wise, are we talking large object or small?"

"Small . . . ish," I say, making a circle with my hand to demonstrate the size of the necklace. But I'm just guessing, actually. I don't think the king said if that drawing was done to scale or not, now that I think about it.

"All right," Dryn says, nodding, "that gives us a place to

start. Now, is this going to involve stealth or deception in any way? Sneaking around, probably?"

I'm so relieved to finally know the answer to a question that I practically shout at her. "Yes!"

"Okay," she says. "Follow me."

We make our way across the room, past a knife-throwing range where several large handles are embedded in small wooden targets, and past a large cushioned ring where two men are sparring. Dryn pushes away a large black partition and waves me through to the other side.

I'm in a small rectangular space, set off by six-foot-high partitions. And in front of me is a maze.

Except that the walls of the maze are fairly low, just over my head; a tall person could see right over them. Which makes me wonder what their purpose is. They're rather flimsy-looking, possibly cardboard, their edges jaggedly torn.

I'm so distracted by the weird walls that it takes me a second to notice the floor, which is even stranger. At the entrance to the maze, the rock floor of the cavern is covered in dark, even circles, spaced neatly next to each other, with only glimpses of rock visible between them. Unlike the walls, these don't look flimsy at all. They're made of some material I'm pretty sure I've never seen before that is most likely very expensive.

"Pressure sensors," Dryn explains, seeing my gaze. "Made by magicians. We stole them from a security company that sells them to banks and noblemen who want to guard their safes. Eventually, you'll learn how to disable them in case you ever come across them, but for now, *I'm* going to use them."

It takes me a second to catch on. "It's a test," I say, dread coiling in my stomach.

"Right. There's a safe over there, on the other side of the maze." She points toward the entrance. "The point of the maze isn't to confuse you, it's to make you practice turning corners and fitting in narrow spaces. Get to the safe without setting off a sensor, and you win."

The way she says "win" reminds me of how competitive she was at the sled race, and I suspect that there's nothing in the safe, no prize to be reached. The goal is just *to win*, to beat the game.

"And how exactly do I keep from setting off the sensors?" I ask, knowing I'm not going to like the answer.

She gives me that sharp grin again, the one that reminds me, in the same way that Durban's voice does, of razor blades. "You have two options. Either you walk on your toes and manage to step in the spaces between the sensors, or you walk so lightly that the sensors don't even detect your steps."

She cuts a sideways glance at me, and I understand. I really only have one option. The point of this whole exercise is to teach me how to be stealthy. Stepping in between the sensors is possible, but it would take ages to precisely plant each step, and it wouldn't really teach me anything. The goal is to learn how to walk lightly, to be silent and quick, unheard and unnoticed. The pressure pads aren't really meant to be obstacles. They're for measurement. Light enough, or not light enough.

"Okay," I say. "Let's do it, then."

Dryn gestures with one hand toward the entry. "Go ahead," she says.

I take my shoes off—there's no way this will work with them on. The cavern floor is chilly against my bare feet. I step forward, toward the entrance—the absolute last normal step I can take from here to the end.

"Oh, and Rosco?" Dryn calls. "You have two minutes."

That's okay. In order to succeed, I'll have to be fast anyway. Slow means heavy.

I will myself to be light. I am a cloud, floating away. I am nothing but air. My bones are like Dryn's, weightless and small. I am hollow.

I take a step, my foot landing on the first sensor.

I don't know if it goes off. I'm not paying attention to that. I'm flying, barely allowing my feet to land before lifting them again, springing on my toes. I'm a bird, soaring. I don't need to touch the ground.

The walls curve rapidly, back and forth, the turns so narrow that I nearly stumble into them. My cursed arm bangs the walls more than once, and the pain is excruciating. At one point the passage is so tight I have to squeeze through sideways, and it seems impossible that anyone larger than me has ever successfully managed this. Maybe Dryn is playing some kind of elaborate hoax, and this isn't a test at all but a prank designed to make me look ridiculous. If so, it is wildly successful.

But then I round the last corner, and the end veers into view. I leap off the last sensor and land hard, my heels thudding to the ground for the first time since I entered the maze. A small gap between the maze walls and the natural rock makes a sort of doorway; I step through and walk back up the length of the maze to the front again, where Dryn is waiting impassively.

"Time?" I ask.

"You were fast," she says, inclining her head. "And you only set off two sensors."

"Only?" I can't believe it. "Then I failed."

"Well, technically," Dryn says. "But nobody ever passes their first try. You did well." She says this casually, in the way you might say *the sun is bright* or *Ruhia is cold*, but I suspect that Dryn is not the sort of person to hand out compliments unearned. I smile. I might actually be good at this.

"So, I'm done with this one?" I ask, trying not to sound too relieved.

Dryn nods. "We can move on for the moment. Now we know you can step lightly, but can you do it without making a sound?"

I really don't like where this is going. "Silence has never been one of my favorite things," I warn her.

She grins her razor-blade grin again. "Oh, Prince is going to *love* you."

★ ★ ★

Prince, it turns out, is a very large dog.

A very large dog with very impressive hearing, and even more impressive teeth.

A good-sized pen in one corner of the cavern is entirely devoted to Prince, who sleeps on a large pile of blankets in a far corner. A high chain-link wall firmly squares off his territory.

"Only Kierr can go in there," Dryn says to me conversationally. "Prince snaps at everybody else, even if they bring food."

Kierr, it turns out, is Tattoo Guy, the one I met ice sledding. Dryn drags him away from the boxing area and commandeers his services. Which must be a regular occurrence, since he's fairly good-natured about it.

Kierr opens the gate and slips into Prince's pen. The dog's head jerks up, teeth bared, but then he drops it back down and closes his eyes again. Kierr walks casually up to the dog, then slips off his watch and sets it near the pile of blankets.

This time, I don't need anyone to explain to me what I have to do. I have only one question. "What happens if he mauls me?"

Dryn shrugs. "Kierr stops him in time. Usually."

I can't tell if she's joking. But surely the Guild doesn't want all its new recruits to die on the first day of training, or there wouldn't be anybody left. This is as much a test of bravery as it is of my thieving abilities, and it's one test I don't intend to fail.

Kierr makes a sweeping gesture toward the open gate. I square my shoulders and walk inside.

I'm glad we did the pressure-sensor thing first, because it really does help. Moving both quickly and lightly, I take a direct route across the pen, my toes barely hitting the floor with each step.

I hold my breath as I get closer to Prince, not wanting the sound of breathing to give me away. It's probably a useless gesture, though; I'm sure he can hear my heart hammering.

Keeping my eyes on the sleeping dog beside me, I reach down and scoop up the watch.

Prince doesn't move.

Still holding my breath, I move back across the pen, victory within sight—

There's a low growl behind me.

I run.

I charge through the gate, and Kierr slams it shut behind me. Prince reaches it a second later, teeth snapping, and lets out a loud bark.

"Oh, shut up," Kierr says. Prince peers at me through the fence and gives one last warning growl, then retreats to his bed. Breathless, I hand Kierr his watch.

"That was close," Dryn says, her eyebrows arched, but I think she sounds a little impressed.

Dryn tells me I've earned a "break," which means I get to watch other people train for a while instead of doing stuff myself. We sit down by the fighting ring and watch a couple of matches. While we watch, Dryn points out things about each fighter's techniques and movements, giving me instruction on what to do—and, more importantly, what not to do. Though Dryn never gets up there herself, it's clear that she knows what she's talking about—she calls half of the fighters' moves before they make them. She doesn't always offer a prediction on who will win a match, but when she does, she's always right.

Most of the fighters are older people who I don't recognize, but Bray steps up for the third match, and Kierr goes against him. Kierr suddenly appears impossibly small in comparison to Bray's bulk. Bray looks so intimidating standing in the ring that he seems nothing like the friendly guy I met at dinner and raced in the ice caves.

"Pay close attention to this one," Dryn says as Kierr and Bray circle each other. "Chances are most of your opponents are going to be larger than you, which means you'll have to be faster and smarter. Watch Kierr's technique here."

I still don't know much about this, but it's clear right away that Bray is very good. He uses his size and force to his advantage, but it's not the only thing he relies on. Kierr immediately goes on the defensive, weaving in and out of Bray's attempted strikes. At first Dryn points out all the things Kierr's doing right that I should try to imitate, but then she starts shaking her head in disapproval. Kierr is getting worn out, his movements growing slower. Bray mostly stands in place and forces Kierr to do all the work avoiding him. Even I can tell who's going to win this one.

By the end of the fight, Kierr's sporting a nasty bruise on his face but grinning broadly. He and Bray shake hands and leap down from the ring.

"Learning anything, Rosco?" Kierr says to me.

"She learned how to get knocked out," Dryn says dryly.

"So what's next for you?" Bray asks me. "Want to learn how to swordfight?"

Sword fighting with Bray sounds like fun, actually. I look imploringly at Dryn, but she shakes her head. "Just basics for her," she says. "She's getting a crash course for her trial."

"Another time," Bray says. "After you pass your trial, of course." He winks at me.

"Definitely," I say.

Bray claps me on the shoulder like we're old friends, then nods at Dryn and saunters off. Warmth fills my chest again. I'm starting to feel like one of them, like a young Guild member myself. I have to earn their respect, but I seem to be doing okay at it so far. Maybe it won't matter that I didn't grow up here, like Beck and Mead and Peakes and them. Maybe being brave and a good thief and more than a little reckless are all it takes to fit in. If so, I've just got to work on the "good thief" part. But given my progress so far, I might actually be good at it.

"Where to next?" I ask Dryn. I beam a little, unable to contain how pleased I'm feeling.

She lifts her sharp eyebrows again, and this time it's not in approval. "All we have time for is the final test," she says.

"Save some of that energy, 'cause you're going to need it."

"And the final test is . . . ?"

"You're going to steal," she says, "from me."

Unfortunately, she wasn't joking.

She makes me leave the cavern and tells me to count out five minutes. When I return, I have to locate her in the crowded space and figure out how I'm going to steal the knife that's sheathed at her right hip. The technique I use to steal it is entirely up to me—stealth, speed, confrontation—but I will win the challenge if I can get the knife away from her in under ten minutes.

The problem, of course, is that she knows I'm coming.

Direct confrontation obviously isn't an option, since I have no real fighting skills. I decide to treat Dryn like the sleeping dog—a combination of stealth and speed might allow me to get close enough to grab the knife. But the dog was asleep, and Dryn certainly won't be. She may not have Prince's hearing, but she'll be watching for me. Maybe I can hide behind something, get in as close as I can, and then . . .

My five minutes are up. I reenter the cavern.

I spend a couple of minutes walking through the archery and weapons ranges. I want to move quickly, but I force myself to take it slow. If Dryn sees me before I see her, I'll have lost my only advantage. I try to blend in with the crowd of Guild members instead, all the while keeping a lookout for the dark brown color of Dryn's jacket.

Which is why I don't recognize her right away. I've almost passed by her entirely when I catch a glimpse of her face. She's taken her jacket off, so she's now dressed in black. Cheater.

I duck down behind one of the partitions. Dryn is on the other side, but I don't think she's noticed me; she's deep in conversation with Kierr. Maybe she doesn't realize my five minutes are up, or maybe she doesn't think she has to try very hard to stop me. I grit my teeth. Either way, she's wrong.

I close my eyes. I visualize pressure sensors covering every inch of the floor between her and me. I creep to the other side of the partition, so I'll have a direct shot. I take a deep breath.

And run.

She sees me coming and tries to turn, but Kierr's in the way and I'm fast. She can't quite spin away quick enough. As I run past her, I grab the knife. I have so much momentum that I can't stop running, and now I've overshot it and I'm about to crash into an archery target. . . .

I skid, trying to slow myself down, but I slam into the side of the wooden target and land with a rather loud thud on my back, all the air whooshing out of my lungs. The knife is clenched in my hand.

I hear laughter. And applause.

Someone walks over to me, and a tattooed hand appears. "Get up," Kierr says. I accept his help and let him pull me to my feet. Nothing seems to be broken, but I think my back is going to be bruised, and fresh waves of pain are shooting up and down my cursed arm.

Dryn almost smiles. "Not bad," she says to me. "Not bad."

"Your escape is going to need a little work, though," Kierr says, laughing.

"Agreed," I say, rubbing my back with a wince.

I hand Dryn's knife back to her. "So, what do you think, coach? Do I pass?"

She looks me up and down again. "You're fast," she says, for the second time today. "And you know how to play to your strengths. Keep doing that, and you'll be fine."

"That means you passed," Kierr translates.

Dryn points a finger at me. "But I expect to see you back here for *full* training as soon as your trial is over," she says. "If you don't show up, I'll find you." But she smiles when she says it.

"You got it," I say. "Thanks, guys."

"Be careful," Kierr says, giving me a little salute.

"I will." I wave in farewell and walk out of the training center, feeling lighter than I have in days. My curse suddenly seems irrelevant, a problem that happened to somebody else. It's not going to stop me.

I'm going to pass this trial, and Beck and I are going to join the Guild for real. Those rich people and their balls and their necklaces aren't going to stand in our way.

They won't know what hit them.

Chapter Fourteen

Rosalia?" I moan in disbelief. *"Why?"*

I have returned from my training session only to find that my lunch is cold and Beck has clearly lost his mind. Instead of letting me in on whatever it is he's been doing today, he insists that I need to go see *Rosalia*, of all people. Given how prickly Rosalia seems, I'm not sure this is a good idea.

Beck remains unmoved by my reaction. "Her mother was once a lady-in-waiting for some noblewoman or other, and—"

"Wait, what? Then how'd she end up here?"

"I don't know for sure," Beck says impatiently, "but rumor has it she fell in love with Rosalia's father, who was a commoner, and ran off with him. When Rosalia was little, their father lost everything and they came here, where Peakes was born. Their mother died, but before she did she taught Rosalia all about being a noblewoman. If there's anybody in the Guild who knows about how to behave in a ballroom, it's her."

"So why don't you have to go see her too?"

"I already did. I told her you'd be coming. Besides, I don't need as much training there as you do. You're the one who's going to have to corner Lady Atherton somewhere, so you've got to convince her you're nobility."

"Great, so I'm doing all the work while you're off enjoying the party?"

"Hardly. I'm going to be your bodyguard. I'll get us out of there if anything goes wrong."

I start to ask him what he's going to do if something happens, but the image of him holding a knife to the shopkeeper's throat flashes in my head. I guess I know.

"But if nothing bad happens—which it won't, because no one will see me and I'll totally fool Lady what's-her-name— then you don't have to do anything but smile and look pretty."

I expect Beck to joke back, but apparently he's not in the mood. "Atherton," he says. "Her name is Lady Atherton."

"I know, I know." I roll my eyes. "I've got this."

Beck looks pained. "Go see Rosalia. Please."

"Fine. Where is she?"

"She's got a room in the single living quarters. She's waiting for you there. Halfway down the hall on the left side. Just look for the nameplate."

"Right," I say. "Okay, and then what should I do after that?"

"Go to Olleen's and get ready. By then it'll be time to go."

"It won't take that long," I protest.

Beck shakes his head. "It might take a while. And so will getting dressed. And then there's the flight to Dearborn's. We've only got a few more hours to get ready. So hurry."

"Who left you in charge of this trial, anyway?" I stomp over to the door, just to let him know how I feel about his bossing me around. But once the door closes behind me, I hurry down the hallway. We don't have much time left.

By the time I finally open the door marked ROSALIA PEAKES, she's waiting for me inside, looking impatient.

"Lesson one: punctuality," she snaps as I close the door.

"Um, I don't think that's really an issue," I say. "No one's supposed to notice us enter the ball anyway. And I doubt the lady will care if I'm punctual in stealing from her."

Rosalia looks me up and down, her eyes stern. "We have a lot of work to do."

I think I'm supposed to be insulted.

Rosalia proceeds to lecture me on everything from manners to posture to grammar to dancing. She hands me papers with long, tongue-twisting sentences on them and makes me read them out loud, starting over every time I stumble on a word, correcting the way I say things and complaining about my Azeland accent. She gives long instructions on how to address nobility and how to say things politely and all this other stuff I'll never remember. Every time I point out that this information is useless to me, she just makes me do something harder, glaring the whole time. Irritation prickles under my skin, and before long it sharpens into anger.

Then come the books. Rosalia stacks heavy books on my head and makes me walk across the floor, holding my back perfectly straight and balancing them. I never make it more than a few steps.

After the hundredth time I've dropped the books, Rosalia glares, her eyebrows raised and her gaze cold, and says, "Again."

In response, I grab one of the books and hurl it at her head.

She sees it coming and sidesteps, dodging without breaking a sweat. It barely grazes the sleeve of her dress. I wait for the lecture.

She lunges, grabbing my right arm. A wave of pain rolls through me. I try to spin out of her grasp, but her grip tightens, squeezing hard, and her other arm comes up around my neck. Cold metal presses my skin. She's holding a knife to my throat.

"Don't be a fool," she says. Her voice is calm and deadly. I wish she'd scream at me. I wish she'd act human. Then I'd know she's vulnerable. "If you act too rashly tonight, your recklessness could get someone killed. This isn't a game."

She pauses, her breath slow and steady in my ear. "Beck Reigler has been waiting his entire life for this, and if you don't pay attention now you might ruin this for him. You cannot mess this up."

She pulls away from me, releasing her grip and moving

across the room in one quick stride. "You never know what will happen. You need to be prepared for anything. And if you can't even walk with the correct posture, those nobles will know in a second that you're not one of them, no matter what you're wearing. You don't have much time to get this right. Now try again."

I don't care if she's right. I hate her. I hate the way she tells me what to do, the way she acts like I can't do anything, the way she talks about Beck like she knows everything about him. And the way she tries to make me feel afraid. She's nothing more than a bully.

But I can't deal with her the way I would the orphanage bullies. I don't doubt that she'll use that knife.

The books are still strewn across the floor. Rosalia waits, tapping her foot impatiently. She won't even help me pick them up. She thinks I'm beneath her.

I can't do what she says. I won't.

"Now, Rosco."

I bend down slowly, picking up the nearest book. And as fast as I can, I throw it at Rosalia's face. But this time I don't wait to see her dodge it. I know she will. This time I just run.

As I race down the hallway, I know I have the advantage of surprise. Plus Rosalia will never be able to run as fast as me in her dress and heeled shoes. But as I reach the end of the hall, my footsteps are the only ones beating against the stone floor. She's not following me.

From here, the sewing room comes up quick. I slow to a stop outside the door and catch my breath, hands on my knees.

Now that my heart's stopped racing, guilt churns in my stomach over what I just did. Beck asked me to learn from her and I failed.

The thing I hate most about Rosalia is that she was right.

I ignore that thought. I can do this. This is nothing. This trial is nothing. I don't need Rosalia. And I'll make it in the Guild just to spite her.

While Olleen and her seamstresses work feverishly to put the finishing touches on my dress, another girl does my hair, brushing out the snarls. It's all wet and limp because Olleen insisted I take a bath before the beautification process could begin. Not that it helped much. Beck's tub was tiny, and the water was cold, and my hair was so tangled I could barely get the soap through it. The girl with the brush has been working mercilessly for what feels like hours. She twists my hair up and pins it on top of my head somehow, but I can't really tell how it looks in the mirror. Then she dabs some kind of thick cream on my face and adds a smelly powder on top. I probably look like a performer in the Fool's Parade on Saint Samyra's Day, with a painted-on face that makes me look stupid and ghoulish, so everyone will cheer when Samyra shows up and banishes me. That's how it always goes in those parades.

Before I see if my face looks as bad as it feels, though,

I'm whisked off to the fitting area, where we have to do the whole pricking-and-jabbing process over again as I'm stuffed into a thousand billowing skirts. Someone has finally found a pair of heeled shoes in my size, and I thank Ailara that Mrs. Pucey made me wear heels to church, so I know how to walk in them. Olleen also provides a pair of elegant white gloves, but I don't put them on yet—I'll have to strip off the bandages to do so, and I don't want anyone to see that my hand and arm are turning black.

After what must be hours of Olleen making little adjustments to my dress, I'm finally allowed to step out of the sewing room. Despite my hatred of how Rosalia treated me, I do walk a bit straighter as I make my way across the room and out the door.

Beck's waiting for me in the hallway, wearing a fancy black suit. The formality of it makes him look much older and much younger all at once. And for the first time since I've met him, his hair actually looks like it knows what a comb is. It's shorter, too.

He's staring at me. At the dress, at my face, at my hair. For what may possibly be the first time in my life, I blush. He probably thinks I look like a fool too.

But his mouth quirks up at the corners like it always does when he's smiling and trying to hide it. He looks like he's about to say something, but before he gets it out, Olleen rushes over to him and wraps him in a hug. This time it's Beck's turn to look embarrassed.

"You're so grown-up," she gushes. She steps back and takes in the two of us, side-by-side in our newly fitted clothes. "That's it. Go."

Beck swallows hard. "Ready, Allicat?"

"Ready."

He takes my hand, and we go.

Chapter Fifteen

Ruhia in the late spring looks a little like Azeland does. I've always pictured cozy snow-covered cottages and quaint streets, but the city is sprawling, with big brick buildings. At this time of year there's not even much snow on the ground. The streets are cleaner than Azeland's, though, all of them paved, and less crowded. Where Azeland's size feels chaotic, Ruhia's buildings are laid out in neat, orderly rows, square boxes of brick all standing in a line, their slate roofs dusted with snow.

Our current thilastri, whose name is Jiavar, doesn't speak much as she flies, so we're left mostly in silence. Beck doesn't look out the carriage window. He stares straight ahead, fiddling with his jacket, bouncing his leg nervously against the seat. I pretend not to notice and try to be calm enough for the both of us. This is no big deal. Just go in, take the necklace, go out. Easy.

I occupy myself by stripping off the bandages covering my right arm so I can put on the white gloves. I haven't looked at it since the last time I changed bandages, after I took a bath. It's so much worse than I thought. From fingertip to elbow, deep black lines streak across my arm, crisscrossing and running together so much they almost entirely obscure the skin, as if I'd plunged half my arm into a massive inkwell. Even my nails are darkening.

It looks like death.

I grab one of the gloves and shove it on as quickly as I can, but it's too late. Beck is staring at me, and the horror that's curling in my gut is reflected on his face. I tug the sleeve of my dress back into place and try to pretend I haven't seen what I've seen.

Beck stands and picks up my other glove, which has fallen to the floor. Swiftly he sits beside me and passes me the glove. He helps hold my left sleeve up as I slide it on, then pulls the sleeve back into place.

It's his turn to be calm. "It's okay," he says. "We can do this."

I can't look at him. I can't breathe. "I don't want to die."

"You won't."

"I already am."

I don't think I've ever prayed to Saint Xeroth, the patron of death. I guess now would be a good time to start. But I don't even know what I want to say.

Please. Not yet.

"It'll be fine," Beck says. "I know we can do this, Allicat."

I gulp for air, and eventually my breathing steadies. I look at him. "Why are you always so nice to me?"

He frowns. "Why wouldn't I be?"

I barely restrain myself from rolling my eyes at him. "Do you really think anyone else in the Guild would've helped me like you did? You think someone like Mead or Rosalia would've cared?"

He doesn't answer for a minute. "I don't know. I guess I'm not always a good thief."

He's wrong. I've seen the Guild in him, like when he threatened that shopkeeper when we first met. He knows all the rules, and he always tries to follow them.

But there's something else, too. Some deeper instinct, the one that drew him to help me, a total stranger, in the first place. Because he didn't see a total stranger; he saw a homeless orphaned girl who needed help. He cares about people, in a way that the Guild teaches you not to. He hasn't figured out how to stop.

He stands again, picks up the bandages I dropped on the floor, and stuffs them under his seat. He goes back to fiddling nervously with his jacket, and I go back to staring out the window. We don't speak.

Too soon, the carriage is dropping, and I close my eyes as the ground swoops up to meet us. A massive jolt throws me against the seat, then the carriage wheels scrape stone. I open my eyes.

We wind down a long road, which ends in massive iron gates that have been flung wide. A long parade of carriages, pulled by thilastri, are lined up, making their way through the gates.

All around, the grass is lush and neatly trimmed; flowers and trees and other ornate-looking plants fill well-manicured gardens. The closer we get to wherever we're going, the gardens get bigger, and the flowers get more elaborate, until I'm certain that Saint Ilaina herself must have grown them. No gardener could grow these fancy plants without help from the patron of nature.

The road widens, and the house rises into view. It's exactly what I expected: big and fancy. With massive windows and sweeping turrets and curved balconies, it towers over the surrounding landscape. The carriages curve around a circular drive, then stop one by one and drop off their occupants.

After an agonizingly long wait, it's our turn. Jiavar slows the carriage to a halt. A footman dressed in a sharp blue uniform opens the door and sweeps into a low bow.

"The most esteemed Baron Dearborn extends his deepest welcome. Your invitations, sir?" he says, his voice crisp. He doesn't sound suspicious, just overly polite.

Beck reaches into an inner jacket pocket and withdraws two pieces of paper, which he hands to the footman. The invitations are fresh from the forger and barely arrived in time. They're supposed to be exact replicas of the invitations to this ball, but they claim we are Allianna and Berkeley

Martell, heirs to some estate or other. We don't really look like brother and sister, but we figure we can pass as cousins.

The footman barely looks at the invitations before handing them back to Beck, and I sigh in relief. The footman holds out his hand and helps each of us out of the carriage. I try not to trip over my skirts as I step down. Beck tosses a single jamar to the footman before taking my arm and leading me up the path, following the nobles inside. I'm so glad I'm not doing this by myself. I never would've known I was supposed to tip the footman. Unless that was something Rosalia was going to mention?

In my heels and huge skirts, every step is agonizing. I keep hoping the path will end before I trip, but it winds through one of the large gardens, which is illuminated by flickering lanterns and contains a massive gurgling fountain, before narrowing into a set of wide glass doors.

Beck's breath catches in his throat, whether from nerves or awe I can't tell. I want to squeeze his hand in reassurance, but the way we're walking arm-in-arm like the nobles makes it impossible. "Okay?" I whisper under my breath.

"Okay," he whispers back.

We follow the crowd through the double doors and into the ballroom, and this time it's my turn to choke back a gasp. The room is so much more elaborate than anything I could've imagined. The walls are golden and luminous. Chandeliers drip glass crystals that catch the light and make the whole room sparkle like we're inside a diamond. The walls are striped with windows overlooking the twinkling candlelight of the gardens. In a far corner, musicians sit on a raised platform, playing slow, elegant music. All across the dance floor, the bright flashes of the women's spinning skirts blur as couples glide through the steps.

I should've listened to Rosalia. She could've told me how to deal with this. I have no idea how to deal with this. Oh God, will I have to dance? Saints help me, why didn't I learn this?

Beck looks a little awed, too, but he hides it better than I do. He tugs me down the side of the dance floor before we're noticed by anyone standing near the entrance. He scans the room, looking for Lady Atherton.

We stop in the corner opposite the musicians, where butlers in neatly pressed uniforms are serving refreshments. We turn our backs to the wall. From here we can see the whole room.

I only have a dim idea of what Lady Atherton looks like from the description Beck got from Rosalia, so I look for the necklace instead. A rock that big will be hard to miss, after all. The problem is, most of the ladies here are wearing large necklaces. The one we're after is distinctive, but it's hard to tell right away from a distance—

There. A heavy silver chain, glittering in the light, with a rounded deep blue stone easily as big as my fist. The woman wearing it is the right age. I nudge Beck. "Ten o'clock. Puffy blue dress."

"I see her," Beck says, excitement tingeing his voice. "Okay, what's the plan?"

"You tell me. How do I get to talk to her?"

"Someone has to introduce you," he reminds me. "You can't just walk up and start talking—"

"But no one here knows me!"

"We'll have to fix that." He scans the crowd again, but I have no idea what he's looking for this time. "There!"

"What?"

"That man standing alone, at twelve o'clock. We'll need to get near to him, close enough so he can overhear, and start talking about something. If we can get him to jump into the conversation, we'll introduce ourselves. Once someone knows us, we can start making the rounds until we get to Atherton."

That involves talking to people. A lot of people. Someone's sure to notice that we don't act or speak the way we should, or doubt our identity, or . . . "You didn't mention this part of the plan!"

"Let's go." Beck ignores my protests as he strides away, around the dance floor and toward the only man in the room who's by himself. Maybe the man doesn't even know anyone. Maybe he's actually a serial killer and that's why everyone's avoiding him. Maybe he's going to notice something's wrong with us. Maybe . . .

We're closing in. Beck steps beside me, matching his stride to mine. "Pretend we're deep in conversation," he says. "Laugh like I've said something funny."

I try, but the laugh gets stuck in my throat on the way up, and comes out more like a choked snort.

Beck smiles tightly. "Really? Was that supposed to be a giggle?"

"I didn't do it on purpose," I say through clenched teeth, forcing a smile. "I don't know how to giggle."

"Just smile then. And try not to look so murderous." Beck grins more naturally.

We're only a few feet away now, so close the man can hear us if we raise our voices. Beck looks at me and, like we've been deep in conversation this whole time, says, "I've been telling you, this ball far outpaces the one at the Sheffield barony." His voice is perfect, sounding clipped, brisk, and arrogant.

I try to match his tone and figure out what he wants me to say. "I disagree," I say stiffly, trying to arch my eyebrows haughtily the way Rosalia does. "The Sheffield ball was far more . . . sophisticated." The word pops into my head on its own, and for the first time in my life I'm grateful to Sister Romisha for sharing her big vocabulary.

By now we've clearly caught the man's attention. "Yes, but it seemed to lack something that the Dearborns always provide," Beck says, arguing in that eerily calm and elevated tone that only the rich nobility use, the one that's polite and arrogant all at the same time. "It's a certain . . . a certain . . ." He flounders at the last second, unable to come up with a word.

"The Sheffield ball was so much more refined," I say, trying to smooth over Beck's flustering while sounding as pretentious as possible.

The man chuckles suddenly. "I'm afraid she's right, young

sir. The Dearborns have been letting any old riffraff in this year. This is nothing compared to the Sheffields'."

Beck fakes a sigh. "I suppose I'll have to concede defeat, then. But thank you, sir, for putting an end to our argument."

The man frowns, almost sheepish. I have a feeling he's done something improper by jumping into our conversation. He quickly extends one hand to Beck. "Sir Marius Drozzen at your service, young sir."

Beck shakes his hand quickly. "Master Berkeley Martell," he says without missing a beat. "Allow me to introduce my cousin, Miss Allianna Martell."

Drozzen bobs a quick bow to both of us. "Honored to make your acquaintance." He rushes through it like he's just following propriety. "Enjoying the evening, then?"

"We are," Beck says, "but I'm afraid we don't have many acquaintances in attendance tonight. . . ."

Oh. I get where he's going with this.

"What a shame!" Drozzen cries. "For two such lovely young people! Do allow me to introduce you to someone. I'm sure there are some other young people here—"

Before we can say anything, Drozzen's moving, away from the wall and toward the packed floor where, during a lull in the music, the crowd mills around.

Beck barely hides his wince. We don't want to meet young people, especially since people our age will probably notice we're imposters. Besides, we want to be introduced to people who know Lady Atherton.

But it's too late to sneak away. Drozzen's found a cluster of kids close to our age, and he's turning back to us, gesturing. Exchanging hesitant glances, we step forward.

Drozzen's already introducing us. "Master and Miss Martell, may I introduce Masters Abbott and Touzel, and Miss Ariannorah Atherton."

Atherton. My body tenses involuntarily at the name. Do the Athertons have a daughter? They must. Who else could she be?

Ariannorah is as pretentious as her name. She stands with perfect poise, even more than Rosalia, with her soft chin and delicate nose turned up so she can look down on everyone. She's pretty, though, with rich brown skin and curling black hair that's wrapped up around her head with fancy silver hairpins.

She looks down at me, lips pursed. Her eyes scan the length of my dress, and she smirks. With the smallest flick of her head, she turns away from me. Clearly I'm not worth any more of her time.

Then she sees Beck, and her whole demeanor shifts. She drops her chin a little, batting her eyelashes, and slowly extends one hand and curves it downward, the way ladies are supposed to do when being introduced. The way I should've done when meeting Drozzen, probably.

I've never seen anyone kiss a lady's hand, and I'm guessing Beck hasn't either, but he doesn't hesitate or look unsure. In one swift movement he cups her fingers lightly with one hand, bends down, and brushes a kiss across her fingertips.

My cheeks flush, and heat races through me. It's probably all these skirts I'm wearing. But that doesn't explain my sudden urge to claw Ariannorah's eyes out.

In a second, Beck straightens up and drops her hand, but nobody seems uncomfortable or suspicious, so I guess he did it right. The other two boys, Abbott and Touzel, aren't looking particularly friendly, though. If I didn't know better, I'd think they were glaring at Beck.

"I'll leave you to it, then," says Drozzen, slipping away into the crowd. No one really notices.

One of the boys—Touzel?—is in front of me, bowing his head. Am I supposed to do the same thing Ariannorah just did? Quickly I extend my hand, but it doesn't look demure or elegant; I've practically shoved it in his face. He doesn't seem to notice. Cradling my hand like it's made of glass, he kisses the tips of my gloved fingers, so quickly I barely feel it.

"It's an honor, Miss Martell," he says. He stands up, looking awkward, like he's not used to doing this. Maybe it's okay if Beck and I are a little clumsy, then. Maybe all noble's kids are new at this whole manners thing too?

Ariannorah's glaring daggers at me. She bobs a quick curtsey in my direction. "A pleasure." Her voice drips sarcasm.

I don't really know how to curtsey, but I'm counting on my long skirts to hide this fact. I manage a sort of bobbing movement and incline my head. "The pleasure is mine," I say with equal venom.

Hearing the sharpness in my voice, Beck gives me a sort of warning glance. Oh, right. Ariannorah is somehow related to Atherton. We need to meet Atherton to get the necklace. We have to focus. *I* have to focus.

Not to be outdone by the other boys, Abbott approaches me, and I repeat the hand-shoving motion with him. Then both boys nod their heads toward Beck in a quick bow, which he returns, and the introductions are finally over.

"Is this your first ball?" Abbott asks, looking at Beck but not me. "We haven't seen you at any of this year's large events." He says it politely, but I don't think I'm imagining the thinly veiled insult. Clearly, he doesn't think we're important enough to have attended their fancy parties.

"I've been staying at my uncle's estate in Azeland for the past year," Beck says. He nods at me. "I offered to escort my cousin to her first Ruhian ball."

"You're from Azeland?" Ariannorah says it like it's a dirty word. "How charming. I thought I heard an accent."

I want to point out that Ruhians are the ones with the accent, but I'm supposed to be on my best behavior. "Yes," I say stiffly.

Ariannorah laughs, a sort of cackling sound like a witch, and turns back to Beck. "How awful, that you were estranged from all polite society for so long."

I'm definitely not imaging the insult this time. "Yes," I cut in, "it's such a shame Berkeley never knew polite society until he came to Azeland. He'll have to come visit more often."

Ariannorah's eyes narrow, and she turns slowly back to me. The boys are all looking at me now too. Touzel's mouth hangs open, but Abbott looks offended. Beck's glare suggests he wants to strangle me. I guess I forgot about the whole "best behavior" thing.

"I know this is your first Ruhian ball," Ariannorah says quietly, "and therefore you've never been in such polite society before, so I will not take offense at that remark."

I open my mouth, planning to say something like "Then I won't take offense at yours," but Beck starts talking before I get an insult out. "So tell me, what have I missed while I've been away?"

Ariannorah is all too happy to turn her attention back to him. She launches into a long description filled with noble-sounding names and estates that no one really pays attention to. Halfway through, the musicians strike up a new tune, and couples move toward the dance floor.

Ariannorah watches the couples with a gleam in her eye and turns pointedly to Beck, breaking off midsentence.

For a second I think Beck's going to miss her not-so-subtle hint, but he gets it. Copying a gesture we've seen other men doing, he bobs down in a half-bow, extends his hand, and asks, "May I have this dance?"

It's awkward, but Ariannorah's too thrilled to notice. She places her hand lightly in his and steps forward, her long dress rustling. Her gown is pale pink with a massive skirt that reminds me of a frosted cupcake. She and Beck walk away, revealing that the waist of the gown is cinched with a massive pink bow in the back like she's sprouting wings. She looks so ridiculous I have to bite back a laugh.

I'm distracted by Touzel, who bows in front of me, a bit more gracefully than Beck managed, and says, "May I have this dance?"

I'm about to say yes, but I never learned how to dance. I shouldn't have thrown that book at Rosalia. The first book, anyway. The second was justified. Touzel's just staring still. God, what should I say? Panic surges through my mind.

"I'm feeling a little faint," I manage, which is true, since the bodice of this stupid dress is squeezing all the air from my lungs. "I think I need to, uh, sit for a second—"

Touzel is instantly concerned. "Let me help you."

Without waiting for a response, he takes my arm and leads me over to some chairs against the wall, all the while looking at me like I'm suddenly incapable of walking two steps on my own. I guess playing the damsel in distress was a good move, though. Touzel's jumping at the chance to help. "Let me get you a refreshment!" he offers, way too enthusiastic. "Perhaps some cider, or some sparkling water?"

"Thank you," I say, both to seem polite and avoid the drinks question, since I have no idea what any of them are. I try to remember the last time I had anything to drink but water and can't think of a single time.

Abbott sits beside me, but he doesn't look happy about it. He stares longingly toward the dance floor. I follow his gaze and see Ariannorah and Beck. Luckily it's a slow dance, so it doesn't look like Beck has to know any complicated steps. I don't know how much Rosalia taught him. . . .

Ariannorah's hand is digging into his shoulder like a bird sinking its talons into prey. He's got his hand around her waist, which is awkward, since it's squashing the ugly bow on her cupcake dress. They're standing so close their noses practically touch.

Heat floods my face. Good thing Touzel went to get me a drink. I'm so hot under all these skirts.

Abbott and I sit in silence, glaring at Beck and Ariannorah.

Touzel returns with a drink in each hand. "I wasn't sure which you wanted," he gasps, "so I got both, and I'll take the other. . . ."

I take the nearest drink without really looking at it. "Thank you," I say, trying to smile at him. It probably looks more like a grimace.

Touzel sits down on my other side. He looks at the dance floor like he's watching the couples, but he keeps glancing at me and then looking away quickly. Every couple of seconds, he runs a hand through his light brown hair, making the ends stick up a little. It looks better that way, sort of tousled instead of slicked.

I take a sip of the drink. It's tart and fizzy, burning on its way down my throat. Touzel seems to be waiting for me to say something. He won't stop looking at me, so I say, "That helps, thanks."

He looks relieved. "If there's anything else you need . . . ?"

"Not right now."

We sit in silence.

I try to plan my next move. Beck's obviously hoping to get Ariannorah to introduce him—or us?—to her mother at some point. But what then? I'll have to get her alone somewhere, then take the necklace and run before she has time to call the guards. But how long it will take Beck to win us an introduction? This is so complicated. I'd been hoping we could just walk up to Atherton once we found her. I thought getting her alone would be the hard part. Now I understand why Beck was so worried about this trial. It requires so much more than just thievery. It's all about deception and playing our parts.

The first song leads right into a second, then a third. Beck and Ariannorah dance without stopping. After what must have been hours, the third song ends. Beck's laughing, his face flushed, and Ariannorah looks like she's giggling. She leads him to the other side of the room, away from where Touzel and Abbott and I are sitting. Toward Lady Atherton.

Maybe he's convinced her to make the introductions already?

Abbott's just figured out Ariannorah's not coming back, and he leaps to his feet. "Let's see where they're going," he mumbles, by way of explanation. I don't think he wants to be accompanied, but I latch onto this excuse and follow him. After a second, I hear Touzel's hasty footsteps behind me.

By the time we get across the floor, Ariannorah's gotten

her mother's attention. Lady Atherton turns away from the women she was talking to and looks down at her daughter. We're still too far away to hear what's being said.

We draw closer. Lady Atherton turns to Beck, and he offers her a low bow. She just looks at him. Now, finally, we're getting in earshot.

". . . pleasure to make your acquaintance," Atherton says, but there's no pleasure in the way she says it. It's cold.

Like mother, like daughter. I wince. I guess we have that in common, since Ariannorah might have an awful mother too. Or not. I can only hope my mother and I have less in common with each other than the Athertons do.

We're close enough now that Lady Atherton sees us. "Allow me to introduce my cousin, Miss Allianna Martell," Beck says quickly.

I fake another curtsey, and Lady Atherton inclines her head a fraction of an inch. "Pleasure," we say at almost the same time.

There's a beat of awkward silence. Then Lady Atherton looks at her daughter and says, "Why don't you children go on to the refreshment table?"

Ariannorah winces, and again I feel a pang of something that might almost be sympathy if I didn't hate her. She's clearly embarrassed at being treated like a child. "I was hoping we could take a stroll in the gardens," she says, and something about the way she says "we" makes me think it doesn't include me or Touzel or Abbott. "I was just telling

Berk—Master Martell that you're such an expert on botany, and you could give us a tour?"

Who does she think she's kidding? We all know she doesn't care about botany, and neither does anyone else. But, now that I think about it, this might be perfect. The gardens are more isolated, and there are fewer people around. If Beck distracts Ariannorah, I can grab the necklace and run. "I'd love to hear your opinion," I chime in. Everyone looks at me in surprise. "I've always been so fascinated by botany, and I'd love to hear an expert's take. . . ."

As I was hoping, Lady Atherton swallows the bait. She looks flattered, if mildly inconvenienced. "I suppose I could show you children around for a moment."

Ariannorah winces again, but Lady Atherton doesn't notice. She sweeps away toward the doors. Beck offers Ariannorah his arm, and this time he doesn't even look awkward.

Now. To get rid of these other fools.

"Master Touzel," I say, remembering to add the title before his name at the last second, "do you think you could get us some more refreshments?" Conveniently, I forgot my drink over by the chairs.

Touzel looks a little confused, but he's eager as ever. It's kind of endearing, actually, like a puppy wagging its tail at me. "Of course." He rushes off.

Abbott doesn't take the hint, though, so I'll have to be blatant. "Won't you help him? He can't carry all the drinks by himself."

Abbott looks annoyed, but as I thought, social convention won't allow him to refuse. "Good idea," he says, his politeness not hiding his irritation as he follows Touzel. Grinning, I hurry after Beck and the Athertons, moving as fast as my heeled shoes and sweeping skirts will let me.

There are a few people milling around the gardens, but Beck and I lead the Athertons to more secluded pathways by asking Lady Atherton about the flowers we see there. Apparently we're both thinking the same thing, because we move to do it at the same time. Adrenaline surges through my veins. We're getting closer. This is it. We finally get to steal something and get out of here.

Ahead, the path splits in two. Beck catches my eyes and nods slightly. I nod back, understanding. I hurry down one of the forks like some flowers have caught my attention.

"Oh, Lady Atherton, do tell me what this is." As Lady Atherton walks toward me to examine the flower I've randomly selected, Beck leads Ariannorah around the corner. He whispers something in her ear, and she giggles quietly. My stomach tightens, but I don't have time to wonder what he's saying to her. I keep walking down the path, leading Lady Atherton as she drones on about flowers.

I pause. Lady Atherton's still blathering on, and there're still too many people close by to try anything. If I can steer her to a more secluded spot . . .

Beck and Ariannorah have stopped walking; I catch glimpses of her skirts through the hedges. Close enough that

I can overhear them. Not that I'm trying to eavesdrop, of course. I don't care what they're talking about. I can't help overhearing, that's all.

Someone sighs—must be Ariannorah. Then she says, "It's so nice out here—so quiet. It's nice to get away from these things."

"Really?" Beck's surprise sounds genuine. "It seemed like you were having fun."

"Oh, I didn't mean that," Ariannorah says quickly. "It's not—it's not that I'm not having a nice time. It's just that . . . all the balls and the parties and everything, I just . . . get tired."

"Yeah," Beck says, but he's having trouble hiding his confusion. I have no idea what she's on about either. Unless she means that she's tired of wearing these ridiculous skirts and shoes, in which case I wholeheartedly support her position.

"I know I sound silly," she says quickly. She's heard the disagreement in his tone too. "Complaining about going to parties. Silly. But it's . . . all the people and the noise and the music, and everybody always trying to say the right thing all the time, tripping over themselves to be polite, everybody hating each other but trying to hide it . . . sometimes I just need to get away. I just want it all to *stop*."

I can barely keep the surprise off my face. That sounds like something I would've said myself. I would almost agree with her, if I didn't hate her.

Beck murmurs something I can't hear. Beside me, Lady

Atherton has turned her attention from one flower to another, and moves slightly down the path, away from Beck and Ariannorah. This is good—it's more secluded here—but I inch forward as slowly as I can to follow her, straining to hear what they're saying.

"And then there's my mother," Ariannorah says. "Always drilling me about manners and decorum, criticizing every little thing—and then not paying any attention at all to anything that matters. She doesn't seem to notice that I'm not five anymore." She stops abruptly, cutting herself off from whatever else she was going to say. "Are your parents like that too?"

"Er, yeah. Yes," Beck says. "My mom . . . she can be oblivious sometimes."

He hides it, but I know him well enough by now to know the words are painful. He might be lying, just agreeing with whatever Ariannorah says, just trying to keep her talking and distracted. But then again, maybe not.

"It's like . . . it's like I don't know what to do to get through to her anymore," Beck continues. "Like I just need to get her attention."

"Right," Ariannorah says quietly. "But then when you have it, you wish you didn't."

"Yeah, exactly," Beck says.

There's a pause. Beside me, Lady Atherton is still droning on about "imports from Cerda," but I don't really hear her at all.

Then Ariannorah says, "You're so different from the rest of them. You're the only person here who actually says what you're thinking."

Beck's voice is tense, cautious. "Is that a good thing?"

Ariannorah's reply is so soft that I can't hear it. I glance at Lady Atherton, make sure she's not looking, and take a step backward, closer to the hedge.

"You're really not from around here, are you?" Ariannorah is saying now.

"What do you mean?" Beck answers a little too hastily.

"I mean, the way you talk . . . I knew Azeland was much more informal, but it's just . . . surprising. I thought you said you were only visiting your cousin there?"

"I was. It—It was a long visit," Beck says awkwardly.

Ariannorah giggles. "Is Allianna *really* your cousin?"

I stiffen. Does she suspect something?

"What makes you think she might not be?" Beck asks. He's keeping his tone nonchalant, but it still sounds tight.

"Oh, nothing," Ariannorah says, giggling again. "She's just so . . . so very *protective* of you. The way she glares at anyone who speaks to you, I thought . . . I thought she was going to kill me." She says it flippantly, but it still takes me a second to realize that it's a joke. Of course Ariannorah doesn't live in a world where everyone's keeping a dagger or two up their sleeves. To her, the idea of me committing acts of violence in a ballroom is silly. Laughable.

Beck *does* laugh, but it's a second too late. "Allianna is

fierce," he says, and this time his amusement sounds real. "Protective is a good word for it, yes."

Ariannorah laughs too. "Not to mention *vicious*."

They both burst into laughter, Ariannorah's high-pitched giggles sounding less and less dignified each time.

Ha-ha. How hysterical.

I turn away from the hedge, striding closer to Lady Atherton. Let them laugh, I don't care. *I'll* be the one laughing in a minute, after I steal this necklace and wipe that stupid smug smirk from Ariannorah Atherton's stupid smug face—

"What do you think, dear?" Lady Atherton says abruptly, looking at me.

"Oh, uh, I agree," I say quickly, trying to shake all thoughts of Beck and Ariannorah from my head.

Lady Atherton frowns. "I said, do you prefer the red or the white?" She's gesturing toward two flowering bushes.

"Uh, the red," I say.

Her frown deepens. "Yet there's something so elegant and understated about the simplicity of the white—"

"Oh, definitely," I agree. "Definitely the white."

She's confused for a moment, but then she nods, a sharp dip of chin. Satisfied, she continues on with her speech, leading me up the garden path and farther away from her daughter and Beck, who I am trying very hard not to think about.

The necklace, the necklace, focus on the necklace. . . .

Seeing it this close, I can tell that the drawing we saw in the Guild didn't do the necklace justice. In addition to being massive, the stone is an incredibly rich, deep blue, its hue shifting and glimmering in the candlelight. I don't know anything about jewelry, but I'd bet it's worth at least a million jamars. Enough to buy me a trip to the Healing Springs ten times over.

I scan the garden. We're alone now. There are people nearby who will hear, but no one can see us over the tall hedges, and that will give me an advantage. I look back at the house and guess where we are, based on the blueprints I studied. We're on the opposite side of the lawn from where the carriages are, unfortunately, but we're not far from a side door to the house. Maybe I could cut through, exit the house on the other side, and make a dash for the carriages? But how will Beck make it? Will he run when he hears Atherton scream?

Atherton doesn't wait for me to ask another question. She's already moved on to the next flower, just up the path, and I'm behind her now. She passes beside one of the lanterns, and the necklace's chain sparkles dimly, drawing attention to her neck. A few tendrils of hair escape her spirally bun and cling to her skin.

Which gives me an idea.

"Oh, Lady Atherton!" I gasp as if scandalized. "A bit of your hair has caught in your necklace clasp!"

She freezes. "Oh dear, does it look dreadful?" She brings one hand up toward her hair.

"Here, I'll fix it," I offer. "I mean, if you'll allow me, my lady."

She nods. I step forward, so close that her musky perfume fills my nose. I reach for her necklace. Good thing she's so short. As quick as I can, I undo the clasp, batting at some of her hair for good measure. And as she breathes a sigh of relief, I drop one end of the necklace, grip the other tighter, and run.

There's a gasp as she tries to figure out what just happened. I almost reach the fork in the path by the time she screams, "Stop! Thief!"

Hearing her footsteps behind me, I kick off my shoes, hoping she trips over them, and gain speed. I shove the necklace down my dress, where it's cushioned by the many layers of fabric. I can only hope it doesn't fall out.

"Thief! Get her, she stole my necklace!"

Who's she talking to? I look back.

Two guards. I can't see their uniforms in the dark so I don't know if they're protectors, but they're tall and big and they have swords belted at their waists and they're coming toward me. I sprint, turning abruptly, trying to lose them among the twisting paths, thinking only run, run, run, run—

Dead end. There's nowhere to go but—

The hedge. I throw myself into it, scrambling up, hands scraping on leaves and branches that rain down as I vault up and over, land hard on my bare feet, and keep running.

I can't breathe. My dress is so tight and the necklace is pressed against my lungs and it's too tight and there's not enough air. I gasp, my chest burning as I double over.

For a second, silence. Then their footsteps, right behind me. "I've got her!"

I take off again. There are screams as I shove a path through the partygoers, the guards a step behind me. More guards appear from all directions, pouring into the gardens, screaming "Thief!" and going after anyone who runs because they don't even know who they're looking for.

Another turn, another path. I don't know where I'm going, I'm just going. Away. Got to get away. Faster. Can't breathe. Faster.

Beck. Right in front of me, but too far away, running. He's reaching a turn, he pivots, and—

A guard turns the corner and slams into him. There's a shout, Beck fumbles for something, and I run, trying to help him, but a second guard is already there. He tackles Beck from behind, pinning him by the throat, then the first guard grabs his hands and wrenches them behind his back. He cries out in pain.

I run faster. I will save him, I will.

Beck sees me. The guards are distracted, but he sees me. He looks right at me, panic in his eyes. And he says, "Run."

Chapter Sixteen

I lurch forward, running to Beck. Someone slams into me from behind and I fall to the ground. Weight crushes against me and I flail, trying to break free. I look up into Ariannorah's face.

"Where is it?" she demands. Her hands are shaking like she's scared, but her eyes are focused and fierce. "Give me my mother's necklace!"

The hedges tower around us, blocking us from the view of the guards. If I could just get her off me . . . I grunt, trying to roll away, but her knee is digging into my cursed arm and sending ripples of pain from my fingers to my spine.

"Give it to me!"

"Get off me, you—"

Her gaze falls on my neckline and she freezes for a second. Before I can move she grabs the end of the necklace sticking out of the top of my dress. Hugging it close, she shrieks, "I've got it!

Help, I've got it!" She leaps up to wave to one of the guards, and in that second her weight vanishes. I take advantage of it and roll free, springing to my feet as fast as I can. Ariannorah screams. I start toward her, reaching for the necklace, knowing I can outrun her—

Something flies past my cheek. I turn. A knife narrowly missed my face. It clatters into a tree trunk and falls to the ground. The knife-thrower is a guard, running toward us.

I can't lose the necklace, and there's such a short distance between me and Ariannorah. But by the time I wrench the necklace from her, the guard will be on me, and I can't get away from them both.

I run, away from Ariannorah and the guard, sprinting back toward the house. I need a place to hide.

There's a door, nearly hidden by bushes at the side of the house. *Please let it be unlocked.* I don't have time to pick the lock; *let it be open.*

It's open. I throw myself inside, slam it shut, slide the bolt into place. There's a thud as the guard slams into it, trying to get it open. I don't have much time.

I walk, just to get away from the door the guard's trying to open, and rack my brain for the blueprint. I think this hallway leads across the house and exits near the carriages, where Jiavar is waiting for me. But I can't go back to the Guild without the necklace. Or Beck.

I have no idea who those guards were, or where they might have taken him. But I have to go after him. I won't leave him behind. And I'll probably need his help to get the necklace back.

I follow the hall, choosing turns at random, trying to put distance between myself and the guard. The sounds of the party in the ballroom grow louder, and before long the hall ends in a single door. Judging by all the noise, the ball-room is on the opposite side. I've stumbled onto the servants' entrance, right behind the refreshment table.

There's nowhere else to go without turning around and walking back toward the guard, so I open the door and walk through. As quick as I can I join the throng of partygoers like I've been here this whole time. Maybe no one will notice.

I hurry around the side of the dance floor, back toward the garden doors. If I get there fast enough, maybe I'll see Beck. Maybe I can rescue him, or at least see where it is they're taking him—

"Miss Martell?" says a familiar voice. It's Touzel.

He comes up to me, a couple of drinks in his hands and a puzzled expression on his face. "Where did—" His eyes grow wide. He's looking at my dress. "What happened?"

I look down. Half of the garden hedge is now clinging to my dress. Without my shoes on, the skirts are trailing the ground, and the hem is covered in dirt. I can only imag-ine what the grass stains on my back look like from where Ariannorah tackled me. Why didn't I think of this before?

"Um, I tripped." *Yeah, that's a great excuse. He'll totally buy that.*

"But why—where did everyone else . . . ?"

I have to get rid of him.

"Hey, Touzel, I need your help," I say in my best damsel-in-distress voice. I consider batting my eyelashes the way Ariannorah did when she talked to Beck, but it'll probably just make me look ridiculous.

"All right. Just tell me what's going—"

"I can't explain here." I indicate all the people around us. "Put those drinks down and come on." I start walking back the way I came, not checking to see if he's following. I know he is.

The servers at the refreshment table are so busy dealing with the demands of the nobles that they don't notice when I pull open the servants' door. Touzel follows me in, and I close it quietly behind me.

Touzel can't seem to decide if he's confused or excited. He's looking at me like I might have lost my mind, but he's as eager as ever. "What are we doing?"

I ignore his question. I'm still trying to guess where those guards might have taken Beck. Would they have handed him over to protectors, or to Dearborn? If I knew who they worked for . . . Oh. I'm a fool. Touzel might know.

"Have you seen the guards working at this party?" I ask.

Touzel, who may have been in the middle of saying something, frowns in confusion. He runs a hand through his hair. "I—um, yeah, Baron Dearborn hired them. Most of the nobles here hire private security, especially for balls, but I guess since you're not from Ruhia you wouldn't—"

"So if there's a security issue, they'll report directly to Dearborn?"

"Yeah, most likely—um, where are you going?"

I'm already moving back down the hall. Time to get rid of Touzel.

I pick a door at random. It's a laundry room, with washbasins, clotheslines, and a table and chairs in the corner. Perfect.

Touzel follows me, running his hands through his hair but, thankfully, keeping his mouth shut. I grab one of the chairs and carry it out into the hall.

I open the next door down. It's a closet. This will work. I wish I didn't have to do this, but I need to find Beck and get out of here.

"Do you see that?" I say, pointing to a darkened corner of the closet. It's less than subtle, but on someone as simple-minded as Touzel it works.

He steps forward, peering into the closet. "See what?"

I step right behind him and shove. He's heavier than I expected, but I've caught him by surprise and he falls forward. I grab the door handle, and as soon as he's completely inside the closet I slam the door shut. He shouts something, but it's too muffled to make out the words.

I grab the chair and angle it under the handle, blocking it. Probably won't keep him for long, but it's the best I can do.

"I'm sorry," I say. "You were my favorite."

I shouldn't feel guilty. One of the servants or guards will

find him soon enough. Anyway, members of the Thieves Guild don't feel guilt, and I'm on my way to becoming one. I have to shove it down deep and bury it. I need to find Beck.

I can't keep running around in this dress. Olleen and her seamstresses sewed a second disguise, one I hid in the carriage. I can run back there and change, tell Jiavar what's going on and ask her to wait for us, and come back inside to get Beck.

I run through the servants' hall. At least everyone's so busy with the party that nobody's around to see me. Surely I'm almost there by now. The house isn't *that* large. Only a few more steps—

A voice comes through the wall, a voice that might be Beck's. No words, just a low moan. Ahead is a door that's cracked slightly open. I slide over to it and peer out.

I'm looking into some kind of fancy sitting room, with plush sofas and woven rugs and fluffy decorative stuff. A balding man in a suit who's clearly come from the party stands in my line of sight, looking down at the floor. In front of him and to the left, one of the burly guards stands tensely like he's holding onto someone, his back to me. His uniform is blue, not red like the protectors. A private guard. Touzel was right.

I can't see Beck, but he must be what the man's looking at. He must be in there.

I want to lunge inside, grab Beck, and run. But I don't have any weapons, and I'm still wearing this stupid dress, and if Beck's hurt he might be incapable of running. The thought makes my insides tighten.

"Who is he?" the man in the suit says. He turns his head, looking to the side of the room I can't see. "How do you know him?" His voice is sharp.

"Sir Drozzen introduced both of them to me and Master Abbott and Master Touzel." Ariannorah. I can't see her, but I know the voice.

Anger burns me. The urge to claw her eyes out is stronger than ever. I considered bringing a knife, like Beck did, but couldn't find a place for one in all my skirts. Now I wish I had. I would've made Ariannorah Atherton sorry she ever met me.

"Drozzen?" the man says. "Do you think he had anything to do with this?"

"I don't know," Ariannorah says. "But he wasn't with us in the garden, nor were Abbott and Touzel."

"And he tried to take the necklace?"

"Well, no." For the first time, Ariannorah sounds timid and unsure. "Mother said it was the girl who took the necklace, and she was the one I took it from. The boy wasn't . . . he was talking to me. He didn't do anything. But as soon as Mother screamed, both of them started running. But I caught the girl and grabbed the necklace from her." She sounds a little smug at the end. I want to punch her.

"And what did they say their names were?"

"Berkeley and Allianna Martell."

"Martell?" The man pauses for a moment, considering. Then he looks at the guard. "Have someone find Drozzen and bring him in here. If he left already, have someone track him down."

"Yes, sir," says a gruff voice. "And what would you have me do with this prisoner?"

The man, who must be Baron Dearborn, hesitates for a second. "Lock him in one of the servant's rooms and guard the door. When he comes to, get him to reveal who he and his partner are, and where she's hiding. And who sent them. If he hasn't said anything by dawn, call the protectors and have them pick him up."

"Yes, sir." There's a shuffling sound as the guard moves out of my sight. A sound like he's dragging a body across the floor. My chest constricts. Beck.

"Thank you, Miss Atherton," Dearborn says. "Your mother is being tended to by one of our healers, and your father is with her. Let's return her necklace to her."

Footsteps and the shuffling of skirts. Dearborn moves away in the same direction as the guard. A door closes.

I exhale for what feels like the first time since the conversation began. At least now I know the Athertons still have the necklace, and Beck will be here until dawn. I just have to find him.

I don't have much time, but changing my clothes is still a good idea. No one will question a girl dressed as a maid walking around the servants' quarters. And Ariannorah's probably given the guards a description of what I'm wearing. Plus, I'm covered in hedge and dirt and can't come up with a better explanation than the one I gave Touzel.

Right, Touzel's seen me too, and someone will find him in that closet soon, probably, and he'll be telling everyone about the maniac who locked him up. Time to change.

I turn away and keep running down the hall.

Eventually I find a door that takes me outside. On this side of the house, it's a short walk to the massive circle drive where all the carriages are waiting. I find ours without too much trouble and hurry over to Jiavar.

"What happened?" she asks immediately. "Where's Beck?"

"Long story." I wrench open the carriage door and climb in. I glance through the front window at Jiavar, who tenses. Does she think I'm trying to leave Beck behind? "I have to change. Beck's been locked up in one of the servant's rooms. I'm going to put on my servant disguise and go get him."

"How did this happen?" There's no mistaking her tone now. She blames this on me.

"This stupid ball is crawling with guards. And Lady Atherton has a bratty daughter who attacked me right when I was trying to help Beck. I barely got away."

Jiavar's silence is accusatory.

I lift up the seat cushion, revealing the hollow space where Beck hid our extra clothes. I yank the soiled red dress off over my head and stuff it inside, followed by several other layers of skirt. Finally I can breathe. Down to only a shift, I glance at my right arm again. In just the few hours that have passed since I last looked at it, the dark lines have progressed even farther. Thick streaks of black race from my elbow to my shoulder, and veins of it curl and twist around my collarbone. Luckily Olleen remembered what Beck said about giving me a dress with sleeves, and included some cleaning gloves to hide my hands. But there's nothing I can do about the pain, which has only gotten worse since Ariannorah tackled me. If it keeps going like this, I might not be able to move my arm anymore.

I throw the maid's dress over my head and button it. It's a plain cotton gown the color of dirt. An apron, the gloves, and a simple pair of shoes complete the look. At the last minute I remember to grab Mead's lock picking tools from the discarded dress and slip them into my pocket. Then I rub at my face with one of the skirts, trying to get the makeup off. There's no time to fix my hair, so I leave it up. When everything's stuffed under the seat, I replace the cushion and hop out of the carriage.

"I heard Dearborn say Beck will be moved at dawn," I tell Jiavar. "So if we're not back by then, you can leave."

"I'll wait for both of you at the Miagnar Gardens. There are usually many thilastri there, so I won't be noticed. When is the deadline for the trial?"

"The first."

"I will wait until the second, then, just in case."

I don't think she was instructed to do this. She can return to the Guild any time she likes. She doesn't have to help us.

"Thank you," I say. It doesn't seem like enough. But I'm

pretty sure she's not doing it for me, anyway. I'm not the one she wants to bring back to the Guild.

"Go," she says. "Hurry."

I take her advice and run.

Back inside the house, I walk slowly through the servants' halls, trying to act casual. I don't know which room Beck's in, of course, but it will be guarded, so I'll figure it out easily enough. My only concern is running into Touzel. What if he managed to free himself from the closet and is roaming the halls? What if he recognizes me? The distract-shove-and-run trick is the kind of thing that only works once. But maybe it will work on whoever is guarding Beck.

I turn a corner and my heart stops. A guard in blue is leaning against a door. There's a sword at his waist, and I have no doubt he's got other weapons hidden away. I sort of hope he's the guard who threw a knife at me earlier. Maybe that was his only knife. And I'll get some satisfaction from shoving him into a closet.

But as I inch closer, it's obvious he's too big to be shoved into a closet. I need a new plan.

He notices me, his eyes locking on my face. I try to fake an innocent look, but I've never been good at it. Oh God.

I'm five feet away. The guard speaks. "What's your business here?"

I remember what Dearborn said about Lady Atherton being with healers, and the lie gushes out. "Baron Dearborn sent me to see to an unconscious prisoner?" I try to say it questioningly, like it's doubtful that there's any such prisoner. "I'm a healer."

He whistles, loud and sharp, and to my left everything explodes. Something slams into my left side, and I collide with the wall on my right. Everything spins. Blue blurs across my vision as a second guard, emerging from the smoke on my left, shoves me face-down on the floor. I breathe in the smell of the rug—lint and bleach and mold. Cold metal snaps against my wrists as the guard chains them behind my back.

"What'd she say?" someone right above me says. His voice is muffled, like we're separated by glass.

"Said she was a healer," another guard says, even more muffled. "But the healer's already been here."

A hand grabs my chained wrists and pulls. "Stand up!"

Everything hurts so bad my eyes water, but I force myself to stand. *Must get to Beck. Focus. Find him.*

I wrench away from the guard, struggling with everything I have, running to the door that contains Beck—

Something hard connects with my head, and I hear a distant scream as everything goes black.

Chapter Seventeen

My head hurts. I open my eyes slowly, not sure what I'm going to see. I don't remember where I am. . . .

"Alli."

Beck's voice brings the memories flooding back—the ball, his capture, the guards . . . and Ariannorah getting the necklace from me. "Are you okay?"

I close my eyes, trying to pinpoint the pain. "My head hurts." And my whole left side is sore, but manageable. My right arm, on the other hand, is searing with pain from the shoulder down. I wiggle one finger experimentally and wince; it feels like I've been stabbed.

"They hit you pretty hard with something," he says. "When you didn't wake up, I tried to heal it as best I could, but like I said, I don't have much healing magic—it's pretty useless. I used most of it to heal myself before you got here, since the healer they sent wasn't much help, and then I spent the rest trying to wake you up. . . ."

I stare at the plain gray ceiling above me, not daring to look at Beck.

"What's wrong?"

I turn slowly, pain shooting from the back of my head and my right side with every movement. I'm lying on some kind of sofa, and Beck's crouched beside me, looking confused and concerned all at once, but he's here, he's mostly unhurt, he's alive. And he'll probably kill me when I tell him. But maybe he's figured it out anyway.

"I lost the necklace," I say. "I had it, but then Ariannorah shoved me and I couldn't get up and she took it back—I'm sorry."

Beck shakes his head impatiently. "Don't worry about that now. Are you sure you're okay?"

How can he shrug off the loss? The Guild means so much to him, and I lost it. Without the necklace, we can't go back. Unless . . .

He hasn't given up yet. He'll keep trying until we get it.

"What day is it? How much time do we have? How long have I been out?"

"I don't know. I haven't been out of this room since they put me in here. Two guards dropped you off a while ago, but they didn't tell me anything."

I sit up, clutching my head as pain stabs me, and take in

our surroundings. We're in a maid's quarters or something, with only one door and not much furniture. It's so drab it reminds me of the rooms at the orphanage, but not as cramped: thin, dingy rugs on the floor, dim lighting, and a few personal possessions—clothes, a bag, a hairbrush—peeking sadly out of a bare wardrobe with a broken door. No windows, so there's no way to plan an escape or even tell if it's dark or light outside.

Lying on the floor beside Beck are two metal chains—the cuffs the guards used to bind our hands. "How'd you get those off?"

Beck grins. "Oldest trick in the book. Remind me to show you later."

Later. He still thinks there will be a later.

"I came after you as soon as I could," I say. "I overheard Dearborn. Said he'd turn you in to the protectors at dawn, but that they'd question you first."

"He must've changed his mind. I think it's past dawn now, and nobody's questioned me." He pauses. "You really came after me?"

"Well, yeah, how'd you think I got caught? I changed clothes at the carriage and told Jiavar about everything. She's still waiting for us at—"

"Don't tell me here," Beck says quickly. "Someone might overhear."

He's right. I have to be more careful if I'm going to be good at this thieving thing. So far I'm not doing very well.

If I'd been captured and Beck were the rescuer, we'd already be out of here.

"So it's probably the fifty-eighth by now," Beck says. "Counting today, that gives us three days until the deadline."

I do the math in my head. I have about four days until the curse kills me. Maybe five.

"What's the plan? Do you think it'll be possible to—?"

"If we can escape, definitely. Ariannorah told me she and her parents are going to the big Samyra's Day festival on the north side of Ruhia. And since it starts at midnight, they'll be leaving on the night of the sixtieth." He glances at the door and lowers his voice. "Which means they won't be at home, and Lady Atherton's personal chambers will be empty."

My eyes widen. "You're not serious." But he is. He wants to break into the Atherton manor, find Lady Atherton's rooms, and snatch the necklace. "How would we get in?"

"The same way we got into the ball. Disguise ourselves." He looks at the maid's costume I'm still wearing. "You can totally pass for a maid."

I scowl. "Oh, thanks, Beck, what a compliment."

His grin widens. "Sorry, Allicat." But he doesn't sound sincere at all.

I glare at him. "Don't make me regret coming after you, or I won't even try next time."

A china dish sits on the floor beside Beck, and my stomach rumbles hopefully. "Is that—?"

"Food," Beck says, passing the plate to me. He already

helped himself to half of it, but there's still some kind of bread left. "Figured whoever left it here wouldn't mind."

I didn't realize until now how hungry I am. I practically shove the bread into my mouth, swallowing chunks without chewing. "So," I say around the mouthful, "what happens now?"

Beck shrugs. "We wait."

We wait. And wait. And wait.

I am *not* good at waiting.

With every minute, I'm more and more restless, more and more trapped in this little windowless room with no light and no food and no water and no air. I try not to think about the fact that the seconds of my life are ticking away, and I might not have many of them left. But the pain in my arm is making it difficult to forget.

"How long has it been, do you think?" I say for what might be the hundredth time.

Beck lies listlessly on the floor, watching me pace without really looking at me. "I dunno, let me check the watch that magically appeared in the two seconds since you last asked."

"Why aren't you wearing a watch? Don't noblemen wear watches? Isn't that, I dunno, a status symbol or something? That's, like, necessary to your disguise."

"Sorry, next time I'll make sure to include a really fancy noble's watch, that just so happens to be lying around, in the disguise that I only had a few hours to come up with," he says without looking at me.

My sarcasm is really starting to rub off on him.

I reach the end of the room, spin around on the balls of my feet, and start back the other way, counting the steps. It takes fewer steps to reach the opposite wall this time. Does that mean I'm walking faster? Or are the walls creeping in on us? Is Dearborn planning to crush us between slow-moving walls of death?

"How much longer?" I groan.

"Two seconds less than the last time you asked," Beck says.

Finally, finally, *finally* the door opens. I expected Dearborn or one of his guards to enter, but the man who walks in is unmistakably Lord Atherton. He has the same superior haughtiness as his daughter. I'm so glad to see *someone* walking through the door that I don't even care it's him.

He's followed by two blue-uniformed guards, who keep their hands on their sword hilts and glare at us like we're a suspicious slime they stepped in.

"Don't even think about trying anything," Atherton says, his voice clipped. He doesn't really look at either of us—at least, not like he *sees* us. He's taking in every detail of our appearances, but he's not looking at us like he's talking to another person. "Baron Dearborn has hired an excellent guard service that will undoubtedly counter any foolish escape attempts."

I glance at Beck, but he's keeping his mouth shut, so I do the same.

"Now," Atherton says, "both of you will be handed over

to the protectors and imprisoned. You will be charged for attempting to rob a noble and assaulting my wife, who is still recovering from her injuries."

What? I never hurt Lady Atherton. Startled her, probably, and maybe she even fell into some prickly bushes or something, but I never hurt her. I open my mouth, about to call Atherton out for being a filthy liar, but Beck's watching me, and he shakes his head slightly. I bite my tongue, grimacing as the pain shoots up into my head.

Atherton doesn't seem to notice. "Unless." He draws it out real long and dramatic, like we're supposed to hang on his every word and beg him to not throw us in prison. I bite my tongue harder. "Unless you cooperate, and tell me what I'd like to know."

A long silence stretches out between Beck and me and him as he waits, probably expecting us to jump on his offer. Beck's expression is closed and cold, colder than I've ever seen him. I just keep biting my tongue and wincing and ignoring the urge to slap the smirk off Atherton's face.

"I'll not be making this offer again," Atherton says, like we're too stupid to understand. "Now, answer me immediately. Who sent you?"

Beck doesn't even blink. I try to imitate his blank expression and give nothing away.

"Who are you working for?" Atherton says, raising his voice. Like asking us louder is going to make us more likely to answer.

Atherton's eyes flit from Beck's face to mine, waiting for us to give something away. "Was it Wyatt? Brookshead? Yvonn Ilira?" He pauses after each name, hoping for a reaction. With every guess, his voice rises. He doesn't even mention the Guild. Even though he seems to have countless enemies, he probably thinks he's too important for ordinary thieves to target. Or maybe he doesn't believe the Guild exists.

"I know you had help. You didn't plan to infiltrate this barony and make disguises by yourselves." He pauses, waiting. We give him nothing. "Or was it Sir Drozzen? Is he in on it?"

When we don't say anything, he starts throwing out motives instead of names, waiting for a reaction. "Is it my politics? Is that what brought on this attack?"

I want to laugh at the word "attack." All we did was grab a necklace, not blow up the barony.

Finally he runs out of steam. His voice quiets again, but grows more ragged, like he's worn out. He glares for a long moment.

His voice low, he asks, "Why did you speak with my daughter?" And something about the way he says it tells me this is the real problem, the real question that brought him here. It's the thing he doesn't understand, and the thing that scares him most.

The fear comes through in his voice, even when he makes it threatening. "If either of you so much as comes near my daughter again, I'll kill you."

Chills run up my spine. There's fear in his voice, but also anger, and those two things together make me believe he's not bluffing about this part.

That's the convenient thing about dying, though. Death threats don't really mean much.

He straightens up, throwing his shoulders back, and his curt, haughty voice returns. "Very well. I'll report to the protectors that you've been quite uncooperative."

He starts for the door, and the guards shuffle after him. Halfway there, he turns and looks back. "I'll give you some time to think it over and change your minds."

He sweeps from the room, and the guards stomp after him. The door locks with a loud click.

"Well, that was interesting," Beck says casually. "Doesn't seem to understand simple motives, does he? Never occurred to him that we'd steal a valuable necklace just because it's *valuable*." He laughs.

I don't. He turns, seeing my expression. "What's wrong?"

"I never hurt Lady Atherton," I say. "I barely touched her, I swear."

Beck's brow creases. "I believe you. I know you didn't."

"Why would he say that I did?"

"To make us think it's going to be worse than it is. To make us answer his questions." Beck scoots closer to me until we're sitting side by side on the floor. He hesitates for a second, like he's thinking about something. "It's gonna be okay, Allicat."

I force a smile. "I believe you."

We stay that way for a while, not saying anything, just sitting beside each other and wondering if this is the end.

We wait for the protectors to arrive, but they don't. I stare at the door, waiting, waiting, but I can't keep my eyes open any longer and my head is throbbing.

"We might as well get some sleep," Beck says finally, breaking a long silence. His voice is tired. He didn't get much sleep back at the Guild. It's amazing he's lasted this long.

"Probably," I agree. "You can take the couch."

"No, you. You're more injured than me."

This isn't totally true. Beck swears he used some of his healing magic on himself before I got here, but I'm not sure I believe this story, since he winces every now and then when he turns his head fast. But I want the couch anyway, so I don't argue.

As soon as my head hits the sofa cushion, I start drifting. Everything sort of swirls around, getting all tangled until it's hard to think straight and I don't remember, exactly, what I was thinking about . . .

"Alli?" Beck whispers.

"Yeah?"

He rolls over, looking up at where I'm lying. "Do you think . . . do you think people become like their parents?"

"I dunno. Why?"

"I was just thinking," he says quietly, "about Ariannorah,

and how she's so much like her parents already—all rich and arrogant, I mean—but only because she didn't know any better. I was wondering what she'd be like if . . . I dunno. I was just thinking."

I hesitate. "About your mom?"

For a second I think he's not going to answer, but he does. "I mean—I wouldn't mind being like my mom. She was the smartest person I've ever met, and a way better healer than I'll ever be. And she was funny, too—she could make anybody laugh."

"Really?" I say. "Even all the scary thieves in the Guild?"

He almost smiles. "Even them." He looks down at his hands. "Ariannorah talked to me about her mother today, when we were in the garden, and it made me think of mine. And . . . I dunno, it was like we really weren't all that different deep down. And it made me wonder what we'd be like if we swapped places—if she were in the Guild and I were rich. Would she still be snobby? Or would I be? Would we be just like our parents?"

"You think too much," I say. But he still seems to be waiting for some kind of answer, so I give him one. "I really wouldn't know. Whether I'm like my parents, I mean."

He nods. "You were three when you went to the orphanage, right?"

I can't believe he remembers that. I said something about how long I'd been at Sisters of Harona, but I never told him about that day.

"Do you . . . do you remember anything?" he asks. "From before?"

"Not much," I say, which is true. The memories I have are flashes, incomplete thoughts, and sometimes I wonder if I made them up. A small bedroom with a dirty window draped in lacy white curtains. A kitchen that smelled like cinnamon, with dishes piled in the sink and cupboards that were all empty. The stickiness of summer, the windows thrown wide to let in a breeze.

And my brother. I can't see much of him at all, just this vague thought of white chocolate and a single image: a boy with shaggy black hair whose face I can't see, who throws me up into the air—I shriek, but it's from excitement, not fear—and when I start to fall he catches me, spinning me around.

There's nothing else of him, but I guess it doesn't matter. It's not like I'm ever going to see him again. He's just another thing my mother took from me.

There's not much else of her, either. Only one full memory, a scene that plays itself over and over in my head, no matter how hard I try not to think about it. The last day. Even as my eyes slip closed, the picture's still sharp and fresh in my head like always, playing out against my eyelids.

I was asleep, mostly, while she carried me. I woke to feel water on my face. Rain? My mother set me down but held my hand as we walked toward a stone wall, through a gate, and up a garden path. An old gray house sat at the end, covered in trails of ivy. We waited on the porch for a long time until the door opened. The woman at the door was dressed all in white, the Sisters' color. I hid behind my mother's skirts.

I don't remember what the Sister said, if she said anything. But I can't get my mother's last words out of my head.

"I can't."

Out of everything, that's the part that makes me hate her. She didn't say anything I needed to hear. Not "I'm sorry," not "I love you," not even "good-bye." It's the only thing I know for sure she ever said to me.

To Beck, I say, "I don't remember my mother."

He must be looking at me, but I don't open my eyes. I know there will be pity in his face and I don't want it. "But it doesn't matter. She can't have been worth remembering, right?" My voices catches at the end, and I hate how whiny I sound.

Beck doesn't say anything for a second. "What do you mean?"

I try to swallow the lump in my throat. "I mean, I'm glad I don't remember her. She obviously wasn't much of a mother."

I keep my eyes clamped shut, wishing he'd stop looking at me. I want to stop talking about this.

"You don't know that," he says quietly. "Maybe she was just trying to—"

"Trying to give me a better life, yeah, whatever. That's the orphanage's line. The thing they say to everyone who gets dropped off to try and make us feel better. Doesn't make it true." I never really understood their point anyway. Saying "you'll be better off without me" is also saying "I'll be better off without you."

And even if it's true, it doesn't change the fact that she picked my brother over me. That she wanted him more than me. I've tried to guess why a hundred times. Did she not want me at all, or did she want me the least?

"What I was *going* to say," Beck says quietly, "is maybe she couldn't be what you needed her to be. So she tried to give you someone who could."

He's talking about his own mother, not mine, but I don't point this out to him.

"Anyway," I say, in a casual voice that doesn't belong to me, "that was a long time ago, so . . ." I roll over, facing into the sofa, so I don't have to see Beck watching like he's seeing me for the first time.

He doesn't say anything else.

Sleep comes quickly after that, but it doesn't last long. Every time I close my eyes, I see my mother's face. Or what I think it might look like, anyway. It's all kind of fuzzy.

"It's me," I say, trying to get her attention. "I'm your daughter."

She doesn't recognize me. She just stares.

"I never stopped being your daughter," I say, but she's gone. I think I hear her footsteps echoing around me. I wake in a cold sweat.

It felt, for a second, like she was really here, in this room.

If we saw each other now, for real, what would we say? I don't even know her. Would she try to explain? I guess it doesn't matter. No excuse would fix it. We couldn't ever be what we should be.

I guess that's the thing about dwelling on the past. You can't go back. You can just keep running forward and try to escape it.

I close my eyes again and she's there, a ghost against my eyelids. As I drift back to sleep, I wonder if she's thinking of me, wherever she is. I hope so. I hope the ghost that haunts her dreams is me.

Chapter Eighteen

I wake to a thud. I open my eyes just in time to see two armed protectors barrel through the open door toward us. Beck's still lying on the floor, and before we have time to move, they're on us.

I lunge away from the one who reaches for me, but he's fast and I'm stumbling. He grabs my gloved right hand and pulls, yanking me until I fall off the sofa, and my knees hit the floor hard. My right arm burns as I try to escape his grip. He wrenches my arm behind my back, and I can't help but let out a squeak of pain.

As one protector grabs my other arm and reaches for the handcuffs on his belt, the second shoves Beck to the ground. Beck's stronger than me and manages to rip away for just a second, but the protector grabs him again, shoving him to his knees. I hold back a scream.

My hands are chained together behind my back with metal

cuffs that rub against my gloves and click as they're clamped into place. The protector grabs the chain and pulls, throwing me backward. I try to scramble to my feet but fall again, landing hard on my side, unable to get up with my hands tied. Everything flashes red and black and white as the room spins around me.

The protector grabs my arm and jerks me up. I kick at him, but he keeps me at arm's length as he walks out of the room, dragging me after him.

Outside the door, Lord Atherton is watching everything, his mouth set in a hard line. I glare at him, anger flooding through me, flashing redder than the protectors' uniforms. I wait until the protector has passed by Atherton, dragging me closer to him. I look straight into Atherton's eyes and smile. I'm rewarded by his confused look.

I spit in his face.

Atherton roars, the protectors whirl around, Beck looks back at me and I can't tell what he's thinking, then the protector yanks me away from Atherton and slaps me across the face. Fire burns my cheek and I try to blink away the red spots that cover everything.

Beck lunges for the protector who slapped me. I can't see them, but suddenly they both hit the floor. I run, but everything blurs and spins and flashes red. Atherton yells again. I stagger, disoriented. Where's the door? I need to get out, I need to—

A strong hand grabs me from behind, locking around my

arm. I turn and see that Beck lost the fight—the other protector hauls him to his feet, and blood runs down his face.

"If either of you tries anything else," Beck's protector growls, "we'll get out our swords. Now *move*." He shoves Beck in front of him and starts walking, keeping a tight grip on the chain of Beck's handcuffs. My protector follows after, dragging me along. As we move away down the hall, I look back at Atherton, who still stands there, looking stunned. It would have been worth it, just to see that look, except for the blood that Beck spits from his mouth, leaving a crimson stain against the bright white floor.

Prison is exactly what I remember—cold, bare, and gray. I've never been in a Ruhian prison before, but it's practically identical to the Azeland one where the protectors took me after one of my attempts at running away. Only this time there's no Sister Morgila to come pick me up.

Beck and I are shoved into adjacent holding cells, the barred doors are slammed shut and locked, and the guards' footsteps retreat down the hall, leaving us alone in the cold silence.

The wall between our cells is so old it's practically crumbling, and there's a sizeable gap in the mortar through which, if we position ourselves correctly, we can still see each other. "Are you all right?" Beck asks, peering in at me. He looks at my cheek.

"Never better," I say. "And you?" The blood's dried around

his mouth and nose, making it look gruesome, but he's not bleeding anymore, and nothing looks broken.

"Could be worse," he says cheerfully. He turns and peers down the hall, in one direction, then the other. He lowers his voice. "You don't still have your lock pick on you, do you? They searched me, but I thought maybe . . ."

I feel the spot on my dress where the lump of the pick used to be. "I still have the tension wrench!" I say triumphantly. "But . . ." I shift more of the fabric. "No pick. Must've taken it off me after they knocked me out."

Beck curses under his breath. "We'll just have to wait them out, I guess. They'll have to let us out of here sometime."

"And when they do?" I ask skeptically.

"We fight them off and make a run for it."

"Really? *That's* your brilliant Guild strategy? Right, that worked so well last time."

"Have any better ideas?"

"Not at the moment."

And now we wait some more.

Great. I'm *so* good at waiting.

It feels like several years later when Beck and I doze off, resting against the bars, angling our heads so we can see each other's faces. We haven't said anything to each other in hours, but there hasn't been much to say.

I slip in and out of sleep, jumping awake at every little noise outside my cell. Beck's restless too, constantly shifting positions. When I manage to fall asleep, my dreams are mostly black and white. First, I'm in the orphanage, except the walls and floors are a starker, cleaner white than they've ever been, and the Sisters, dressed all in white as usual, are kneeling on the floor, scrubbing it clean. I step forward, peering over their shoulders. What mess could they be scrubbing?

It's the same hallway I once vandalized to frame Striker, but there's no red graffiti this time. A black stain, darker in the dream than it could ever be in real life, spreads like water all over the floor. And the more the Sisters scrub, the more it grows, until everything—the room, the Sisters, me—is black with it.

In the second dream, I am in Dearborn's house, and a protector is chasing me. I run, ducking down halls, but all the hallways look the same, with prison-gray walls and white marble floors. I reach a doorway and run inside. The door slams shut behind me, and I'm pitched into total blackness. I turn around and try to open the door, but it's locked and they've taken my lock picks. I shove myself against it but it won't open, won't open, won't open. And now Beck's on the other side of the door, his voice pleading. "I need you, Allicat. We have to get in the Guild."

"Wait," I scream, "wait." I bang my fists against the door. A strong hand grabs me from behind. I scream, whirling around, seeing nothing but the red of a protector's uniform. I kick and claw and scratch at it, trying to get away—

There's a knife in my hand, a shadowy outline in the darkness, and I stab blindly.

The room is flooded with light. The weapon clatters to the ground, its silver-white blade bloody. Standing in front of me, wearing a protector's uniform, is my mother. She is holding the bloody wound with one hand—the wound I gave her—and she is dying. She looks at me, expressionless, and says, in a cold voice, "I knew it all along."

Someone screams, but I don't know who, and I jerk awake, shaking.

Beck cracks one eye open. "'Kay, Allicat?" he mumbles through sleep.

"Just cold." I fold my arms against my chest to stop the shaking. I don't go back to sleep. I lean my head against the bars of my cell door and watch Beck, who looks so much younger when he sleeps, his head lolling against his own cell door. I track the rise and fall of his chest and try to match my breaths to his, thinking about nothing but breathing to chase away whatever's haunting me. We stay like that, breathing, until I'm not sure if it's been an eternity that's passed, or no time at all.

I'm still awake when Beck opens his eyes again. He blinks for a second, confused, before his gaze focuses on me. "Still here, Allicat?"

"Where else would I be, stupid?"

He just smiles.

"You're awfully happy for someone in prison," I mutter.

He shrugs. "Well, I could be cranky and depressed like you, but that won't help us much, now will it?"

"I am *not* cranky and depressed."

"Oh, right, I forgot, you're just naturally unpleasant."

I scowl. "You're lucky you're behind bars, Beck Reigler, or I'd—"

Beck laughs, interrupting my threat. I wait for him to say what's so funny, but he just keeps looking in my direction and *laughing* at me.

Anger flares beneath my skin. "What's so funny?"

"Sorry," he says, "it's just—your hair—"

I lift a hand to the top of my head. My hair's still done up all fancy, but a big chunk of it is falling, and when I laid my head against the cell bars some of it puffed out, I guess. But I still don't see what's so funny.

"It's sticking straight up on one side," Beck says, still infuriating me with his grin. "And the other side's falling out of its pins—" He's laughing so hard he can't finish the sentence.

I glare at him. "Don't make me come over there and hurt you."

Hastily, I reach for my hair again. Maybe if I take out the pins, it won't look so—

The hairpins.

"Saint Samyra help me, I'm a fool," I say.

Beck stares at me blankly. "What are you talking about?"

I turn around, scanning the hall, then look back at Beck and lower my voice. "*Pins.* They took our lock picks, but can't we pick the lock with my hairpins?"

I'm not sure I can do it; I've never practiced with something so flimsy. But Beck's eyes are wide with excitement.

"I can," he whispers. "And you probably could too, eventually, but it will take you longer. You'll have to practice with Mead later. Anyway—what time is it?"

"I don't know, Beck, why don't I check the watch that you neglected to wear with your fancy nobleman suit? We've been over this."

He ignores me. "The best time to leave is at night. How long do you think we've been in here?"

"How should I know?"

"Think," he says impatiently. "It was light outside when they brought us here, right? Maybe right after noon, d'you think?"

"Really?" I say, but now that I think about it, he's right. "No wonder I'm so hungry, it's been like a day since I've eaten anything—"

"Focus," he interrupts. "How long was I asleep for? Best guess?"

"I don't know. At least a few hours, probably, but it's not like I have anything to go by—"

"So that makes it, what, ten hours or so since we got here?"

"How'd you figure *that*?"

"While you were complaining about waiting and being hungry, I was paying attention to the guard shifts. There was one. So that took a few hours, at least. And then you and I were both asleep for a while, and at one point when I woke up the guards were different, so there must've been another shift, and then—"

"Okay, okay, I get the point. I'll take your word for it. So, if it's been ten hours since noon, at your best guess, that would make it—"

"Ten. So we can afford to wait a little longer. I say we wait until the next shift. Every time the new guys come in, they walk around some and pass right by here, but then they don't come back. So, we wait until the new guys finish walking by us, then we leave. And that way, even if the calculations are a few hours off, it will be dark either way. Don't you think?"

I blink at him. "You're kind of a genius."

He looks confused. "Um, thank you?"

"But don't forget, you were the one who got caught first, not me. This mess isn't my fault."

"Uh, yeah, I didn't say it—"

"I wouldn't want you to get a big head or anything," I say, "so I just thought I'd remind you."

"Okay . . . so, anyway, I'm thinking they'll probably leave another guard at the desk by the front, so maybe we can . . ."

I sort of tune out the rest of what he's saying. I get the idea. I'll pass the hairpins to Beck, he'll unlock our doors, we'll make a break for it when no one's looking. Just the kind of plan I like: simple. Overly complex strategies aren't really my thing, obviously, and I don't have Beck's compulsive need to outline every single moment of our lives in advance. And the whole impulsive no-plan thing works well for me, mostly. Now being the obvious exception.

Of course, Beck's plan means more waiting. Every second I think I hear the guards' footsteps getting closer, but they never show up. My stomach rumbles, and I try not to think about what I'd give for some of the disgusting Guild food right about now. If the guards would just *show up* already—

"Stop looking at the door," Beck whispers. "Act natural."

"How am I supposed to act natural in a jail cell? Should I be sobbing or something? Want me to fake it?"

"No." He's losing patience with my sarcasm now. "Stop looking at the door. Pretend to be asleep, if that helps."

If I close my eyes, I might actually fall asleep, and then I might have that nightmare again. I know I will see her when I close my eyes for too long. I spin around so the door is to my back, staring at the wall between Beck's cell and mine.

"Thank you," Beck says.

I scowl at him.

There. This time I'm not imagining it. Footsteps, coming closer. Beck tenses, and I can practically hear what he's thinking: Act natural. I lean my head against the bars and close my eyes, just like I did when I was asleep earlier. With every second, the steps get closer and closer until they must be right beside me, yet somehow they keep coming. I fight the urge to open my eyes. *Don't look, don't look, don't look . . .*

Finally, the footsteps fade. I open my eyes and stand. Beck

waits for a second more, then nods to me. I reach for my head, locate a hairpin, and yank. Clumps of knotted hair fall down into my face as I unfasten the rest of the pins.

"Do you need the tension wrench too, or just the hairpins?" I whisper.

"I could do it with just the pins, but a real wrench will be faster," he whispers back.

I pull the wrench out from the pocket of my skirt. The gap in the wall isn't large enough to stick my hand in, so I move to the very far corner of the cell door and shove my hand through the last bar. I have to yank my gloves off to make my hand fit, but it hardly matters if anyone sees the mark at the moment. "Can you reach them?"

Beck's out of my line of sight now, though we're basically standing next to each other with a wall between us, but I imagine he's doing the same as me, squeezing one arm through the bars. "Almost . . . there," he grunts.

I bend my wrist, trying to get the pins inches closer, reaching, reaching— "There!"

"Shh!" His fingers brush my palm as he manages to grab the end of the wrench and a few of the pins. "Got 'em."

I slide my hand back inside my cell. "Good thing we're both so scrawny, or this would never have worked."

"Speak for yourself." I hear the clicking of metal on metal. "I'm not *scrawny.*"

I return to the other end of my cell where, if I angle it right, I can see Beck at the other end of his. He's got both of his hands through the bars, shoved up against the lock, but at that angle he has to hold the tension wrench in the wrong hand.

He swears. "I'm not left-handed."

"Hurry!"

"I would if I could *reach* the stupid thing—"

I turn to the hall where we last saw the guards. Will they come back? Is that their footsteps?

"Can't you hurry up?" I whisper.

"Next time I'm in prison, I'm finding a more patient cellmate."

"Shut up."

There's a sharp *snap*, and Beck curses. "The hairpin broke."

"You've got a second one?"

"Yeah, hang on."

Agonizing seconds pass as Beck grabs a second hairpin, bends it into shape, and slides his arm back through the bars again. It barely squeezes through.

"Next time I'm in prison, I'm finding a cellmate with thinner arms," I say.

"I thought I was scrawny?"

"You are. But apparently your arms aren't."

"It's called muscle. You wouldn't know anything about it, obviously."

"Wow, that was almost a good insult. I think I'm a bad influence on you."

Click. It's so soft I might not have heard it if I wasn't listening closely. It's followed by the heavy thud of the bolt sliding free. Beck pulls his arm from the bars again and pushes gently on the door. It opens.

"Oh my God," I mutter, "you actually did it."

"And *that*," Beck says proudly, "is how you pick a lock left-handed without looking."

"Mead would've done it faster."

"You know, I could just leave you in there. Rule number nine: Fall behind, get left behind." Beck slips out of the cell, moving the door as little as possible. Even so, it squeaks, and we both cringe.

For a second—only a second—it occurs to me that he *could* leave without me. Mead would. Any other Guild member would. But Beck?

No. He helped me once, before he even knew me. He wouldn't stop now.

Besides, I went back for him, and clearly that worked out so well for me. He owes me. Right?

"You wouldn't leave a damsel in distress," I say sarcastically as he crosses from his cell to mine.

"Are you saying you actually need my help?" Beck slips the hairpin into the lock on my door.

"No, I'm saying if you left me in here I would track you down and beat you so bad even a healer couldn't help you."

A few minutes later, the lock turns. Beck smiles. "Let's go, Allicat." He tugs the door open, shoving the wrench and hairpin into an inside pocket of his jacket.

"It's about time," I say.

We tiptoe toward the door the guards always enter from, in the opposite direction of where we last saw them heading. Beck cracks the door open a slit and peeks through. "It's just the front room," he says.

"I know." I roll my eyes. "I was paying attention when we were brought in here."

"Would you like to go first, then?" Jail has really made him more irritable than usual.

"No thanks," I say with false cheer. "When they catch us, I think my odds of escape are better from back here."

Beck peers through the crack in the door again. "We're behind the desk. One guard there with his back to us. Two sets of doors to get outside. The guard has the key to open the first set, probably."

"So the plan is . . . ?"

"Surprise the guard, take his weapon, get the key, run for it."

It only takes me a second to consider this. "Is it just me, or are your plans getting worse?"

"Would you just shut up for a minute, please?"

I glare at him. "Well, since you said 'please.'"

Beck's still not really paying attention to me. "Okay, one of us is going to distract the guard, keep his attention at the front of the room, while the other sneaks behind him to grab his weapon. . . ."

"Let me guess. You're the weapon-grabber, and I'm just the distraction, right?"

"It's only a knife, I think, no sword, so it shouldn't be too hard, unless he's got another somewhere. . . ."

"Most likely."

"Okay, and remember, once you've got him talking, don't let him look back here or he'll see me. If he does turn toward me, you'll have to go for the weapon instead."

"Uh, yeah, no problem."

"Okay, ready?" He steps back from the door.

"Wait, what?" I have no idea what I'm doing.

"On three." His hand is on the doorknob before I can protest. I swallow hard and wipe my palms on my dress.

"One."

I take a tiny step forward. Distraction, distraction, how can I be a distraction?

"Two."

Beck's expression is serious, focused, in full thief mode. My pulse quickens.

"Three."

He opens the door.

I take a deep breath and walk through it.

Chapter Nineteen

The guard doesn't look like a guard.

He's young.

His back is to me at first, as he faces the doors at the front of the room, but I'd guess he's older than me, about sixteen. He turns around at the sound of my entrance and looks even younger, with shining eyes, floppy hair, and the innocent face that the orphanage kids always had, before they learned better. In this second, with his eyes locked on me, he is all the boys I used to pull pranks with and fight with, all the newcomers I used to trick into stealing me things from Sister Romisha's room. And now, instantly, I am that girl again.

He frowns, confused and startled all at once, then he opens his mouth and says, "Hey!" like he's not sure what's happening but wants to sound authoritative. He stands and moves toward me, and all I can think is *get away from the door.*

I rush to the front of the desk so he has to turn away from

the back door to look at me. At the same time, I start talking. "I can't *believe* this took so long to get straightened out," I say, inching toward the desk. I fake a Ruhian accent as best I can. "I told them Baron Dearborn would come for me, I did, I told them, but you know how it is, all accusations and no explanations, and d'ya know, they made me wait around like a common criminal. Simply unbelievable. When Baron Dearborn hears about my treatment, let me tell ya, he will have something to say about this."

The boy turns again, following my progress around the desk, so that he's facing the front, with the inner prison door behind him. "What? You can't be out here—"

"Didn't they tell you? Baron Dearborn already arranged for my immediate release and return to the barony. Of course there's been a big misunderstanding, I told them that, Baron Dearborn knew it was all wrong, I've been with the family for years. So of course he came for me soon as he heard, I think, as soon as he could, anyway, and they said they'd release me straight off. I'm sure he'd be horrified to know what kind of conditions I was kept in! I'm no common maid, and no common criminal, neither—"

The boy's brow furrows. He's just another Striker, another kid at the orphanage, the kind I can manipulate. I know everything and he knows nothing. He's all innocence and eagerness still, easily used and easily broken.

"They didn't tell me anything about a release. . . ." He takes a step toward me—

And goes flying, slamming into the floor, Beck pinning him to the ground, one knee pressed into his back. The boy shoves his arm back, connecting with Beck's chest, but Beck just yanks the guard's knife from its sheath and lays it against his cheek.

"Don't move, don't speak, don't scream." Beck's voice is low. Like the first time I ever heard him speak, protecting me by threatening that shopkeeper.

The boy makes a sort of whimpering sound as Beck presses the knife against his skin, but he doesn't move.

"Get the key," Beck says to me. "Quick, they may have heard that."

I kneel down beside the boy and reach into his pocket, pulling out all the metal things my fingers find. I dump the objects onto the ground and sift through them—an old candy wrapper, handcuffs, handcuff key, ID badge, coins—quickly, quickly, looking for any key that's big enough—

"Try the other pocket," Beck says.

I move to the boy's other side, and he stares at me, his eyes wide and scared and so ridiculously young. I reach for his pocket, and he just keeps staring at me with those eyes that are terrified and begging but trying to be strong, too, trying not to cry. I know the feeling well enough, and it makes me want to snatch the knife from Beck's hands, to tell the boy that it's okay, that we won't hurt him.

He's a guard, not a boy. I have to remind myself. It's one of the rules on my list: There's no place for guilt in thieving.

And rule number one: Stealing is necessary to survive.

My fingers wrap around the key. "Got it!"

"Quick, get the door," Beck says. I run for it, not daring to look at the boy—no, the guard—again. I hear movement behind me, hear Beck order something in that low voice that's not his, but I don't turn around. I stuff the key in the lock, wait for the click that means freedom, and shove the door open.

I turn around. "Come on!"

Beck walks the boy back over to the desk. Still keeping the knife up against him, Beck uses his other hand to clip one end of the handcuffs to the desk and the other around the boy's wrist.

"Count to one hundred before you yell for help," Beck says, "or we'll come back for you." He runs, reaches me in a few quick strides, and we both pass the outer door and run, run, run. We reach the street outside the prison but we can't stop. We can never stop. There will always be someone chasing after us.

I'm kind of okay in my maid's uniform, but Beck's way too conspicuous in his torn, dirty suit, so the first thing we do is find a clothing store. Beck's calculations must've been close to correct, since it's obviously dark outside and all the shops are closed for the night. We find a small clothing shop and break a window in the back, then slip inside. Beck looks like he's done it a thousand times, and I pretend like I have too.

Once we both have clean clothes on, we head back out to look for food. Beck seems to know his way around the marketplaces. Everything's closed, of course, but there's no one to stop us from picking the padlocks on a few stalls. We snatch a little bread here, a little fruit there, and by the time we reach the end of the market the ache in my stomach has dulled, even if it's still not quite full. Maybe it will never be completely filled again. I can't remember the last time it was, actually. Has it ever been?

"So," Beck says quietly as we reach the end of the street, "I've been thinking about the plan."

"Oh no."

"I think we're going to want a pretty fast getaway this time. I don't know about you, but all this running is really wearing me out. And I think it's the fifty-ninth by now, and the Athertons aren't leaving until the sixtieth, so we've got a day to wait. So we should find Jiavar and ask for her help. You said she was waiting for us, right?"

"Yeah. She told me she'd be in the Miagnar Gardens."

"Okay. So we go there and plan everything out, let her know what's going on and where we'll need her to be."

I look down at my feet. "Beck?"

"Yeah?"

"Do you really think we can still do this? We only have a day to figure it out, and we have to break into the Athertons'. . . . I mean, the last plan didn't really go so well."

"I think we did all right, though, don't you? I mean,

yeah, going to prison wasn't part of the plan, but we got out, thanks to you."

At least it's dark so he can't see the heat flooding my face. "And thanks to your expert left-handed blind lock-picking skills."

"And that. Anyway, we're really not doing too badly at the moment. And we have time. A whole day and a half, really. We'll just go in, grab the necklace, and have Jiavar fly us back to the Guild. We'll be back before morning on the first."

"Right. It will really be that simple."

Beck looks at me. At my right hand. "We have to try."

"Yeah, I guess." I don't know if we can do it. But I don't have any other choice. The pain in my right arm is spreading well past my shoulder. I don't have much time.

"And, Alli?"

"Yeah?"

"Thanks. For coming back for me, I mean."

"Yeah, whatever. Let's go find our thilastri."

Miagnar Gardens is some kind of fancy noble's place, with a big fence bordering the property that we have to climb. It's too dark to see much, but the grass is thick under my feet, and in the distance fountains gurgle and wind chimes ring. It's like the gardens at Dearborn's, but on a much larger scale.

"There are stables around here somewhere," Beck

explains. "Some of the nobles who live nearby keep their carriages and thilastri here. Easier than building their own stables."

We wander around in the dark for a while before we find it—a large wooden building in a far corner, right up against the fence. The path outside is studded with wheel ruts that we stumble over in the darkness. There's no one around, and the doors aren't even locked.

Inside, we find row after row of snug little rooms filled with massive plush cushions that a bunch of thilastri are sleeping on. They may just be the chauffeurs, but these thilastri are treated like royalty, apparently.

"How do we know which one's Jiavar?" I whisper. "I can't tell in the dark." There are a few lamps suspended from the ceiling, but it's still pretty shadowy in here.

"Most of the rooms have names," Beck says. "Look for one of the guest ones that doesn't have a nameplate."

A few rows over, we find the guest rooms, which are all empty except for one. When we walk in, Jiavar's eyes snap open. Then she sees Beck and smiles.

"I thought you were a goner, Reigler."

Beck smiles back. "But you waited."

"I didn't have anything else to do at the moment," Jiavar huffs. "So. What now?"

"The Athertons are leaving their estate tomorrow night," Beck whispers, "so we're going to sneak in and grab the necklace."

Her eyes widen. "You're going to break into Shoringham." She says it like she doesn't quite believe it.

"We were hoping you'd provide the getaway transportation," Beck says.

Jiavar looks at him for a long moment. "You've thought this through."

"Of course. And it's the only way."

She hesitates for a second. "You could walk away now."

"No." Beck's voice is firm.

The thilastri turns to me for the first time. "Don't do this. You don't want to do this."

"Why not?" I say, genuinely confused now.

"I'll do it by myself if she won't," Beck says, but his voice wavers.

"Then you'll get yourself killed." Jiavar glares at me, as if I have any idea what's going on.

"What else do you want me to do?" Beck's voice rises in agitation. "I can't just quit."

"What's going on?" I say. "Beck?"

He doesn't meet my eyes. "The guards at Shoringham have a reputation for being ruthless. They have magic, and they'll aim to kill."

"They killed a Guild member two years ago," Jiavar says harshly, "just for being on the property without permission. Atherton tells them to kill any trespassers on sight."

I swallow hard. "You seem to have forgotten to mention that, Beck."

"You can't do this," Jiavar says. "Be reasonable."

Beck's jaw tightens. "I have to do this. And I'll do it with or without help from either of you."

"It's suicidal!" Jiavar says, her voice rising too.

"Okay, okay, let's calm down," I say quickly, my voice hardly above a whisper. "Let's not wake everyone else up, all right?"

Jiavar glares at both of us. "Fool," she says, and for a second I'm not sure which of us she means. "You're going to get her killed, do you understand? Not to mention yourself."

"Nobody's getting killed." I try to keep my voice calm and soft. Beck glowers at her, defiant and stubborn. "If Beck's going to do this, then let's do it. The Athertons won't be home, and we'll disguise ourselves so the guards won't notice us. We'll only need a couple of minutes to get in, grab the necklace, and get out. But we'll need your help, Jiavar."

Beck looks at me gratefully, but Jiavar grimaces. "You're both fools," she says.

"Thanks," I say. "I really appreciate your optimism."

Beck makes a sputtering sound that might be a smothered laugh.

"Fine," Jiavar says coldly. "Fine. Tell me where I need to be when, and I will be there to pick you up. But that's all I'm doing. I won't help you get yourselves killed."

"We're not asking you to," I say. "Now. If Beck and I were in Lady Atherton's chambers stealing the necklace, could you wait for us nearby? Outside the window, maybe?"

"What would I tell the guards? If I just land there, they'll kill me before I have a chance to get away."

"The Athertons own thilastri," Beck says. "We can repaint the crest on the carriage to make it look like one of theirs, and then they'll let you in, no questions asked. You can wait in the stables until it's time."

I raise an eyebrow at Beck. "Do you know how to paint? Because I don't."

"We have a whole day to get ready," he reminds me. "We'll just hire a painter."

"With what money? The protectors took everything we had on us."

"I left some money in the carriage under the seat," he says, "and I stole thirty jamars from the cash register in that clothing shop just now."

I try not to look impressed. Why didn't I think of that?

Jiavar sighs. "So what time do you want me to be outside Atherton's window?"

Beck considers this for a second. "Around twelve thirty."

"How will she know what time it is?" I ask. "How will *we* know what time it is? You still don't have a watch."

"We'll get two," Beck says, "and sync them up. Then Jia can keep one, and I'll wear the other."

"Oh, so now we have the funds to hire a painter *and* buy expensive watches."

Beck rolls his eyes. "We'll *steal* the watches, Alli."

Jiavar interrupts before I can say anything. "And how will

I know which window is the right one? I've never been to Shoringham."

"I have a map in the carriage," Beck says. "I'll show you."

"Wait, what?" This time I raise both eyebrows at him. "Now you magically have a map of the Atherton estate in the carriage?"

Beck shrugs. "When I got the blueprints of Dearborn's, I asked for any material on Atherton's too. I always figured this would be our backup plan. I didn't really have time to look over it, so I put it in my bag with the money and left it in the carriage, just in case."

Jiavar and I both stare at him. "Beck Reigler," I say, "you are a criminal mastermind." I'm not sure if that's a compliment.

Beck either doesn't notice how impressed we are, or pretends not to. "Right, so I'm thinking we should all study the floor plans tonight. Then when it gets light out, we can get everything we need: a painter, the watches, and another servant disguise for Alli. Then we'll meet you back here, Jia, and get you hooked up to the carriage so you can head out ahead of us. The Athertons should leave sometime between ten and eleven to get to the festival in time, but I think we should wait until midnight, just in case. If we know where we're going, it shouldn't take long to find the necklace, get to Jia, and get out. Simple."

A long pause. "Right," I say. "Simple."

"All right," Jiavar says finally. "But right now, I think all of us need to get some sleep. Both of you look like you're about to drop. Anyway, you can't do much until the morning, so you may as well rest."

She's right, of course, but I still don't want to go to sleep. Who knows who will die in my dreams tonight.

"Yeah, you should probably sleep, Allicat," Beck says.

"*Me?* What about *you?*"

"I already slept in the jail, and anyway I've got to study the—"

"*Both* of you will get some sleep," Jiavar says, "or I will lock you in the carriage until the first and you'll miss your deadline. I should do that anyway, to keep you from going through with this idiotic plan."

"I thought the plan was pretty clever, actually." Beck pretends to be wounded.

"Sleep," Jiavar orders. She shifts back on her cushion to make room. And the cushion is so soft, so plush, that against my better judgment my eyes close, and I fall into sleep before I can open them again.

The boy from the prison is in my dreams. He wears a guard's uniform, but it's white instead of gray. And I have to run, I have to run—something tells me I will die if I don't—but he's everywhere I turn, blocking my path. Thousands of him surround me. And once more there's a knife in my hand. I can't think, all I know is I have to run, I *have* to, and

I bring the knife down. Right before it strikes his heart, his eyes meet mine. Pleading, innocent, confused. And even as he dies, the confusion never leaves his face. He cannot comprehend what I have done to him.

His blood is a red stain on his uniform and a black stain on my hand.

Chapter Twenty

When I wake up, my arm is on fire.

Frantically I open my eyes, squinting in the darkened stable. I try to bring my hand up close to my face to take a look at it, but I can barely lift it without doubling over in pain.

It is burning me, searing me. My whole arm, and reaching into in my shoulder, creeping around my collarbone and down my back. The ache of it is even touching my spine. I am on fire.

Dying.

I take a shuddering breath and sit up, pressing my back into the wall of the stable, and cradle my arm against my chest, willing it to feel normal again. It burns.

It burns it burns it burns. I can't think. I can't move.

I imagine the curse seeping through my blood, burning me as it goes. Rushing through my chest, pouring into my heart, wrapping tendrils of death around it. My heart thrashes wildly in response, but the curse chars it, blackens it, burns it into ash.

I can't breathe. My lungs are burning, my heart is burning, everything is dying dying dying—

"Alli?"

Beck is awake, staring at me as I shudder and gasp for breath. His hair is all tangled from sleep and sticking straight up. I focus on this detail, on how silly and mundane it is, to bring myself back to reality. To life.

I am still alive. The curse hasn't stopped my heart. Not yet.

I take a deep breath. "The curse. It hurts. Like it's on fire."

Beck sits up. "Are you sure?"

I muster the strength to roll my eyes at him. "Of course I'm sure, idiot."

He sighs, staring at my hand. "Did something happen? Do you know what caused it?"

"Nothing happened. I'm just getting worse."

"Here," Beck says, "hold out your hand."

He wraps his fingers around mine, and I barely feel it. He closes his eyes, concentrating. A bright blue light pulses around his hands, and a steady chill spreads down into my fingertips and all the way up my arm into my shoulder. Then Beck opens his eyes and drops my hand. The coolness fades, and when it's gone, some of the pain is gone too.

"Did that help?" he asks.

"Yeah, it's a little better," I say, clenching my hand experimentally. It's still hurting, but it's more of a dull ache.

"It didn't affect the curse itself," Beck warns me. "I'm not strong enough for that. I just tried to numb the pain and make it feel better."

"It does," I say. "Thanks. But . . . Are you sure your estimate was right? About how much time I have?"

"I think so. It's not in your chest yet, right?"

"Not really. My collarbone and shoulder, mostly."

He nods. "I think you're okay, especially since it's on your right side—farther from your heart. As long as we do this today . . ."

"But we don't have any time to waste."

"Right."

"Well," I say, "let's get busy, then."

When Jiavar wakes up, we follow Beck's plan. First, we find a painter who takes one look at the coins in Beck's bag and doesn't ask any questions. While he works on the carriage, Beck and I go into the marketplace, where I distract a number of people so Beck can snatch things—watches, an outfit for me (a dress, gloves, and shoes), some food, and everything else Beck thinks we'll need. We spend most of the afternoon in the Miagnar Gardens, snacking on some stolen apples and studying the floor plans of Shoringham. Finally, when the painter's finished, Beck pays him, making sure to include an extra-large tip and a reminder to keep his mouth shut.

By late evening, Beck and I are dressed in our servant disguises, and any evidence that might incriminate us has been hidden away inside the carriage, which now bears the Atherton family crest. Jiavar, who spent most of the day either napping or reminding us how much she disapproves of this whole idea, is strapped into place at the front of the carriage. After telling her the meeting place for the thousandth time, Beck nervously adjusts her watch, which is attached to the side of the carriage where she can see it, since she doesn't have a wrist to wear it on, and sends her off.

"Be careful," she says. Then she runs down the path and leaps into the air, pulling the carriage after her, becoming a distant pinprick of shadow until the sky swallows her up.

"So, we're going to pay someone for a ride now, right?" I ask.

Beck nods, reaches into his pocket—and freezes.

"What's wrong?"

"I put the money in the carriage." His face is frozen. "All of it."

I curse. "What're we going to do now, steal a whole carriage?"

"Don't be ridiculous." Even when he's afraid, he still manages to scoff at me. "We're just going to steal the money."

I roll my eyes. "Oh, *I'm* ridiculous? And where, exactly, are we going to get this money from? Are we going to rob the whole bank?"

"We don't need *that* much money. I'll just pick some pockets. A little loose change should do."

"Right," I say. "But if we needed more money—if, say,

we needed *a lot* of money—you wouldn't rule out robbing the bank, would you?" I already know the answer to this, actually. But I wonder if he's aware of how ridiculous he is.

"If we needed that much money, I wouldn't have forgotten it on the carriage." Without looking at me, he starts walking away, toward the entrance to the gardens.

"That's not the point." I run after him. "You didn't answer the question, Beck."

He's already at the garden entrance, peering out into the street. "Everybody's closed up shop for the holiday. Not many people around."

"So, at what point do we resort to bank robbery?"

"No time for that," he mutters distractedly. "I'll bet some of these shops have full cash drawers, though."

"Great," I say. "Fantastic. I always look forward to breaking and entering."

"If you don't have anything helpful to add . . ." Glancing around, he veers down the street, cuts into an alley, and circles around to the back of the shop.

I follow him. "If you finish that sentence by telling me to shut up, I will punch you in the face."

"I'm not finishing that sentence. I think the implication was pretty obvious." Beck pulls the tension wrench and hairpins from his pocket and picks the lock on the back door of the little shop.

"I happen to think everything I say is helpful. I think it's very helpful to have someone remind you, through witty and intelligent sarcasm, that some of your ideas—like robbing a bank, for example—are really, really bad ideas."

"Robbing a bank was your idea. You brought it up."

Click. Beck shoves the door open, and we enter the darkened shop.

After a minute of fumbling around in the dark, I find some matches in a drawer and light a candle. I'm about to hold the light up for Beck so he can pick the lock on the cash drawer when he holds the hairpin out to me. "You do the honors."

Beck has bent the hairpin into the right shape, but it's still harder to use than a proper pick. I take a lot longer than Beck would have, and Mead probably would've had the thing opened in two seconds, but I finally turn the lock and slide the drawer out. Beck holds the candle over the drawer as I count the coins quickly.

"Thirty-three jamars," I report. "Is that enough?"

"Probably," Beck says, but he doesn't sound sure. "I don't know what the fare is to go to that side of Ruhia."

"That would've been helpful to know." I pocket half of the coins and hand him the other half.

Beck slips the coins into his pocket. "Yeah, why didn't you think of that?"

"Let's get out of here."

Before either of us can move, the door flies open, and someone holding a lantern enters the shop. "Stop! Don't move."

We run.

Behind me, the protector swears, her footsteps thudding, but I don't turn around. I duck under a rack, turn a corner, try to find my way through the maze to the door—

Crash. The protector fumbles through the shop, knocking shelves over as she goes, sending everything toppling to the ground. A shelf falls right beside me. I lunge forward—

I barely make it out of the way as the shelf collapses. Its merchandise spills to the floor, and something lands on top of my foot and pins me in place. The protector sees and rushes toward me, ten feet away—but there's a mountain of stuff between us standing in her way, I might be able to make it before—

A hand grabs my arm and yanks me up. My foot slides out from under the dead weight and I find the ground again.

Beck's voice is in my ear. "C'mon!"

I don't let go of his hand as we run out the door, the protector right behind us but struggling, not as nimble as we are. We sprint down the street, take a sharp turn, then another, trying to lose her. One alleyway bleeds into the next, and there's just the pounding of my heartbeat and footsteps, thudding out a rhythm in time with our gasping breaths.

We can't go on anymore. We stop, lean against a wall, drop hands. Breathe.

"You okay?" I gasp.

"Yeah, you?"

"Fantastic."

"Did you hurt your foot?"

I'd forgotten all about it, so I guess it's okay. A little sore, now that I think about it. But compared to the pain of the curse and the bruises on my left side and head, it's nothing. "No."

"All right, let's go." Beck steps forward, peering first in one direction, then the other.

"You do know where we are, right?"

"Um." Beck walks to one end of the alley and looks out at the street. "I'll figure it out once we get to a main street."

"You mean you've spent all this time studying maps of Shoringham and Dearborn, but you never memorized every side street and alleyway in Ruhia? What good are you?"

"Sorry, I was too busy memorizing a map of Azeland. Knowledge which saved you from a protector, as I recall."

"Whatever. Like I needed your help." But he *did* seem to have an uncanny knowledge of Azeland, come to think of it. "Wait, you didn't really memorize a map of Azeland, did you?"

"Come on, Allicat," he says, disappearing around the corner.

"Is that a yes or a no?"

Beck's knowledge of Ruhia's streets isn't too bad, all things considered, but I continue to berate him about it as we wander through some more tiny alleys. Finally, we find a more populated area, and Beck figures out where we are. In no time, we've located a carriage service and are on our way to Shoringham.

Beck doesn't speak much during the ride, no matter how often I try to get him talking. I guess he knows this is really it this time. If we fail tonight, it's all over. No chance to try again. Everything we've done—the ball, the prison escape, and every successful theft along the way—will have been for nothing.

And what will I do if we don't make it? It's not like there's some other way to get the money, even if I have time, which I don't. How many days do I have left? Last time I looked, the black lines had spread still farther, and it seems like every second the pain is growing. And I'm starting to feel weaker all over—dizzy and tired. I probably have three days at most. What if I . . . what if I die?

I've come so far. I've maybe even found a home in the Guild, the thing I didn't even know I wanted until I found it. But if I fail . . .

I can't even think about it, can't even think beyond where I'm going to sleep tomorrow or what I'll do if I make it into the Guild, or what I'll do if I don't. Everything is too far away to worry about. I've got to take it one thing at a time, like I always do. It's the only way to survive.

And Beck? What will he do? Has he thought about it all? Something tells me he has—he's too meticulous not to have a backup plan. But then again, he's been in the Guild his whole life. Not being in it is probably unthinkable to him. He didn't even consider giving up after we lost the necklace the first time. Was that just determination, or refusal to admit the inevitable?

The funny thing is, I can't picture Beck outside of the Guild, even though I've seen him more outside of it than in. I can't see him living in a clothing shop and stealing food from marketplaces in ten years, let alone twenty or thirty. I guess he could get a job somewhere. He's about to turn thirteen, after all, so employment's an option. I try to picture him in some kind of uniform, working for a boss and getting a paycheck, but I can't—my mind draws a complete blank. There is too much of the Guild in him for that.

"Alli?" Beck says.

"Yeah?"

He takes a deep breath, not looking me in the eye. "You don't have to come."

"What?"

"You don't have to come." Another breath. "Jiavar wasn't totally wrong. This is really dangerous—you know that. And you've almost gotten hurt or imprisoned a dozen times already. This will be worse, if the guards catch us. So if you want to leave, I don't blame you. I—I don't want you to think you have to do this."

"I'm cursed, remember?" I say, forcing a smile. "I don't have much of a choice in the matter. And I'm not scared."

Finally, he looks at me. "I know you're not. That's what concerns me."

"We both have to do this." I don't know where the words

come from, but I know they're true. "We both need to survive, right? And the Guild's our best shot, even if we have to go through all this to get in it."

He doesn't say anything to that. I almost tell him—I *want* to tell him—how much I've come to want the Guild the way that he does. The way I felt at home for the first time ever. The way I felt after ice sledding, after training, like I was finally part of something. And the truth is, I'm not sure I want to be anywhere without Beck. But I don't know how to say any of that without sounding totally sappy. After a few beats of silence, I say, "I'm doing this because I want to, all right?"

His lips twitch. "Okay."

"No other reason. None at all."

"Right." The twitch again.

"What's so funny?"

"Nothing."

Shoringham is completely isolated from the rest of Ruhia. We pass what must be miles of rocky, snow-covered countryside without seeing another building. The land out here is bleak, nothing but gray stone and slushy spring snow that slows down the carriage's wheels. Aside from the occasional skeletal tree, the landscape is nothing but long stretches of gray, like being inside a raincloud. The dark, overcast sky is practically indistinguishable from the ground.

Eventually we stop at a set of large iron gates. The guard on duty just glances at our uniforms and waves us through.

Beck lets out a relieved sigh. "Well, that was easier than expected."

The house looms before us, dark and ominous. Beck gives the carriage driver instructions, and we veer onto a small path off the main drive that wraps around the side of the house. We've reached the back when Beck stops the driver and we hop out.

Beck slips the driver a few extra coins for his silence and sends him back the way he came. We're left standing on a pathway between the gardens and the back of the house.

The back door to the servants' kitchen is locked, but that's no problem, of course. This late at night, the kitchen is dark and empty. We fumble through the blackness, trying not to bump into anything as we walk to the west wall, where there should—according to our map—be a door.

Bang. Beck curses. "Watch out."

I narrowly avoid whatever-it-was and press up against the wall beside Beck, feeling around for a lock, latch, anything. . . .

"Got it," Beck whispers, and the door swings open.

The next room is the main kitchen—though why two kitchens are necessary I have no idea—and it's as dark as the last one, but twice as big.

"At least the dark means there's nobody in here," I whisper.

"Yeah, but it also means we have no explanation if we get caught. What reason do we have for sneaking around a dark kitchen?"

"Let's say we're servants stealing food. Then they'll just

hand us over to the protectors, instead of killing us."

"If we're lucky," Beck mutters.

This kitchen is shaped like a funny L, with the door to the dining room in the recessed part, opposite where we came in. We make our way down the long side of the room and turn the corner.

A light flickers from the doorway. It's the only door on that wall, according to the map, so it's got to be the dining room. "Would you like to curse again, or should I?" I mutter.

"There can't be anyone eating at this time of night," Beck whispers, "and the Athertons have left. Someone just left a candle burning, probably."

"Probably. But how are we going to find out for sure?"

"Someone should check," he says, but he doesn't move.

"All right, I'll do it." I tiptoe forward, press myself against the wall, and slide toward the doorway. Slowly, slowly I angle myself until I'm facing the next room and peer in.

A massive table dominates the space. In one corner, a little serving board sits, with the flickering candle on top of it. Empty.

I exhale slowly, relieved. "No one's here."

I slip into the room, Beck following me. On the wall opposite us are two doors, just like the map.

"When we get out of here," I whisper, "remind me to send the mapmaker a personal thank-you."

"We want the one on the right," Beck says.

"I *know*," I say. "I read the map too."

I make my way across the room, being careful not to bump into any chairs. I put my hand on the doorknob, about to fling the door wide—

"Wait. Make sure no one's in there."

"Right." I open the door a crack and try to sneak a glance inside. "Nope. It's all dark."

Since the large parlor and sitting room on the other side of the house were just not enough, apparently, we're now in another small parlor, the only access point to Lord and Lady Atherton's chambers. This time, it's Beck who finds the door and peers through the crack. "All clear."

We cross the threshold. And in this moment, it's truly the first time I've felt really, deeply unsettled. This has been easy. Too easy.

"Okay," Beck says, "look for anyplace she might put a necklace. Jewelry boxes, dresser drawers. . . it might even be in a hidden safe. Check everywhere."

There's enough moonlight from the window to see the outlines of things. We tear the room apart. No need to hide what we're doing. They'll notice it's missing soon enough, and we have no good excuse for being in this room anyway, if we get caught. Might as well move quickly.

Beck checks the closet while I tackle the dresser. There's a jewelry box on top, but no necklaces at all inside. I pull all the clothing out of the drawers, sifting through it as I go, but there's nothing there either.

As Beck reenters the room from the closet, I abandon the

dresser and pull the cushions off the sofa. I jump as a clock on the wall above me chimes. Midnight.

It's officially the first day of the month. Deadline day. Samyra's Day. And . . .

"Hey, Beck," I say. "Happy birthday."

He looks up from his search long enough to grin, then both of us resume the hunt.

The sofa is completely worthless. Not even a few lost coins or something buried beneath the cushions. I pick a new target—the nightstand.

A quick inspection reveals a candle, a book, a few papers, a quill, and—a small box with a lid. I fumble for the clasp, slip it open—

The necklace is curled up inside, its jewel winking in the dark.

"Beck."

"Yeah?"

"Beck, I've got it. I—I've got it!"

He's at my side instantly. "All right, Jia should be here any minute."

The necklace is a heavy weight in my hand, heavier than it should be. I can feel the pressure of it—this is it, our ticket to the Guild, resting on my palm.

I should feel relieved, but my insides are tight and my knees are shaking. Something feels wrong. Something *is* wrong.

The necklace should have been harder to find. It should

have been in a safe, not in plain sight on Lady Atherton's nightstand. Especially since the Athertons knew someone tried to steal it—

The guard at the gate. He shouldn't have just let us through like that. That was too easy.

The Athertons know exactly what we look like, and they know exactly what we're after.

The guard at the gate wasn't looking at our uniforms. He was looking at *us*.

Beck's at the window, throwing it open. Our signal to Jiavar.

"Beck," I say, but I can't get the rest of the words out. "The—the gate—"

Bang. Light bursts everywhere, and the world goes white. The door's been flung open, and a cluster of figures are standing in the threshold. A high voice screams, *"Stop them!"*

Chapter Twenty-One

I run for the window at the same time Beck does. I don't bother to see who's in the doorway, but I recognize Lady Atherton's voice, saying something I can't make out. Then, with a calmness and authority that sends shivers up and down my spine: "Kill them."

Everything explodes. I duck, hitting the floor and crawling forward. To my left, green flames sprout from nowhere and eat a hole in the rug, only a few inches from where I was standing. On the other side of the flames, Beck crawls across the floor.

Lady Atherton screams again, but I can't make out the words. I focus on crawling, each movement bringing me closer and closer to safety—

Heat bursts right behind me, unbearable—I lunge forward as the flames engulf my foot—

Not fast enough. I can't contain my scream as my foot burns white-hot. I roll across the floor, away from the second explosion of flames, but my foot's still on fire. Oh God, the flames won't go *out*—

And all at once, they *do* go out. I stop rolling and examine my foot. It's glowing blue. The color of healing magic.

Beck.

"Run!" I yell. "Get out of here!"

But the blue glow fades, and it's not enough. Searing pain is still shooting through me, and I don't know if I can even stand. I might be able to drag myself to the window. . . .

I'm wedged up against the bed now, with the fire roaring between me and the window, so I can't really see Beck, I don't know where he is—

A man in a guard's uniform whose hands are glowing green stands on the other side of the flames. Lady Atherton is behind him in the doorway, still screaming. Beside her is Ariannorah.

The guard walks toward me, extinguishing the flames between us as he goes. Why is he targeting me? Beck's closer to the window, and I'm clearly not going anywhere—

The necklace. Somehow I didn't drop it. The corners of the box dig into my palm, but I can't even feel it over the pain in my leg.

The guard is going to kill me, there is no doubt about that. The only reason I'm not dead right now is he's afraid to char the necklace to bits along with me. But he's coming for me, and I can't run, and he will kill me.

Beck could leave, get to safety.

But he won't leave without the necklace.

I turn. Beck is scrambling toward me, skirting the edges of the flames.

I pull the necklace out of the box. "Beck!"

He turns, and I throw. The necklace arcs through the air and falls, skidding across the floor.

The guard and Lady Atherton both lunge for it at the same time, but they're not fast enough. As they stumble into each other, Beck grabs the necklace and loops the chain around his neck.

Ariannorah rushes over to Lady Atherton, who fell dangerously close to the fire, but she's uninjured and yelling at her daughter to stay back.

The guard ignores them. Ignores me. His eyes are locked on Beck.

I push myself forward, but my foot won't move at all, and it hurts so bad that tears stream from my eyes. I drag my leg behind me and crawl, toward the guard and the Athertons and Beck. I've got to do something, got to cause a distraction so he can get away. He's only a few steps from the window. . . .

But Beck's not running for the window. He's standing in place, watching the guard. Why doesn't he run? Why doesn't he—

Me. He won't run because of me.

"Go!" I scream. "Run!"

Beck looks at me, but he doesn't move. The guard steps

closer. The necklace is the only thing protecting Beck from a sudden and fiery death. But the guard will just use a different spell, once he gets close enough, and then it will all be over.

"Go, you idiot, *leave!*"

The guard spreads his hands, and green light glows on his palms, spreading bigger and bigger, forming a massive ball of light, of death—

Beck backs up a little but there's nowhere left to go, the window's just to his left but he won't make it—

The guard throws his hand back, aims—

The magic is headed straight for Beck. He's not going to make it.

Until Ariannorah leaps forward and shoves Beck to the floor.

Lady Atherton screams and lunges between Ariannorah and the ball of light that's now headed straight for her—

And the ball of light hits Lady Atherton squarely in the stomach.

For a moment she's frozen, hanging, her mouth dropping open, and with her frilly gown and painted face aglow in the green light, she looks like a ghastly doll. A puppet, permanently suspended.

Then she crumples to the floor.

Ariannorah shrieks. The guard stands there, looking at Lady Atherton's unmoving body, like he's not sure what just happened. He looks at Ariannorah. In one swift movement, he extinguishes the flames and runs from the room.

"Beck!" I yell. "Are you okay?" He's not moving. God, why isn't he moving?

"Okay," he grunts, sitting up slowly.

Ariannorah lets out a cry of pain. She's still lying on her side, and it's only now I realize she's hurt too. Part of the blast must've hit her arm. She's clutching it tight.

I don't want to look at Lady Atherton, but at the same time I can't stop. She can't be dead, she can't be, but my eyes are telling me she is. She lies still in a way that only the dead can. Her eyes are open.

Beck has picked himself up off the floor. He's not injured. The necklace is still around his neck. But his face is twisted with pain as he sees what I see—she's definitely dead.

Wincing, I drag myself forward and crawl over to Lady Atherton's side, just to confirm what I already know. She's not breathing.

Ariannorah sobs hard and clenches her arm. She's losing blood—a *lot* of blood. It must be some side effect of whatever spell the guard used.

Ariannorah whimpers when I get close but doesn't say anything. She squeezes her eyes shut against the pain, or maybe she's trying not to cry. "It's okay," I say, because I don't know what else to say. "It's okay. Beck can heal this. Beck, can't you . . . ?"

But he's shaking his head. His face is frozen, and his eyes are painful to look at. "I used up all my healing on your leg. I don't have anything left."

He told me he was a bad healer, but I never really believed him until now. He didn't even heal my leg all the way, for God's sake. "Can't you *do* something?" I know he can't, but I keep repeating the words anyway, like my brain's stuck on them: "Can't you do something?"

There's nothing to be done. Lady Atherton's dead and Ariannorah's bleeding to death all over the plush white carpet. Maybe if I can bandage the wound . . . ?

Ariannorah's wearing a lacy white dress with lots of padded skirts that are already bloodstained. She doesn't say anything as I rip off a bottom layer of the dress and try to use it like a makeshift tourniquet around her arm. God, why didn't I pay more attention to Sister Perla's first-aid lessons?

Finally, Ariannorah seems to realize I'm there. She looks up at me, then down at her ruined dress. "I need a healer." Her voice is firm, but also pleading. She says it again, like it's the only truth in the world she knows: "I need a healer."

"No kidding," I say. "What in Saint Ailara's name did you do that for, anyway?"

I wasn't expecting an answer, but Ariannorah seems to be seriously considering the question. "I don't know," she says, and her voice is small. "I just . . . I didn't want him to die." Her face contorts in pain, and she chokes out the next words. "I didn't want anybody to die."

"Neither did I." I look her straight in the eyes, hoping she'll know that I mean it. And I *do* mean it. I don't like the Athertons, but I didn't want them to die. And it's kind of hard to hate Ariannorah right now, when she looks so lost.

It's too late for Lady Atherton, but maybe not for Ariannorah. Not if we get her a healer in time.

"Beck," I say, "do you think you can run and get—"

Beck is by the window. He whistles—our signal to Jiavar, who should be waiting just off the pathway. The necklace glitters around his neck.

"What are you doing?" I say, even though I know what he's doing. "We have to help her."

"How?" His voice is desperate, wanting an answer and knowing there isn't one. And it really hits me. We cannot help her and ourselves. Beck knows this. He's already thought it through and arrived at the logical conclusion. We cannot help her.

But we have to. My poor bandaging effort was useless. Everything is stained: the bandage and her arm and her dress and the floor and me. My palms are red. Her death is all over my hands.

Jiavar pulls up to the window, and Beck looks at me. "Can you walk if you lean on me?"

In the near-darkness of the room, the bloodstains on the floor are black.

"She's dying," I whisper.

"Alli," he says, and I can hear how much this hurts him. He knows what I know and it's hurting him as much as me. But Beck is nothing if not practical. He will follow the rules. He knows how to survive. "If we go for help, they'll arrest us. They might even kill us. There are other guards around."

"If we don't, she'll die."

"Someone will come in here any minute now. Someone will find her." I can't tell if he really believes this. It's a possibility. But that's not enough.

I want to just leave through the window. I don't know what they'll do to me if I go for help, but it doesn't matter. I'll die. I'm out of time. I don't even like Ariannorah anyway. . . . It would be so, so easy.

But I know what the right thing to do is.

And I can't look at Beck because I already know what he will do.

Rule number nine: Fall behind, get left behind.

I remember the first time I met him, in the shop where he saved me from a protector. How he held a knife to an innocent man's throat like it was easy, like it was nothing. And I admired that. I thought it was strength.

But what Lady Atherton just did for her daughter, *that* was strength.

Maybe sometimes loving someone means you have to leave them. Or let them go.

Beck's at my side now, taking my hand, helping me to my feet. I can't put any weight on my injured foot, so I lean against the nearby nightstand. "Come on," he says.

"No."

He stares at me for a long moment. Fear and pain and

desperation are all wrapped up in the silence, in his eyes. "Don't be stupid. You can't even walk."

"I don't have to go far. Just far enough to call for help and have someone hear me."

"Alli, you'll die. Don't do this."

I have to do this. A mother who tried to save her child is dead, and it's our fault. And that child is dying, right now. But there's no point in saying this to Beck. He already knows it. It's all over his face. But for him, that's not enough. He wants the Guild too badly, and he will never get another chance. Someone who's spent his whole life trying to survive won't throw it all away now, when escape is only a few feet away, through the open window.

You must be willing to take from anyone. From everyone. That's the first rule of survival. Someone's loss is another's gain. Someone's death is another's life. The king knew this would happen. He was trying to warn me, to tell me what it would cost, but I didn't understand until it was too late. I knew there would be a price, and I knew Beck's first rule. But I didn't know the price would be so high. I didn't know I, and innocent people, would have to pay it.

My right hand is black.

I will die if I don't go to the Guild now, but I could never live with myself if I did.

"Beck!" Jiavar's voice, from the window. "There are guards coming!"

Beck looks into my eyes. "I don't want to leave you behind."

"Then don't leave."

"Alli—"

"If you're going, you'd better go."

"I'll carry you into the carriage." It's more of a threat than an offer of help.

"Beck." My throat's all choked up. "I'm staying."

He pauses. "I'll come back for you."

It doesn't matter. It will be too late.

He hesitates, like he's going to stay something else. Then he reaches up and brushes his thumb against my cheek, softly, for the briefest of seconds. "Good-bye."

He turns and walks away.

He climbs through the window. He does not look back.

And he's gone.

Chapter Twenty-Two

I still can't stand, so I have to hold on to the bed with one hand and shuffle along on my good foot. My right hand isn't working anymore, and I'm dizzy. From the bed, I grab hold of the sofa, then a dresser, then I'm finally at the door.

This whole time, Ariannorah hasn't moved. I almost point out to her that there's nothing wrong with *her* legs, but then again she's bleeding so heavily that movement probably isn't a good idea. Not to mention the fact that she doesn't seem to have the firmest grip on reality at the moment. Her face is frozen, blank, like she's just shut herself off.

"It's okay, I'm going to get help," I say, but I don't know if she hears me.

I limp through the little parlor and barely reach the dining room before I'm all out of energy. And I have to go all the way around the dining table to get to the door. So I do the only thing I can do. I scream.

"Help!"

The sound echoes around the room. I can only hope it drifted through the door to an inhabited part of the house.

A few beats of silence.

Footsteps.

I scream again, no words this time, just holding it out as long as I can so they'll know where I am. I scream until my throat threatens to rip apart.

The door crashes open, and bright lights shine on my face, blinding me.

"What the—?"

"Ariannorah. In the bedroom. Needs help." My throat's so raw the words scrape against it and come out in a rasp.

Blurry lantern lights dance as the room sways.

Voices surround me, but I don't know if they're in the room or in my mind. I am too tired to look. Too tired to move.

The injury to my leg has only made all the cursed parts of me hurt worse, and now everything is burning. Pain racks my legs and my arm and my throat and my eyes.

I wonder, detachedly, if this is what it feels like to die.

It's funny, really, in a pathetic sort of way. I spent my last few days of life trying to outrun death. If only I'd known it would catch me anyway, I would've spent my time differently.

From the direction of the bedroom comes a woman's scream.

Then, a familiar face appears in the doorway. Lord Atherton. I expect him to recognize me, but he doesn't even look. He's running for the bedroom.

There's shouting and running in all directions as hundreds of people, it seems, pass by me, running to and from the room, and in all the shouting I catch words like "healer" and "bleeding" and "dead." Somewhere, someone is sobbing.

My good leg is giving out. I don't have the strength to drag a chair all the way out from the table, so I collapse against it, falling on the armrest, not caring that it hurts. I just want to sleep; why won't they be quiet?

A man rushes in from the parlor and past me. He's holding a little girl in a lacy white dress. And she's awake. She's alive. I don't remember why that's important, but something tells me it is, or it was. . . .

Someone's yelling. A man. Lord Atherton. Yelling in a way that's angry and scared and confused all at once. The room floods with light. And guards, all around me. Their lanterns throw light everywhere. The walls of the room are red.

In front of me, a woman. A maid, I think. "Here she is. The girl who was screaming."

Lord Atherton looks at me for the first time. His eyes widen. "The thief."

He walks over to me, practically shoving the maid out of the way. "What have you done?" His yell stings my ears. "What have you *done*?"

Before I know what's happening, he slaps me across the face.

"Lord Atherton." A low voice at the door. Disapproving.

Atherton spins around. "Is she all right?"

"She is weak," the voice says, "but she will live."

Atherton sinks back against the wall, a balloon that's been deflated. "You're sure?"

"Yes. She's lost a fair amount of blood, but the wound is not fatal, and I was able to stop the bleeding. She will recover. Now, I was told there was another . . . ?"

Atherton looks at me, half collapsed against a chair, unable to stand. "Never mind." Almost in a whisper, he adds, "She killed my wife."

I try to protest—it wasn't me, I didn't kill her—but I can't remember why those words aren't true. Maybe I did, maybe it was me, that's why I had to stay behind. . . .

"What would you have us do with her, sir?" asks another voice. A guard?

Atherton hesitates. He's going to tell them to kill me. He wants to, I can tell. But he looks at the doorway, toward whoever is standing there, and he won't say it.

"Call the protectors," he orders. "And no one let her leave this room."

There are murmurs of assent.

"Sir," the voice says, "she does not look well. I could heal her—"

"I wouldn't have you waste your magic on a murderer."

The voice says something, but I can't catch the words. The room swirls around me, the lanterns throwing shadows against the walls, and all I can see are flashes of light against the darkness before it all goes black.

★ ★ ★

I open my eyes and everything is white. The walls, the ceiling, the floors, the sheets, the thin gown I am wearing, the curtains over the window that filter in white sunlight. The bars of the bed I am strapped to.

I yank back the sheets and look at my injured foot, which doesn't hurt anymore. It's completely wrapped in white bandages.

I try to find things in the room that are not white, but the only thing I find is me.

I will not think about Beck. I will not think about how his mouth twitched at the corners when he tried to hide a smile, or the way he called me Allicat, or how he annoyed me with all his plans and his backup plans and his smirks and his rules. I will not think about the way he touched my cheek or wonder what that meant. I will not think I have lost him.

A nurse comes in, wearing, of course, a white uniform and apron. "You're awake," she says cheerfully. Like waking up a prisoner in a strange place is worth being cheerful about.

"Where am I?"

"The House of Healing, of course," she says.

The House of Healing. In Cerda. At the Healing Springs. "How . . . ?"

"You were hit with a fairly nasty curse, dear. Xeroth's Blood. Only the healing waters of the Springs will put it right again. Another curse hit you in the leg, but that one should heal up quickly."

"I know," I say. I look down at my chest. The dark lines of the curse are there, peeking above the neckline of my nightgown, almost to my heart. I haven't been cured yet. They must've already done something to help with the pain, though, because it doesn't hurt as much as it did before. "But . . . I can't afford it."

"Oh, no need to worry about that. You've been paid for."

"What? By who?" No one would do that for me.

"It was an anonymous donation," she says. "You were in a hospital in Ruhia, and someone just dropped off the money, with a note insisting that it go toward a trip to the Springs."

Beck.

He must have made it, then. He must have taken the necklace to the Guild, passed the trial, collected the money . . . and given most of the money to me.

"Okay," I say. "When do I get to leave?"

She laughs. "When you're healed, of course."

"And how long will that be?"

"The Springs will only heal one person at a time. You're next on the list. Should be any moment now." She pushes over some kind of cart with lots of funny objects on it. "In the meantime, let me check your bandages."

"I don't need bandages. I'm not bleeding or anything."

She raises her eyebrows at me. "Who's the healer here?" But she doesn't say it like she's angry, just amused.

I glare back at her, but I'm not really angry either.

"Now," she says, bustling around her cart, "time for you to eat." She plops a huge tray of food onto my lap.

I stare at it for a couple of seconds without saying anything.

"Everything all right?" she asks, looking at the tray like there's some kind of problem.

"This is just for one person?" I say. "I can eat *all* of it?" This must be some kind of joke.

Healing Lady looks confused. "Yes, of course," she says.

I pick up a fork, but I'm not sure where to begin. There are so many choices. There's steaming soup and brown rice and meat covered in creamy sauce and a pile of little blue fruits and a bunch of other unfamiliar things I can't name.

"I can have them make you something else," Healing Lady says uncertainly.

I lift a massive roll of bread off the tray. It is whole and fresh and perfect. I am afraid to take a bite of it. I just hold it for a second and inhale the fresh-baked-bread smell. My stomach rumbles.

Healing Lady's watching me like she wonders if I should be in the mental ward instead of hers, but I don't know how to explain it to her. I'll sound pathetic if I confess that I've never had a whole roll of bread like this before. Not one this big, anyway, or this fresh.

Finally I set it down at the far end of the tray, saving it for last. Then I devour everything else. Healing Lady, apparently satisfied that I am eating like a normal person now, leaves the room, promising to return in a few minutes to take the tray.

Everything is delicious, but when I get to the bread I'm glad I saved it for last. It's the best thing I've ever tasted.

A few hours later, they bring me another whole roll with dinner.

★ ★ ★

It's finally my turn to visit the Springs, and Healing Lady pushes me out in a wheelchair. Outside, it's even more beautiful than I imagined. The water is deeply, beautifully blue, bubbling softly in pools that stretch on as far as I can see. Smooth white rocks frame the pools, and around them tufts of bright green grass pop up. The vivid expanse of sky overhead stretches on uninterrupted, seemingly endless.

Healing Lady lifts me from the wheelchair and gently places me at the edge of the water. Without hesitating, I push off from the rocks and submerge myself. The water is the most amazing thing I've ever felt, so soft and cool against my skin. I close my eyes and feel the blackness of the curse seeping out, feel what remains of the pain in my leg and arm and hand slowly ease. Healing.

"Alli Rosco?" someone says.

I do not want to move.

"Alli, dear," Healing Lady says. "You have a visitor."

I lift my head from the water, blinking. "What?"

Mead stands at the edge of the pool, holding a small brown package in his hands. "Hey, Rosco, how's it going?"

As Healing Lady leaves us alone, I stare up at him in disbelief. "It was *you*? You paid for this?"

Mead laughs. "Don't be ridiculous. I'm only the delivery boy. For some reason he wanted to see you—why I have no idea—but your friend Atherton's got every protector from Ledrea to Ruhia looking for him, so you get me instead."

"He made it, then? Beck passed the trial?"

"Yeah, he's in."

His tone isn't what I expected. "You sound disappointed."

"Not at all," he says, but this time his flippancy is fake. "I was just surprised, really. I thought Reigler was too good for the Guild." He says it with derision, but there's a hint of something else, too. Admiration.

It makes sense now. Why people in the Guild like Ser and Mead and Jiavar and Rosalia all seemed protective of Beck, and treated me like a threat. They saw something in him that the Guild members had lost. The kind of goodness that motivated him to help some orphan girl from Azeland just because she needed it.

But I was never the threat to Beck. It was always the Guild.

I wish I'd known it sooner. I wish I'd saved both of us from it before it was too late. But maybe it was already too late for Beck. He made his decision long before that night at Shoringham. There is goodness in him, but the Guild is in him too.

How long will it take for Guild life to change him? To suck out all the good? I hope it can't, but I don't know. He will have a hundred more Ariannorahs.

"I dropped off the money right away, as he instructed," Mead continues, "but I needed to deliver this personally, so I had to wait until they said you could have visitors." He holds out the package.

Slowly, I lift my hand from the water. For a moment, I marvel at how smooth it is. The black veins are gone.

I take the little package from his hand, and he steps back. "Well, if that's all."

"Wait." I meet his eyes. "I've been dying to know—why did you steal that ring from Jarvin?"

He holds my gaze for a long moment. "You want the truth?"

"Please."

"I didn't want the ring. I just grabbed something that I knew would trigger the spell. I gave it back to my sister the next day." He pauses, waiting to see if I get it.

I think I do. "You didn't need to steal anything from Jarvin. It was . . . it was part of the tour."

He wanted to show me what the Guild was like. What being in the Guild meant. It was a risky, reckless thing to do—it really could have killed me, probably. But that was the point. He was willing to take a risk with my life, and willing to leave me behind to save his own skin. Any Guild member would, if it came down to it.

The king wasn't the only one who tried to warn me.

"Why? Why would you do that for me?"

"It wasn't for you." He doesn't meet my eyes.

Oh.

It was for Beck. He'd taken a risk bringing me there; Mead said as much before. And he wanted to make sure I wouldn't be scared off at the first sign of danger. That I knew what I was getting into. Because Beck was risking so much for me, Mead wanted to make sure I was worth it.

"Thank you," I say. "For everything."

He nods, turning away.

"Hey, Mead—I still have your tension wrench. They gave me back the stuff that was in my pockets when they found me; I guess they didn't know what the wrench was. Do you want it back?"

He rolls his eyes. "You're trying to return my property to me? Honestly, Rosco, you're a *terrible* thief."

"Thanks."

"You can keep it. I'm sure you'll want something to remember me by."

I snort. "Don't flatter yourself."

"I don't need to. You're doing a fine job of it."

"Look after Beck, okay?"

"Sure. See you around, Rosco."

Long after Mead's disappeared, I reach for the package sitting at the edge of the pool. I yank the wrapping off and set it aside.

A small bronze key lies in my palm, wrapped in a slip of paper. Moving carefully so as not to smudge the writing, I unfold the note.

Allicat:

45 W. Carriage Street. If you ever need someplace to go. Tell them I sent you.

—B. R.

It's a Guild hideout. It has to be. Beck told me they're everywhere. Members of the Guild who are on assignments need places to stay, he said, and there's at least one in every major city.

If I ever get out of prison . . .

If I ever need a place to stay . . .

I could go back to the Guild, and Beck would help me. They won't give me another trial again—they were clear about the fact that you only get one chance—but maybe . . .

No.

My fingers close over the key.

I can't rely on the Guild anymore. There is always a price, and the Guild isn't worth it.

I don't know where I will go when—if—this is all over. But I will not go back there.

I fold Beck's note up in my hand and slip back into the clear coolness of the water. I drift down, down, down, to the very bottom. I close my eyes, and I open my hand.

The key drops away, taking the sodden paper with it, lost to the depths.

I push upward, my head breaking the surface of the water. Slowly, I reach the edge of the pool and climb out.

I am healed.

Chapter Twenty-Three

A few more days pass by, though I'm not sure exactly how many since I spend most of the time sleeping or "resting," which is Healing Lady's term for being bored and not being allowed to do anything. Even though I'm healed, Healing Lady says it may take some time for the magic of the Springs to fully take effect, and any activity in the meantime might make things worse. I am not even allowed to go to the bathroom by myself because, according to Healing Lady, physical activity could further injure my foot. Plus the bandages are too lumpy to walk on. But I suspect I also have to be escorted because I am still, technically, under arrest, and they think I might try to escape or something. I might, if not for my bad foot making running impossible.

Despite my annoyance at being treated like a baby, I grow to like Healing Lady because she brings me lots of food. Although I can't have as much as I want anymore. I made myself sick the first day, when I was served three huge meals. After that, Healing Lady figured out I'll eat anything she puts in front of me, no matter how full I am, so she made my portions a little smaller. But she still said I could always ask for food if I got hungry. I never do; three meals a day is like feasting.

The other good thing about being here is that it's given me time to think. About the things I did and the decisions I made. I'm still not sure exactly where I crossed the line, where I stopped doing what I had to do and started doing what I wanted to do. But I know I have to be better in the future. I'm not very good at following rules, but I think it's time I write myself some new ones. Rules about consequences and selfishness. About how sometimes other things are more important than your own survival.

I don't know if I'm ready yet.

But it's release day. I am given clothes that look like hand-me-downs donated to charity, placed in an unnecessary wheelchair, and escorted out of the House of Healing by an unsmiling protector. I am put into a carriage pulled by two thilastri. An armed guard accompanies me back to Ruhia, where I am wheeled into the courthouse.

I guess appearing in court in a wheelchair can't hurt my chances, can it?

But we don't go into the courtroom. We go into the judge's chambers. Which is weird. Is this like a pre-trial interview? How does the Ruhian court system work, exactly?

The judge is a really old, wizened-looking man with

spectacles. A typical judge, then. That can't help my chances.

After wheeling me into place across from the judge, the protector leaves, slamming the door shut. It's like I've just been thrown in a prison. Probably because I'm about to be.

Judge peers over his spectacles at me for a minute, like I'm a puzzle he's curious about. His eyes are sharp and perceptive. "You know why you're here," he says. "But before I make a decision about what to do with you, I have a few questions."

Now I have to decide what to tell him and how much to lie. There's no point in denying who I am or anything. It won't help me at all to lie about that. But I will lie to protect Beck. I owe him that much.

"What's your name?" Judge asks.

"Alli Rosco."

He pauses for a moment, probably gauging whether or not I'm telling the truth, then continues. "And where are you from, Miss Rosco?"

"Azeland."

He nods. "And you are under the age of thirteen. Which makes you a minor in both Azeland and Ruhia."

"Yes."

He leans back in his chair, relaxing, like we're having a casual dinner conversation or something. "So how did you come to be in Ruhia? Did your family move here?"

"No." I take a deep breath. Honesty. Right. "I ran away from an orphanage in Azeland."

This information doesn't surprise him. "I see. So tell

me. Who was the boy you were with when you entered the Atherton residence?"

Time to start lying.

I try to shrug like it's no big deal. "Some boy I met after I got out. Berkeley somebody. He said I could stay with him for a while. Guess he felt sorry for me or something."

I don't know if Judge is buying it, but he doesn't press the issue. "Did you meet him in Azeland?"

"Yes."

"So how did the two of you come to be in Ruhia?"

"We met this guy. He said he'd pay us big if we stole this necklace for him. He said it was in Ruhia, so he gave us a carriage and everything and flew us there. We lived in some house he owned, or said he owned, for a few days."

"And this necklace he wanted was the one owned by Lady Atherton?"

Hearing her name out loud makes me want to cringe. "Yes."

"Why did this man want it?"

"I don't know. We didn't ask why. We needed the money."

"And what was this man's name?"

"He didn't say."

Now Judge looks disbelieving. "And what made you so certain this stranger you just met was telling the truth about paying you?"

"He was loaded. He gave us some money just for the trip. Lots of it. And, okay, we didn't know for sure he was legit, but we figured we'd make him show us the money before we gave him the necklace, you know? And if he didn't have it, we figured someone else would pay us for the necklace."

"All right. So this strange man pays for you and Berkeley to fly to Ruhia and instructs you to steal Lady Atherton's necklace. Now, perhaps you can walk me through the night of the Dearborn ball."

I shrug. "Not much to tell. The guy said Lady Atherton would be there. We just sneaked in and tried to grab the necklace from her."

"And where did you get the disguises you were wearing?"

"Stole them."

Judge raises an eyebrow. "Such fine clothing isn't available in stores. It would have to be custom made."

"Stole them from a tailor shop," I clarify. "Took them to a different tailor shop to have them fitted for us. Paid with the stranger guy's money."

Judge's eyebrow sinks back down into place like he's buying this. "All right. So you go to the Dearborn ball in disguise, planning to target Lady Atherton. Why did you spend time talking with Atherton's daughter?"

"You can't just walk up to somebody in a ballroom, right?" I say, like I've been to tons of balls. "You have to be introduced. So we were sort of walking around, talking to people, trying to get someone to introduce us to her. And this one guy introduced us to Ariannorah Atherton. We had no idea she was Atherton's daughter until that point. Anyway, so Ariannorah introduced us to her mother, then we convinced them to walk out to the garden with us, where there weren't so many people, and grabbed the necklace."

"But Baron Dearborn's private guards caught you, yes?"

"Yeah."

"And you were taken to a Ruhian prison to await sentencing."

"Uh, yeah."

"So how did you escape?"

Instinct tells me to lie about this, but I can't come up with a good one. Anyway, I guess it can't hurt to tell the truth. I'm already in trouble. "We picked the lock."

Judge leans forward, making a sort of startled splutter. "On your cell?"

"Yeah."

"With what? Weren't you searched?"

"Uh, yeah, but I had some hairpins in. . . ."

"You picked a lock on a prison cell door with a *hairpin*?"

"Well, I didn't. Berkeley did. I don't really know how to pick locks." Not totally true, but close enough.

Judge seems to buy that part of it, at least. "And the guards?"

"There was only one guard, and we overpowered him. Two against one, right? Anyway, it wasn't much of a prison. Not, like, high-security stuff."

Judge frowns and scribbles on a parchment on top of his desk. "All right, Miss Rosco. I need you to walk me through the events that occurred around midnight on the first day of Mirati's Month."

"Okay. Berkeley and I rented a carriage and rode up to Shoringham. Then we just went in through a back door."

"Was this door locked before you entered it?"

"Um, yeah."

He scribbles something else on his parchment. *Breaking and entering*, probably. Right next to *prison escape* and *theft* and *general stupidity*. "Please continue."

I tell him the truth. When I get to the part about being hit with the magician's fireball, I gesture dramatically to my bandaged foot for emphasis. It's here that I pause, unsure what to say next.

Judge is still scribbling. "And then?"

And then. I still don't know what happened. "And . . . and the guard guy was going after Berkeley, right? And he's throwing this fire stuff all over the place. And then—I think—I think Ariannorah jumped right in between Berkeley and one of the spells. So then Lady Atherton tried to jump in front of her. And all three of them went down. And then I don't even know what happened, but Lady Atherton was dead and Ariannorah was bleeding all over the place."

"So it was definitely the guard who attacked Lady Atherton?"

"Well, yeah. I mean, he's the only magician in the room, right? I didn't even have any weapons at all. But the guard didn't attack her on purpose, or Ariannorah. He was aiming for Berkeley, but they got in the way. And after he did it, he looked real scared and he ran off."

There's a long pause as Judge writes on the parchment. "And then?"

I tell him the rest, up through wandering the house looking for help.

Judge stops scribbling. "And help came."

"Yeah. I mean, I guess. Everything's kind of a blur after that."

Judge drops his pen and leans back in his chair again. "Well. Luckily for you, Miss Rosco, most of your account lines up with what Ariannorah Atherton told me a few hours ago."

"It does?" I don't mean to sound surprised, but I do.

The corners of Judge's lips twitch. "Is there some reason it shouldn't?"

"No, no, I didn't mean it like that. It's just—I guess I just expected her to say that I killed her mother or something. I mean, I didn't, but Lord Atherton said that. Before the guards took me. He called me a murderer."

Judge frowns. "Well, Miss Atherton was quite clear that it was an accident. She was rather inclined to blame herself, as a matter of fact. She also said that you saved her life."

Well. How honest of her.

He sighs. "Well, Miss Rosco, since your account lines up with hers, I believe you are telling the truth. Therefore, I have two options. Option one: I can send you to prison on charges of escape from a holding facility, breaking and entering, theft, and attempted theft. However, because you are under thirteen, you will be sent to a juvenile facility—a high-security one, to prevent another breakout attempt—and your sentence will be considerably lighter. If you behave yourself, I expect you'll spend the next three months—one hundred and eighty days—in prison. Upon your release, you will be sent to a Ruhian orphanage, where you will stay until you turn thirteen or are adopted.

"Option two: I send you back to Azeland and place you in the custody of Azeland's protectors, with a full account of the crimes you committed here, and allow them to deal with you as they see fit."

Which city I'm imprisoned in makes no difference to me. But I already have a record in Azeland. And they probably won't want to send me back to Sisters of Harona since I escaped from there once already. They'll keep me in prison until I'm older so the orphanages won't have to deal with me anymore.

"If it's all the same to you, sir, I'd prefer to stay in Ruhia."

Judge leans back in his chair, thinking it over. "And your desire to remain in Ruhia wouldn't be because you're planning some kind of escape attempt? Or expecting someone to help you escape?"

"No, sir. The only person I know who was here is Berkeley, and he's probably halfway to Ledrea by now."

Judge's mouth quirks up a little. It reminds me so much

of Beck that it hurts. "Yes, I expect so." He taps the end of his quill against the table. "All right, Miss Rosco, you may remain in Ruhia. I will send you down the hall for processing, and then you'll be taken to the juvenile center to serve your sentence."

He stands up and makes his way out from behind his desk. He opens the door and speaks to someone on the other side. "Get Barelli for processing."

He returns to his desk, looking at me thoughtfully. "Rosco," he murmurs. "You wouldn't happen to be related to Ronan Rosco, would you?"

Ronan. That same long-buried image swims to the surface—the boy with shaggy black hair throws me up into the air and spins me around. But this time I remember what I said, when I shrieked in excitement:

"Again, Ronan! Again!"

The name tastes like white chocolate.

You wouldn't happen to be related to a lawyer's apprentice in Ruhia, would you? Bray asked me that, in the Guild.

Something between a laugh and a cry bubbles up from my throat. Ronan. I'd almost forgotten.

"Yes," I say. "He's my brother."

Acknowledgments

I am endlessly thankful to the many people who helped bring this book into the world.

To my brilliant editor, Alyson Heller, who understood Alli's story so well and knew exactly how to tell it better. I am so grateful for her guidance and wisdom. And many thanks to the entire team at Aladdin, including Jessica Handelman, who designed the jacket, and Eric Deschamps, who created the incredible cover art.

To my amazing agent, Victoria Doherty Munro, who believed in this story from the beginning. This book would not exist without her hard work and insight, and I couldn't ask for a more passionate advocate. I am also grateful to Daniel Lazar, who helped bring us together.

To Alexandrina Brant and Rachel Done, who read the earliest draft and have supplied feedback, advice, and encouragement at every stage since. And to C.G. Drews and Allison Pauli, who provided invaluable insight and support.

To the teachers who guided and encouraged me, including Sheila Hayden, Sharon Jones, and Claudia Nogueira.

To Kate Brauning and Bethany Robison, who have taught me so much. And to the members of Team Brauning: It's truly an honor to work with all of you. To everyone in the writing community who provided advice along the way, including Taryn Albright, MarcyKate Connolly, Tracy Holczer, Sabrina Oliveira, and my fellow 2017 debut authors.

To my extended family, for their love and enthusiasm for this book. To Mom and Dad, who always believed in me, and help me pursue my dreams every day. And to my sister, Katie, who was the first person to listen to my stories, and who has supported me in countless ways ever since. I love you all.

Turn the page for the next
installment of Alli's adventures

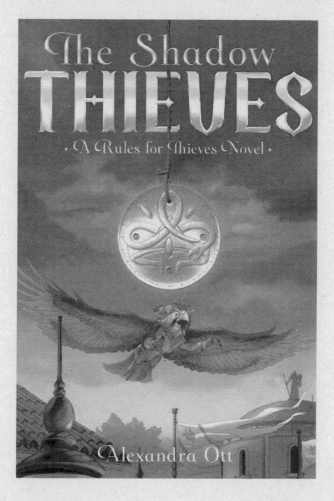

The sunlight glinting off the silver barbed wire makes my eyes water. I always forget how bright it is outside. Prison is nothing but gray.

"This way," the warden says impatiently. She clutches my release papers in her left hand. I blink to clear my eyes and follow her across the courtyard toward the gate.

My heart flutters in my chest. This is it. I've been waiting one hundred and eighty days, and now I only have to wait for them to open the gate. Freedom is on the other side.

It's taking way too long for the gate to move. Maybe the magician is napping on the job or something. They claim that there's one up in the tower who's enchanted the gate and has to lift the spell before anyone can pass. I have no way of knowing if that's true, but it could be. This place is supposed to be the most secure juvenile facility in all of Ruhia. It turns out that once you've broken out of prison the first time they try to lock you up, they don't take any chances the second time around.

Luckily, I'm the only one being released today, but the wait is still agonizing. The warden shows my papers to the guard, and I stare down at the chalky gravel of the court-yard. I'm going to see real grass in a second. Real grass and real trees and . . . my brother. My real, actual brother.

Finally, in one long, excruciating motion, the gate swings open.

Will he really be there? They told me that he'd agreed to pick me up. Surely he wouldn't back out now. Unless this has all been some kind of horrible joke. A mistake, like everything else.

And even if he is here . . . what will he think of me?

The warden strides through the gate and peers down the drive. "Are you Ronan Rosco?" she asks.

He's here.

My feet shuffle forward on their own, leading me across the threshold of my new life.

I've waited one hundred and eighty days for this, but I'm not ready.

I stop beside the warden, just on the other side of the gate. The long drive up to the prison is lined with brown-ing grass and stark, barren trees. It was early summer when I went in, but now it's Vyra's Month, and winter is already settling in for a long stay. This will be my first Ruhian winter, my first experience with heavy snows and freezing temperatures and weak sunlight. I can't say I'm looking forward to it.

A few feet down the gray gravel drive sits a carriage. A cheap rent-by-the-hour one, painted a shockingly bright orange and pulled by a skinny brown horse. The driver looks half-asleep on the front seat, his elbows resting on his knees.

And walking up the drive toward us is my brother.

Ronan is tall, tall enough that I have to crane my neck to look at him. I remember him being about five years older than me, and I don't think I was too far off the mark—he looks eighteen or nineteen. Like me, he has shaggy dark hair that resists all efforts to comb it. Unlike me, he seems to have made an effort to tame it anyway, having tied the loose bits back at the nape of his neck. He's wearing a real, actual suit, with a tie and everything.

But if he's trying to make a good impression on the warden, she doesn't care. She barely glances at him as she riffles through my papers. Having finally arrived at the correct one, she reads a statement in a flat monotone: "As a representative of the glorious state of Ruhia, I now release this ward—Alli Rosco, age twelve, originally of Azeland—to you, Mr. Ronan A. Rosco, hereby establishing you as her legal guardian until she comes of age. In accordance with the law of the glorious state of Ruhia, her guardian must ensure her attendance at all forthcoming probationary meetings and/or hearings until such a time when her probation ends. Failure to comply will result in penalties for both ward and guardian. Do you understand these terms?"

"Er, yes," Ronan stammers.

"Right then." The warden shuffles a few more papers and holds one out to Ronan. "Sign here."

He signs his name with the pen she offers, and then it's done. Just like that, I'm free to leave.

"Best of luck to you," the warden says briskly as she turns back to the gate, but I'm not sure if she's talking to me or to Ronan.

My brother smiles at me. He has a kind face, with soft eyes, and he looks even kinder when he smiles. "Ready to go, Alli?"

No, I think I'll just hang out at the prison a bit longer. The sarcastic response rises up automatically, but I bite it back. "Yeah," I say instead.

He leads the way back to the carriage, each footstep raising a puff of gravelly dust that clouds his shiny black shoes. His suit isn't anything super fancy, like the nobles wear, but it's still a suit. He really *is* a lawyer's apprentice.

I glance down at my feet. They let me change out of the prison-issue jumpsuit, but the only thing I had to change into is what I was wearing when they booked me: a baggy, moth-eaten sweater, and pants that are too small for me, the cuffs hanging too far above my ankles. These clothes are prison-issue too, something they gave me to wear during my meeting with the judge after I got out of the Healing Springs. Probably donated by some charity, just like the stuff we used to wear at the orphanage. It never would've bothered me much before, but they seem shabby now. Do lawyers' apprentices always wear nice clothes? I'm not sure how much money they make or what kinds of houses they live in.

Why didn't I think about any of this before? I've been so busy worrying about what Ronan would be like, I forgot to worry about the rest of it.

Ronan yanks the carriage door open. The whole thing groans as we climb in, and I wouldn't be surprised if it's held together by only glue and prayer. But still, it was nice of him to bring a carriage at all, instead of just walking.

"Nice" is a word that I'm beginning to associate with my brother, even though this is the first time I've seen him in person since I was three. I mean, there really isn't any other word for a guy who apparently agreed to take in his estranged sister after she managed to get herself thrown into juvenile prison before she turned thirteen. I can only imagine how that conversation went over on his end. *So, hi. I know you haven't seen me in a decade, but I'm your long-lost sister. Hurray! Oh, and also, I'm homeless and in jail on multiple charges. Think I can come live with you when I get out in a few months?*

Yeah, way to make a good first impression.

It's only made worse by the fact that Ronan had, apparently, been leading a very successful life until I came along. The list of facts I know about my brother is short, but it includes a few key details.

Number one: His name is Ronan A. Rosco.

Number two: He's a lawyer's apprentice currently living in Ruhia.

Number three: He must be a good apprentice, because the judge handling my case thought well enough of him to recommend I be released to live with him once my sentence was up.

Number four: He owns a real suit.

From these facts, I can conclude that things have been going well for him. At least until his long-lost sister was dumped in his lap.

The carriage lurches, almost throwing us against the far wall. Ronan winces. "Sorry about the bumpy ride. I had to save a few weeks' allowance for this."

I don't think he means it to be cruel, but I cringe. Only the first of many expenses I'm going to cost him.

He glances out the window, fidgeting with his tie. His fingers are long and ink-stained, his nails neatly trimmed. A ray of sunlight cuts across his cheekbone and nose, throwing half his face into brightness and the other half into shadow. On the surface, he looks a lot like me—messy dark hair and tan skin and brown eyes. But lots of other people have those features too. There is a deeper resemblance between us, but only if you look for it: His face is fuller than mine, but he still has hints of sharper angles in the same places I do—chin, nose, cheekbones. His eyebrows are as shaggy as his hair, giving a more serious tone to his playful, bright eyes. He looks like my brother only in the smallest of ways. Fitting, I guess.

I should probably say something now, but I don't know what. We sit mostly in silence as the carriage clatters its way down Ruhia's streets. Judging by the way Ronan keeps cutting glances at me and then looking away, I don't think he knows what to say either. We've missed so much of each other's lives that we could never run out of things to talk about, but the gulf is too wide. We don't know where to begin.

Plus, I don't exactly have a great track record when it comes to saying the right things. I've sworn to myself that I'll be on my best behavior, that I won't smart off, that I won't lose my temper. But I don't know how to go about doing that, precisely, and right now everything I want to ask seems too perilous.

Well, I guess we can start small. "What's the *A* stand for?" I ask.

"Hmm?"

"In your name. Ronan A. Rosco."

"Oh." He smiles again. "I have no idea. I made it up."

"Really?"

"Really. I don't know my middle name. Don't know if I have one. But I needed something that sounded official."

"For lawyering?"

"Right." He grins wider, the corners of his mouth twitching, and it looks so much like that *other* grin that it makes my heart stutter. The way his lips always used to quirk up at the corners . . .

Get out of my head, Beck.

"So, I probably don't have a middle name either," I say.

His smile fades. "I don't know. I'm sorry."

I shake my head. "Not your fault."

We go back to staring out the windows.

The city of Ruhia looks so much different from the last time I saw it. Before, in the late spring, the trees were full, the flowers blooming, the streets crowded with pedestrians taking advantage of the mild weather. Now it's the start of winter, and the trees are already bare, the grass brown. Fewer people walk the streets, and those who do wear thick coats, scarves, and hats.

Carriages now clog the roads, most pulled by ordinary horses like ours. But I catch glimpses of thilastri guiding the fancier carriages and crane my neck to get a better look. I hardly ever saw thilastri back home in Azeland, but they're much more common here. They tower over the horses in the streets, their golden beaks and bright blue feathers standing out against the landscape of grays and browns.

Our carriage finally stops, and the driver thuds twice on the wall behind my head. We're here.

Ronan climbs out first and helps me down. As he pays the driver, I glance around. The street is cobbled and quiet, neat brick buildings lining it in rows. So different from Azeland, where everything is a haphazard cluster of different sizes and materials and people. There, the building's materials would tell you how wealthy its owners were. Ruhian architecture makes it impossible to figure out what kind of neighborhood this is. While this street certainly doesn't belong to the nobility, I can't determine much else about it.

"This way," Ronan says, leading me down a sidewalk and toward a tall redbrick building. I memorize the number—the only way to distinguish it from its neighbors—as Ronan unlocks the front door and leads me inside. We enter the mostly empty front room of the apartment complex, and then climb three flights of stairs before arriving on Ronan's floor.

The hallway is narrow and dim, but everything seems nice enough. There are only a few apartments per floor, and Ronan leads me to the second door on the right. 4B, according to the bronze plate.

"It's pretty small," he says, sounding apologetic as he unlocks the door. "And I'm no good at decorating."

I almost laugh. Like I care about decorations.

Still, I have to admit he's right. The room we've entered is pretty bare, just a battered sofa, an armchair, and a rug in front of a fireplace. A low, partial wall that runs only half the length of the room divides it from a small kitchen with faded white cabinets and a single paned window. A dark hallway leads to the right. Lots of books and papers are stacked around the room.

And that's about it. But it's clean, it's warm, it's safe. I've lived in worse.

Ronan looks embarrassed, fidgeting with his tie again. He tosses his keys onto the table in the kitchen and grabs a matchbox off the fireplace mantel. "It gets a bit drafty in the winter," he says in that same apologetic tone. "But the building supplies firewood, so we don't have to worry about that."

"That's nice," I say.

Now that I've heard him speak more, the traces of Azeland in his accent are obvious. The past few months in prison, all I ever heard were Ruhian voices, and I didn't realize until now how much I missed hearing other people who speak like me. It's a small thing, but it makes Ronan feel more like my brother.

He strikes a match, tosses it into the grate, and watches the flames catch. "Bathroom's down the hall on the left. My room is at the end of the hall; yours is on the right."

"Mine?" I say, certain I've misheard.

"Yeah, your room. It's down the hall on the right."

My own room. *Thank you, Saint Ailara.* I've never had my own room before.

Except for that one time. In that one place. With that one boy I will not think about.

"So," Ronan says, straightening up from the fire, "how about dinner?"

Dinner. With real, actual, nonprison food.

This day is rapidly improving.

We head into the kitchen, and Ronan lifts the lid on the small white ice chest. "I didn't know what you'd like," he says quickly, "so I haven't really been shopping yet, and there isn't very much . . ."

Ronan's idea of "very much" differs greatly from mine. He's able to produce a loaf of bread, some sliced ham, a bit of cheese, two bowls of fresh berries—the weird Ruhian kind that manage to grow in frigid winter—and two glass bottles of milk. Practically a feast.

He then makes the questionable decision of trusting me with a knife, letting me slice the bread for our sandwiches. I've just cut four slices when he fidgets with his tie again. "So, Alli," he says, inky fingers tugging at his collar, "would it be all right with you if a friend of mine joined us for dinner tonight? She'll be getting off work in a few minutes, and she occasionally drops by . . ."

"Um, sure." He wants his friends to meet his delinquent sister? Might as well just announce it to the whole neighborhood.

I clear my throat. "Does she know . . . ?" I'm really not sure where to go with the rest of that sentence.

"I told her about you coming to live with me," he says carefully. Which is nice-guy code for *I told her you just got out of prison.*

"Okay," I say, because that's what he wants me to say. "So, six slices of bread, then?"

"Right." He smiles. He's a major smiler, my brother.

The knock comes at the door a few minutes later as Ronan is sweeping stacks of paper off the kitchen table to make more room. "Come on in, Mar," he calls.

The front door swings open, and a young woman strides into the living room. She looks about Ronan's age, probably in her late teens. Her skin is a rich, warm brown, and her dark hair is pulled back into a thick braid. She's dressed casually, in pants and a simple red blouse.

She's also very pretty.

Friend. Yeah, right.

"Hey, Ronan," she says, stepping into the kitchen. But she's looking at me. "You must be Alli."

I nod, and she offers me a handshake, smiling. "I'm Mari. I live next door to you, in 4A."

Two things I like about her instantly: One, she uses the same tone of voice with me as she does with Ronan, not that condescending one some people use to talk to children. And two, she said "to you," not "to Ronan." As if this is my house as much as his.

I try to remember Sister Perla's etiquette lessons. "Nice to meet you," I say.

"You're just in time for sandwiches," Ronan tells her, setting the last plate on the table.

"Sandwiches, huh? Did you forget to go shopping again?" she teases.

"I didn't *forget* . . ."

"Uh-huh." She drops into the chair at the end of the

table, and Ronan settles beside her. I sit in the remaining chair opposite Mari, with Ronan between us.

Ronan rushes through a grace, and then we dig in to the meal. It's all I can do not to shove it into my mouth as fast I can. I haven't had food like this in months. But I'm trying to make a good impression and remember my table manners. Not that I had any to begin with.

"So, Alli," Mari says, "Ronan tells me you're new to Ruhia?"

"Right," I say cautiously. "I'm from Azeland."

She smiles. "Well, our winter's going to be a big change for you, isn't it? But I've always thought it's Azeland that really has it rough. I don't know how you can brave those hot summers."

"You've been to Azeland?"

"Once, on a family trip in the summer. Beautiful city."

You must not've seen much of it. I quickly take a sip of milk to prevent that thought from coming out of my mouth. I'm not going to let myself get into trouble like I did before. That was Old Alli. New Alli is going to make this work. If boring, polite small talk with Ronan's girlfriend is what I have to do to live with my brother, then I'll do it.

"So, Alli," Ronan says, in the same cautious way he said it before, "I know you don't, er, have much with you, so I was thinking maybe you'd like to go shopping for some things tomorrow? I have to be at work, but you could go with Mari . . ."

Is he trying to pawn me off? Or trying to be considerate?

Mari leans toward me conspiratorially. "He knows absolutely nothing about clothing. Or decorating."

"Hey, I've furnished this whole apartment," Ronan says, pretending to be annoyed.

Mari winks at me. "My point exactly."

"Okay," I say. I can't quite muster up the enthusiasm for a shopping trip, but I guess I do need some clothes other than these. I smell like mothballs.

Ronan takes a sip from his water glass. "Have you given any thought to where you might like to apprentice?"

"Apprentice?" I repeat.

"You're turning thirteen next month, right?"

Of course. I've been stupid. All this time, when we talked about my coming to live with him, we never discussed how long I would stay. No wonder he's been so kind, so willing to take me in. Because it's only temporary. Just for a month, until I turn thirteen and am old enough to live on my own or be shipped off to someone as an apprentice. He never planned for me to live here permanently.

And part of me is a little bit relieved. Being on my own is what I know how to do. And as much as I wanted this to work out, as much as I still want to be connected to my brother, I've always known this would happen. I'm the sister he doesn't want, and the sooner he can go back to his perfect life without me, the better.

I was never going to get a real home.

But despite how many times I've told myself that this might happen, the reality of it is like being punched in the gut. The conversation moves along without me for a few minutes as I stare at my plate, at the dishware and the table and the floor that no longer belong to me, that never really did.